The Twisting Vine

By the same author

Sea Dust

The Twisting Vine

Margaret Muir

ROBERT HALE · LONDON

© Margaret Muir 2006
First published in Great Britain 2006

ISBN-10: 0-7090-8132-4
ISBN-13: 978-0-7090-8132-6

Robert Hale Limited
Clerkenwell House
Clerkenwell Green
London EC1R 0HT

The right of Margaret Muir to be identified as
author of this work has been asserted by her
in accordance with the Copyright, Designs and
Patents Act 1988.

2 4 6 8 10 9 7 5 3 1

Typeset in 11/14pt Garamond
by Derek Doyle & Associates, Shaw Heath
Printed in Great Britain by St Edmundsbury Press
Bury St Edmunds, Suffolk
Bound by Woolnough Bookbinding Limited

Acknowledgements

To my dearest friend and partner, Peter Ryan, who travelled with me through the writing of my first two novels. For all your love, encouragement and enthusiasm, for reading, critiquing and rereading my manuscripts, and for your wonderful smile which never faltered – what can I say, but thank you.

Peter J. Ryan died tragically 17 Novemeber 2005

For my mother Ethel Leak
With all my love

'The most beautiful things in life cannot be seen or even touched — they must be felt with the heart.'

Helen Keller

Chapter 1

Heaton Hall, North Yorkshire – 1896

'Oldfield!'

'Yes, Mrs Gresham?'

'Your shoe is still squeaking! Didn't I tell you about that yesterday? And the day before?'

Lucy Oldfield nodded resentfully. 'I tried to fix it, Mrs Gresham. Honest I did. I tried whale oil like you said, but it didn't work.'

'Then I suggest you wear another pair.'

'But I don't have another pair.'

'Then you had better do something about it. I will not have you walking these corridors when every step you take sounds as though you are squashing a mouse. We must have quiet in the house! Do you understand?'

As Lucy's chin dropped, she leaned forward and watched her toes disappear beneath the broad frill of her apron. Why had she listened to her mother and bought the new pair when there was nothing wrong with the old ones? Soft as velvet, they were, and comfortable. And, as she never walked outside in them, except to the pump across the courtyard, it didn't matter that the soles were thin as parchment. If she'd had any sense she'd have had them re-soled.

Lucy shook her head. The thought of her mother's advice aggravated her at times. Always telling her what to do, insisting she knew best, treating her like she was still a child. Even after six years, her words rang in her head: 'Mind you always wear your own boots and bloomers!' It didn't

9

matter that the Hall supplied its maids with everything from stockings to caps, and lengths of cloth to make their own under-linen, the widow would hear nothing of it. 'Your own boots and bloomers! No one else's!' Being reminded of this and a dozen other things, every year when she went home for her holiday, Lucy soon realized it was easier to bow to her mother's wishes than remonstrate. If she ever did speak out, she was accused of being ungrateful, told in no uncertain terms, how very fortunate she was to have a good job in a fine house – and made to feel guilty.

But on the subject of shoes, Lucy knew she should have spoken out. The new ones had been uncomfortable when she first tried them on, but, as always, Mother knew best and had insisted they would soften, wear in, mould to her feet. But they never did! The leather was tough, and despite the grease Lucy had rubbed into them, the right shoe still squeaked and the stitching pinched her toes.

The thought she might end up with ugly feet made her shudder. Her mother's feet were dreadful. Smooth round bunions protruded from both feet like pullet eggs ready to crack and hatch a clutch of new toes. And the shame of having to walk outdoors in slippers with half the front cut away – perish the thought!

Though she loved her mother, Lucy wished she would listen to reason and realize she was no longer fifteen years of age. She hated the new shoes. And what made matters even worse, now Mrs Gresham hated them too.

'No point feeling sorry for yourself!' the housekeeper said. 'You can take that glum expression off your face. You have a lot to be thankful for, girl. Now get downstairs and fetch some water. Nurse is waiting.'

'Yes, ma'am.' Lucy bobbed, turned and tiptoed towards the back stairs which led down to the kitchen. Behind her the sound of Mrs Gresham's heels echoed from the corridor's polished boards, *clack, clack, clack, clack*. When the housekeeper reached the main staircase the sound stopped, her footsteps muffled by the Axminster.

'Damn!' Lucy said, as she flopped down at the table.

'There will be no blaspheming in my kitchen, Lucy Oldfield!'

'Sorry, Cook, I didn't mean that to slip out, but it's Mrs Gresham. She makes me mad complaining all the time about my shoes creaking. I'm sure she thinks I do it deliberately.'

'She's got a lot on her plate at the moment,' said Cook. 'And it's the little things that rattle her.'

'But why pick on me and my shoes? Walk on any of the corridors in this house and the floorboards creak. The stairs creak. The doors creak. In fact the whole damned house creaks. I bet if Mrs Gresham leaned over she would creak too! Mrs High and Mighty, she is!'

Cook thumped her fist on the table. 'Have you quite finished with your speech-making?'

Unfastening her right shoe, Lucy kicked it under the table. 'It's her fault if I fall,' she mumbled.

Cook wagged her head and pointed to the kettle. 'You bide your temper, girl. And don't forget what you came down for.' Brushing beads of sweat from her forehead, the woman turned to the brace of game sitting head to tail in the baking dish. 'Think about that poor little mite upstairs,' she said. 'God help her! Trouble is, her being ill is getting to all of us. Even down here in the kitchen.' She glanced across at Lucy. 'You must feel it. You're up and down to the red room more than twenty times a day. And Mrs Gresham spends more time in there than anyone. I tell you, it'd wear a body out trying to behave like there's nothing wrong.' A blast of hot air hit the woman's face as she opened the oven door. 'There,' she said, sliding the baking dish on to the top shelf. 'His lordship is partial to a bit of pheasant and if he don't start eating soon, he's in danger of fading away too.'

Lucy trickled the boiling water into a china bowl, added a jug full of cold and tested it on her wrist.

'Best get up there before they start ringing the bell.'

As Lucy climbed the steps, she was conscious of the odd sounds her feet made with only one shoe on. From the kitchen she heard a bell ring. It had a distinctive sound, different from the others – brighter, clearer, louder. Lucy didn't know if that was because it was the smallest bell on the line or because its brass was shiniest, but she did know it was summoning her, and that Nurse would probably scold her for taking so long.

'I'm coming as quick as I can,' she murmured, balancing the bowl carefully so the water didn't slop out.

The nursery was at the far end of the long corridor. Lucy knocked on the door and took a deep breath before entering.

How the room had changed since '90 when she had first arrived at Heaton Hall. How bright it had been then with its broad south-facing window. How rich and vibrant the velvet curtains, and the strawberry-coloured drapes tied to the bed posts with cords, whose silk tassels hung like bunches of ripe cherries. Everything had glowed with the same succulent shade – cushions, chairs, even the bell pull. It was no surprise to Lucy it had been called the red room before its role was changed to that of the children's nursery.

That was how she had known it, its door always open, light and sound spilling out into the corridor. Inside, the panelled walls reverberated to the high pitched sounds of children's voices, the floor littered with toys and pretty children.

But in the last few weeks since Miss Beatrice had become ill everything had changed. Now the door was kept closed. The room silent. The toys were gone. The rocking horse had disappeared. The floor was now bare to the boards. Even the carpet had been removed. There were no ornaments on the mantelshelf or dresser. No mirrors or pictures on the walls. The heavy velvet curtains were tightly closed, blocking out any evidence of day. From the table, a single lamp flickered, its wick turned down so low any movement of air threatened to snuff it out. The pale light it cast did not penetrate the confines of the big bed, its four turned posts and heavy canopy reflecting only the sombre darkness of the room's walnut panelling.

'Set it down there,' the nurse whispered brusquely, as she twisted the top from a glass jar and sprinkled a generous serving of green crystals into the still steaming water.

Although the air hung heavily with the smell of camphor, the pungent odour caught in Lucy's throat. She coughed.

'I hope you are not coming down with a cold,' Mrs Gresham said disdainfully.

'No, ma'am. It's just the salts. I shouldn't have breathed them.' Lucy sniffed and waited. 'Is there anything else, Mrs Gresham?'

'Doctor Thornton has been sent for. Make sure Simmonds brings him up as soon as he arrives. And for goodness sake, girl, put both shoes on before you fall and break your neck! I don't need any more problems!'

Lucy nodded and tiptoed from the room.

Outside, the corridor was cold, the air still, but fresher than in the nursery. Lucy breathed deeply and shivered. She hated the smell of camphor, the smell of salts and above all, the smell that always came with sickness in a house.

A feather duster flicked across the small squares of glass in the bay window.

Lord Farnley stood for a moment looking up at the swinging sign: *Terry's Toys for the Discerning Child*. And beneath it in small gilt letters: *Proprietor – J. G. Terry Esq.* It was the first time he had visited the shop.

The bell above the door tinkled, but the diminutive lady wielding the duster didn't turn. 'Mister Terry'll be with you in a minute,' she piped.

Lord Farnley gazed around. In his opinion the shop was a veritable Aladdin's cave for any boy or girl, discerning or not. Packed with all manner of playthings, there was barely an inch of spare space for the dust to settle on. Even the floor was cluttered. Behind a solid wooden cart, the battlements of a castle rose two feet from the ground, its drawbridge suspended on two lengths of bronze chain, its mesh portcullis raised. A doll's pram large enough to accommodate an infant stood against the wall. A hobby horse with plaited mane leaned precariously against it. Taking pride of place on the glass-fronted counter was a doll's house, its front wall hinged open to reveal a stately interior. All four floors, from basement to attic, were filled with fine furnishing, each piece, standing no more than an inch in height, perfectly crafted. At the other end of the counter a regiment of toy soldiers was assembled in formation, in front, a row of archers kneeling, behind them two lines of infantrymen and, at the rear, mounted cavalry, swords drawn, poised for the charge.

After a few moments, the shopkeeper emerged from the back of the shop blowing his nose loudly. On seeing his customer he stuffed the red handkerchief into his pocket. 'How can I be of assistance?'

Lord Farnley stumbled over his words. 'A doll,' he said. 'For my daughter.'

'What sort of doll, sir? Terry's Toys stocks quite a selection.'

The proprietor was not wrong. Dolls were the predominant items on the shelves. There were dolls of every description: rag, wooden, felt. Fashion dolls with heads of bisque, composition, Parian. Some with cork pates. Japanese dolls. Leather bodies. Fixed eyes. Feathered eyebrows. Sleeping dolls. Talking dolls. Teddy bears. Golliwogs. Even a doll with a string-pull arm capable of throwing kisses.

Being little more than five feet tall, Mr Terry regarded the world and his customer from over the top of his gold-rimmed spectacles. 'Might I enquire how old the child is?'

'She will be eight on her next birthday.'

'Ah,' the man said, his face broadening in a smile. 'Then this will be a birthday present.'

Lord Farnley ignored the comment. 'I want your very best.'

'The best?'

'The best doll you have.'

'Sir, I can boast a small selection of dolls from the finest workshops in France. Bru, Jumeau, Thuillier and Steiner. But I do not display those particular items on the shelves. Too valuable. If you would give me a moment.' Without waiting for an answer, he shuffled towards the door. After a whispered word with his wife, the pair scurried into the back room.

Lord Farnley admired the metal soldiers while he waited.

Mrs Terry returned first. After hurriedly clearing the counter, she flicked over it with the feathers. Her husband followed carrying a long box.

'What I have here,' he said, as he laid it carefully on the counter, 'is probably one of the finest fashion dolls in the world. A truly exquisite Bru, from the atelier of Paul Girard. It only arrived last week.'

'Then I would like to see it.'

'Certainly, sir.' The shopkeeper stroked the lid affectionately before lifting it. Inside, the printed label confirmed the toy's French origins. Mr Terry appeared nervous as he peeled back the layers of paper.

Lying on its back, the doll's eyes were tightly closed. The upper lids, framed beneath feathered eyebrows, were shadowed with a hint of blue. Thick dark lashes rested on delicately blushed cheeks. The round bisque face was full, the mouth, as if to smile or speak, slightly open. The rose coloured lips turned upwards softly at the corners. Beneath the hat trimmed with feathers, dark locks fell in soft waves. The doll's expression was wistful and gentle.

'Real human hair,' the woman said. 'And pearls,' she added, pointing to the tiny ear-rings hanging from the pierced lobes. 'Perhaps you would like Mr Terry to take it out so you can see it properly.'

'Thank you, I have seen enough. I would like it delivered to Heaton Hall.' Lord Farnley hesitated. 'On second thoughts I will take it with me.'

Mr Terry glanced at his wife. 'Begging your pardon, sir, but am I serving his lordship himself?'

Lord Farnley nodded.

The man behind the counter appeared flustered as he bowed his head. His wife tucked the feather duster into the folds of her serge skirt and dropped several curtsies.

'Is there anything else I can assist you with, your lordship?'

'No, thank you.'

The remainder of the business was transacted with a degree of obvious nervousness on the part of the shopkeeper. His wife assisted him with the packaging as he was hardly able to tie the ribbon around the box. When he presented the parcel to its purchaser he appeared both pleased and relieved. Mrs Terry dropped several more curtsies as she opened the shop door.

Outside, the pavement was wet. The driver, who had been sheltering under the wooden awning, took the box from his master and opened the carriage door.

'The Hall,' said Lord Farnley, pulling the tartan rug across his knees.

The servant nodded and laid the box on the seat opposite him. It took up almost the full width of the carriage.

The late afternoon sun cast long shadows across the lawns, as the carriage rumbled past the old coach houses and up the driveway of Heaton Hall. The wearied poplars were turning rust and gold. A few had already started to shed. Soon the ground would be littered with leaves, and smoke curling from the gardeners' fires would drift into the stately house. Lord Farnley never minded the smell of autumn, or the chill of winter, providing there was still some sunshine.

'Shall I take that for you, your lordship?' the butler asked, as his employer stepped down from his carriage.

'No, I shall take it myself.'

'Doctor Thornton is upstairs in the red room. Mrs Gresham is with him.'

'Thank you, Simmonds. I will go straight up.'

'Of course, sir.'

The square staircase, dating back over 200 years, was decorated with elaborate carvings of twisted vines, fruits and exotic flowers. From the ornate ceiling, hung a huge glass chandelier. As Lord Farnley mounted the stairs, he noticed neither.

The first-floor corridor was shrouded in gloom. It looked longer than usual, and uninviting. The narrow windows offered little of the dying light and the lamps had not been lit. It was not as Lord Farnley remembered it from his childhood.

'Doctor Thornton,' he whispered, as he entered the end room, 'how is she?'

'Resting quietly, I am pleased to say.'

Mrs Gresham got up from the chair and excused herself. The two men waited until she had left the room.

'But what of the infection?'

Standing beside the bed, the physician looked down at his patient. 'If it were only that then we could be hopeful. But the chest infection is but a complication of the major problem and . . .' He hesitated.

'Please say what you must.'

'I have grave fears.'

'Papa.' The voice was weak. 'Papa, is that you?'

Lord Farnley touched his daughter's hand.

'I shall wait downstairs,' the doctor said, closing his bag.

'Thank you, Doctor.'

Lord Farnley waited until the man had gone before he raised the lamp's wick and drew back the curtains. 'That's better,' he said. Sitting down on the bed he spoke tenderly to his daughter, his voice soft. 'Now I can see you.'

Beatrice's eyes were sunk deep in their sockets, her hair was lank, her cheeks sallow, her lips shaded blue.

'I have something for you.' Resting the long box across her legs, he guided his daughter's hand to the ribbon. His eyes smiled sadly as together they unfastened the bow.

'What is it, Papa?'

The paper rustled as he carefully lifted the doll from its nest of wrappings. A pair of luminous blue eyes blinked open and glistened in the light of the lamp. From the silver buckles on the tiny shoes to the tip of the ostrich feathers decorating the delicately flowered hat, the exquisite French doll stood over twenty-four inches tall. The peacock blue of the cloak flowing loosely from its shoulders contrasted strikingly with the room's red furnishings.

Beatrice's face beamed with delight as she lifted her hand to touch the lace stockings and stroke the strip of soft ermine which edged the peacock velvet.

Her father smiled. The shopkeeper had advised him well.

'Papa, she's beautiful,' Beatrice said, then suddenly her expression changed. 'May I keep her?'

'Of course, why do you ask such a foolish question? It's yours.'

'But Mrs Gresham said I couldn't have any dolls because I would make them sick. She said that was why Fred and Bertie had been sent away. She said I would make them sick too.' Her breathing was shallow and fast. 'I hope I will not make you sick, Papa.'

'Hush,' he said, laying the doll beside her. 'No one will get sick and soon you will be well again. Well enough to play in the garden. To watch the bees and butterflies down by the lake, and have tea parties with the other children. Imagine that.'

Beatrice smiled as she wound her frail arm around the doll's waist. On the pillow, her cold grey face rested against the doll's blushed cheeks, their brown hair melding together. Within seconds her eyes were closed.

'Sleep,' Lord Farnley said, as he held her hand. 'Sleep, my angel.'

'She warned me, if I didn't keep my hair under my cap she would cut it off!'

No one in the kitchen answered.

'Honest she did!' said Lucy. 'I swear Mrs Gresham has something against me! First it was the way I spoke; then it was the way I ironed my apron; then it was my shoes squeaking; now she is complaining about my hair. That woman had better not come near me with a pair of scissors!'

'Lucy, enough of that!' Cook was angry. The kitchen maids were familiar with the tone.

Lucy held her tongue – though she knew it was true. The housekeeper did pick on her, even though she was particular about her appearance, and neater than most of the other chambermaids. Unlike some, Lucy liked her uniform. She remembered the times she used to stop at the top of the stairs to admire her reflection in the long window – until the day one of the under-butlers saw her.

'Don't you know vanity's a sin?' he had said, with a glint in his eye.

How embarrassing that had been. Lucy still remembered how she had blushed and had run down the rest of the stairs praying he would not follow her into the kitchen. After that it was a long time before she ever raised her eyes to her reflection again.

Jennie dragged her stool closer and interrupted Lucy's thoughts. 'Tell me about the young fellow who sent you the letter. Who is he?'

'Just a boy I met.'

'Well then, tell us where you met him? What does he do? Where does he come from?'

'I don't rightly know what he does. I only met him twice and that was purely by chance. The first time was at Skipton market about two years ago. The second time was in July when I went home for my week's holiday.'

'And you gave him your address here.'

'Not really.' Lucy's brow furrowed. 'I just told him where I was working.'

'And now he's writing to you. Tell me,' said Jennie, as she drew her stool closer, 'what does he say in his letter?'

'That's none of your business, Jennie Porter,' said Cook.

'Oh, go on. I ain't got no young man writing to me.'

Lucy took off her cap and, not noticing the disapproving look Cook gave, pulled the ribbon from her hair and flicked her dark curls over her shoulders.

'I've only had the one letter and it was quite respectable. He asked me how I was, if I still had the same job and what it's like living at the Hall.'

'Are you going to write back and tell him what you think of Mrs Gresham?'

'Jennie! Get on with those spuds.'

'Yes, Cook.' The scullery maid shifted her stool back and dragged the wooden pail between her feet. 'Go on,' she whispered as she started peeling. 'Tell me again.'

'He asked where I came from. Wanted my address in Leeds. Wanted to know about my mother and if she went out to work. Asked what happened to my dad and if I had any brothers and sisters living at home.'

'You'll be able to write lots,' Jennie said. 'You are going to write to him, aren't you?'

Lucy shrugged, 'Maybe.'

After glancing at Cook to make sure she was not listening, Jennie leaned across the table. 'When are you going to see him again?'

'I'm not certain I am,' Lucy said. 'I won't be going home again till next July.'

'That is if Mrs Gresham doesn't send you packing before then!'

One of the bells on the wall jangled.

'That's mine,' Lucy said, quickly tying her hair and pushing the loose ends inside her cotton cap. 'Do I look all right?'

No one answered.

'Will someone put some more water on to boil? I expect that's what they'll be wanting.' Lucy didn't wait for a response as she hurried towards the back stairs.

'What's this fella's name?' shouted Jennie.

'Arthur Mellor.'

'You can leave the rest to me, Dr Thornton. I will take care of things.'

The doctor washed his hands in the china bowl. 'Thank you, Mrs Gresham. It's been a long and rather exhausting day and I don't mind getting along. Now with regard to advising his lordship. . . .'

'We don't expect Lord Farnley back until tomorrow but you can be assured he will be told as soon as he arrives. Obviously the funeral arrangements will be attended to as soon as he returns.'

The doctor sighed deeply. 'If you ask me, I'd say it's a blessing in disguise. Amazes me she managed to linger as long as she did.' He took out his watch. 'Almost eleven. I'll bid you good night, Mrs Gresham.'

Lucy was about to knock when the nursery door opened. She stepped back and let the doctor pass.

'Blessing in disguise,' he murmured, as he shuffled out.

Lucy hardly dared look towards the bed. 'Has she gone, Mrs Gresham?'

'I'm afraid so.' Mrs Gresham's voice sounded softer than usual. 'Peacefully, I'm pleased to say. I'm sure his lordship will be relieved to know that. But he'll be sorry he wasn't here.'

Lucy could feel the tears in the corner of her eyes. The lamp looked hazy. As she squeezed her lids a warm trickle ran down her cheek. She didn't see the housekeeper looking at her.

'Come and help me tidy this bed. I know it's late, but we can't leave it the way it is.'

Lucy had wondered why she'd been called from her room at such a late hour. Now she wondered why the housekeeper had picked her and not one of the other maids. She was relieved she had been writing a letter and was still awake. Most other evenings she would have been fast asleep before ten.

The pair didn't speak as they straightened the sheet and pillows under the dead girl. They also straightened her legs and arms and nightdress, and combed her hair. Lucy folded the quilt and placed it in the blanket chest. Finally they straightened the top sheet and pulled it to the head of the bed covering Beatrice's face.

'What do you want me to do with this?' Lucy asked, as she picked up the French doll from the floor.

'Burn it!'

'Burn it? But it's near new!'

'Are you deaf as well as daft, girl? I said, burn it!'

Lucy hesitated.

'Things like that carry diseases and we don't want Miss Beatrice's illness passed on to anyone else. Now take it downstairs and burn it! Do you hear me?'

Lucy nodded, tucked the doll under her arm and tiptoed out, closing the door quietly.

Chapter 2

An Ill Wind

The kitchen smelled of meat fat, cabbages and caustic soda. It was empty. The scullery maids had gone to bed and the milk churn standing by the door indicated Cook had also retired – putting it out for the under-footman to collect was the last job she did each evening. The fire glowed in the stove and the kettle standing on the hob heaved puffs of steam and rattled intermittently. On the pine table, a lace-edged cloth covered the silver tray which the butler set out every evening in case his lordship desired a drink during the night.

Lucy was relieved no one was about. She was tired and in no mood to answer questions. In the morning all the talk would be about Miss Beatrice, but for the moment she preferred to keep her thoughts to herself.

The kitchen at Heaton Hall, though large, was a homely place. Warm and comforting. It was the only room the maids could compare with the homes they had come from. Lucy cast her mind back to the house in Leeds where she had grown up. The back-to-back terrace in Loftholme Street. One room downstairs, one up, and a toilet, two doors away, shared between six families. She thought of the cobbled street and the narrow strip of paving where she played as a child. Of the warp of washing lines running from one side of the street to the other, and the tall wooden props which held the sheets high enough for the rag man to drive his horse and cart beneath without getting tangled in them.

She could remember her mother spending hours down on her hands and knees scrubbing the stone doorstep. Remember the fear she felt when gypsies were seen in the street. The joy when she heard the tunes from the tingle-airey and was allowed to drop a farthing in the tin cup which the man's pet monkey rattled.

Lucy thought about her mother, living alone. She had only scant memories of her father. She was only seven when he died. Seven years old. The same age as Miss Beatrice. Instinctively her arms folded around the doll. The porcelain face was cold as marble against her cheek.

From the window Lucy stared out over the courtyard. The moon was full, the wind blowing from the north bending the trees towards the house. The dark shadows danced impishly around the paving teasing her imagination. She turned from the window wishing she hadn't looked, wishing Mrs Gresham's words would stop ringing through her head – *Burn it*!

But how could she burn something so lovely? It was both exquisite and expensive and would have cost more than she could earn in a dozen years.

Burn it! the voice repeated.

How could she burn something she had admired every day when she saw it resting in the crook of the little girl's wasted arm? Something she had secretly longed to hold? Something she had coveted?

The grandfather clock in the hall struck twelve. Lucy knew what she was supposed to do. Inclining her head towards the steps she listened for the clacking of the housekeeper's feet. But the house was silent. Perhaps Mrs Gresham had gone straight to bed.

Laying the doll on the pine table, Lucy cautiously opened the oven's fire door. The metal handle was hot. Inside the flames had died but the embers glowed red. The firebox was almost three feet deep. There was ample room to fit the large doll in.

Stacked up beside the stove was almost a week's supply of firewood, including a smaller pile of sticks and branches. Kindling for the morning fire. Choosing carefully, Lucy selected an armful of fuel. Thick sticks. Long branches. Slender twigs. Breaking them to the size she required, she placed them in criss-cross fashion on the hot cinders. From the drawer in the pine table she took an empty flour bag and from the tool drawer a pair of scissors. Her hands were shaking and the kitchen's warmth was making her sweat.

She avoided the stare of the doll's deep eyes as she untied the cord which held the velvet cloak, and let it fall on to the table. Carefully, she removed the feathered hat, sliding the two miniature hatpins from the shining hair and slipping them into the hem of her apron. Turning the doll, she unfastened the buttons running down its back. The gown, embellished with ivory satin and lace, glowed in the firelight.

The kettle rattled on the hob. Lucy listened acutely, but the only other sound was the rustle of fabric in her hands. She hurried, removing the layers of petticoats, the delicate chemise. Only the shoes and pantalets remained.

When her ears pricked to the sound of footsteps echoing on the first-floor corridor, she stopped. They were distant, but Lucy knew they belonged to Mrs Gresham. The housekeeper was on her way to the kitchen. She had to hurry.

Grabbing the doll's hair she sliced through it with the shears, scattering the dark locks on the table. 'I'm sorry,' she whispered.

The footsteps were getting louder.

By now the wood was well alight. Taking the pile of clothes she fed them piece by piece into the flames, draping each one carefully across the twisted branches. The dress flared instantly in a burst of white hot flame. The cottons were slower to ignite. The human hair smoked and shrivelled before being consumed. The feathers frizzled. Last to go in was the cloak. Lucy draped it carefully across the rest and closed the fire door.

Her hands were shaking as she pulled open the flour bag. The foot-steps had reached the top of the stairs. Only a dozen steps and the housekeeper would be in the kitchen. Grabbing the doll by the neck, she pushed it head first into the bag, rolled it into a bundle and dropped it at the back of the stack of firewood.

Mrs Gresham was at the door.

Looking down, Lucy noticed a fine fuzz of hair still scattered on the table. Praying the housekeeper was not watching, she dusted the frag-ments, like breadcrumbs, into her palm, then pushed the handful of hair deep into her apron pocket.

'Oldfield!'

She could hardly hold herself still. 'Yes, ma'am.' she whispered, not looking at the housekeeper's face.

'Have you done what I said?'

Lucy nodded, unable to answer.

Mrs Gresham sniffed the air. Singed hair has a distinctive smell. Leaning towards the fire she noticed a piece of peacock blue velvet caught in the iron door. Holding a felt pad in her hand, she opened the firebox and inspected the contents. Inside, the fire burned brightly and within the flames laid a mangled shape, covered in the ashen remains of burnt clothing. Satisfied, Mrs Gresham flicked the fragment of velvet into the blaze and closed the door.

'What are you looking like that for, girl? Go to bed! We have a busy day ahead of us tomorrow!'

Glancing at the pile of firewood, Lucy could see the corner of the canvas flour bag protruding from behind it. Surely Mrs Gresham would notice it. And if she didn't, the scullery maid who stoked the fire in the morning would find it. What then? She would tell Cook, and Cook would report it. Lucy knew she had been blatantly disobedient and before long, the housekeeper would know her order had been disobeyed. If the deceit was discovered, she would be accused of stealing and most probably dismissed instantly. Imagine the shame. Imagine what her mother would say.

'What are you waiting for, girl?'

Unable to reply, Lucy bobbed a small curtsy. Her hands, wet with sweat, were clasped tightly behind her back. The doll's hair was stuck to her palms.

That night Lucy did not sleep. At two o'clock she crept down to the kitchen and recovered the flour bag. She was thankful the sky was cloudless and the moon almost full. She didn't need to light a candle. By the time she got back to her attic bedroom, her heart was thrumming in her ears.

She was grateful she had a bedroom to herself. Most of the other girls had to share. Pulling the doll from the bag, she wrapped it in one of her petticoats and pushed it into her wooden suitcase. With its legs and arms bent forwards, it just fitted. Buckling the leather strap around the case, Lucy slid it under the bed. She could only hope and pray no one would open it.

*

It was two months since Miss Beatrice had passed away and every day Lucy had looked at her case and wished desperately that she had not taken the doll. As she lay awake at night, she considered how she could dispose of it. She thought of throwing it into the lake, but wasn't certain it would sink, or burying it in the woods. But if a fox unearthed it or the hounds found it, it might be brought back to the house. What then? One night she dressed herself and was ready to go to the kitchen to burn it properly when she heard voices on the landing outside her room. She was afraid someone might have guessed what she was about to do. But nothing happened, and after that she never attempted to dispose of the doll again.

A few weeks later, rumours reached the kitchen that almost all the staff were to be dismissed. Lucy was shocked. But she was also relieved. At least, when she left she would be able to take the doll with her.

In a letter dated 15 November 1896 the household was officially notified Heaton Hall was to be sold. For most of the staff, their employment was to terminate at the end of the second week in December.

Though no specific reason was given, Mrs Gresham explained that Lord Farnley had decided that the upkeep of the house was too expensive and it was his intention to move to the south coast. The staff, on the other hand, were of the opinion his lordship's decision was not for financial reasons but because the master had lost interest in the house after his daughter's death. Heaton Hall was a fine house, built by his predecessors over 200 years earlier. It was a house Lord Farnley had once loved, and was a viable concern. If he had needed extra funds, which seemed unlikely, he could have sold off part of its 400 arable acres and retained the house with its sculptured lawns and ornamental gardens.

Word quickly passed around that Simmonds, the butler, and Mrs Gresham were to stay on, together with two maids, two footmen and the gardeners. But with talk in the village that the house might be converted into a hotel or hospital, it was likely even those situations would not be secure for long.

It was drizzling the day the staff left. The gloomy weather reflected their mood. Any sense of excitement or anticipation at going home for Christmas was dampened by the worry of unemployment. The number of positions in good houses was becoming fewer and fewer every year and, despite the minor irritations Mrs Gresham caused, the Hall had been a good house to work for. The idea of a mill job did not appeal to any of the girls.

Lucy's suitcase was among the pile of trunks and boxes lashed on one of the wagons. Because the doll had taken up much of the space in her case, she had rolled her extra clothes into a bundle and tied it with string. With the bundle balanced on her lap and a letter of reference, bearing his lordship's signature, in her pocket, Lucy sat between Jennie Porter and one of the other scullery maids in the second carriage. Not a word was spoken as the three coaches and two dray wagons rolled away from Heaton Hall, rumbling down the driveway and out on to the main road which led to York and the railway station.

'Why didn't you let me know, Mum?' Lucy said.

'There weren't much point. I mean, what could you do from the other side of Yorkshire? It weren't right to bother you with my problems.'

'But I could have helped. I could have come home. Asked for some of my wages and sent you some money. Why did you sell all your good stuff and not tell me?'

Mrs Oldfield tapped her daughter's hand. 'Well, what's done's done. Can't cry over spilt milk. And I can get around all right now. Me leg's healed up and I'm not useless.'

'But how did you manage to pay the rent, and what did you do for food money?'

'I've got good neighbours,' she said. 'When I was in bed, they'd bring me a meal and take it in turns to do me washing. Real good they were. Now I'm right again, I've taken on some mending and if any of me neighbours need anything done, I do it for them for nothing.'

Lucy shook her head as she regarded the woman resting by the fireplace. 'But how could you manage on a few shillings?'

'I managed and that's that. And now you're home, lass . . .' she sighed. 'You don't know how glad I am to see you.'

Lucy touched her mother's hand. 'Here, Mum. My handkerchief.'

'Ta, lass,' she said, as she blew her nose and sniffed. 'That's enough about me. But just take a look at you: a fine figure of a woman you are now.'

'Well, I was at the Hall six years and the food was pretty good there.'

'And you talk real proper.'

'I haven't changed, Mum.'

'No love, I don't suppose you have.' Mrs Oldfield lifted her foot on to the wooden stool. 'But tell me about your young man.'

'What young man?'

'The one you've been writing to. Arthur! Arthur Mellor.'

'Arthur Mellor?'

'Such a nice young man. Helped me out no end when I was short of a bob or too. Took some of the things I didn't need and sold them in the market. Always brought money back. I don't know what I'd have done without his help.'

'But I hardly know him! He wrote to me twice and I wrote back to him once. He's not my young man!'

'Well, he makes out he is. And he says he can hardly wait for you coming home. Sounds to me like he has his mind set on you.'

'Well we'll have to see about that.' Lucy got up from the chair. 'Now, what about a bite to eat?'

The advertisement in the antique shop window said: *Experience Essential,* but Lucy applied anyway.

With his spectacles perched on the end of his nose, old Mr Camrass scrutinized the reference, signed by Lord Farnley. Young Mr Camrass, whom Lucy considered old enough to be her grandfather, was more interested in her experience handling silverware. He explained that if she was offered the job she would work six days a week despite the shop being closed on Wednesday and Saturday afternoons. Her duties would be mainly cleaning; both the shop, and the house which backed on to the business premises; polishing metal – namely the second-hand silver and brass items which were purchased from deceased estates, and washing the fine china which was bought by the two gentlemen in bulk lots at the auctions. Both father and son made it quite clear that she would perform her duties in the confines of the house kitchen and that on no account should she step into the shop during business hours.

As to the wages, Lucy thought them to be reasonable compared with her pay at the Hall, especially considering the long hours she had worked when in service. But at least at the Hall there had been no deductions for food and lodgings. Now she had rent to pay, and had both herself and her mother to support. It would not be easy, but she would be paid on a weekly basis and she was convinced she would manage.

'They are extremely fussy,' Lucy told her mother later. 'But I'm used to that. And really both gentlemen are very polite and rather nice, especially old Mr Camrass.'

'I am pleased for you,' her mother said.

As Lucy talked about her new job, neither noticed the house door open and a man step on to the doormat.

'Hello! Anyone home?'

'Oh, it's Arthur,' Mrs Oldfield said, her face brimming with a smile. 'Do come in, love, and see who's here.'

Lucy stood up beside her mother's chair and pushed the hair from her face.

'Yes,' Lucy said less enthusiastically. 'Please come in. Mother has been telling me all about you and I'm grateful for what you have done for her.'

'Well, someone had to help her out and you being away and all. . . .'

Lucy turned to the stove. 'Can I get you a cup of tea?'

'Don't mind if I do.' Without being invited he hung his hat on the coat hook, took off his jacket and settled himself opposite Mrs Oldfield in front of the fire. 'Nice and warm in 'ere.'

'Got two bags of coal delivered this week. Our Lucy's got money and she's got a job too. Go on, lass, tell him about your new job.'

'Not now, Mum. Plenty of time to talk about that later.

'Tell me, Mr Mellor . . .' Lucy said.

'Arthur to you, love. Or Arty, that's what me friends call me!'

'Tell me, Arthur,' said Lucy, 'I seem to be at a bit of a disadvantage. It's a long time since we first met and I can't remember where you said you came from or what you did for a living?'

'Well,' he said, loosening his tie, 'I work with me father. We've got a place the other side of Skipton. Good land out there. Sheep mainly, but there's plenty of game too.' He leaned over to Mrs Oldfield. 'Would you like me to bring you a couple of rabbits or a nice red grouse next time I'm out this way?'

'My! Fancy us eating grouse in this place.' The woman looked across at her daughter. 'What's wrong with your face, lass? You're allowed to smile.'

'I'm sorry. Yes, that would be very nice, thank you, Arthur.'

Lucy was looking at the jacket hanging over the back of the chair. She knew the cut of an expensive suit and recognized a nice piece of tweed when she saw one. 'You and your father must be doing very well,' she said.

'Can't complain.'

Lucy handed a cup to her mother. Arthur helped himself.

'So,' he said. 'You've finished at the big house I gather.'

'Yes.'

'So, you'll be home here at weekends.'

'I shall be home on Sunday, but I will be taking Mother to chapel in the mornings.'

'Then perhaps I should come along and join you, then we can come home here and spend the afternoon together.'

'I—'

'And you and me can take a walk out if the weather's nice. Get to know each other a bit better.'

'Excuse me, Arthur, but I have only been home a few weeks and what with Christmas, I haven't caught up on all that needs to be done around the place.'

'Then I'll come around and help you do it.'

'But I want to spend some time with my mother. I've hardly seen her over the last six years. We've a lot of catching up to do.'

'Then I'll sit quiet as a mouse and not say a word.'

Mrs Oldfield looked across at her daughter. 'Oh, lass, you and me's got every night of the week to chin-wag and it would be so nice to see Arthur around the place. Don't be mean.'

Lucy smiled, though her eyes did not show it. 'Whatever pleases you, Mum.'

'Next Sunday then?' Arthur said, smiling. 'It's a date. And let's hope it's not raining.'

'Mother, put your sewing down. We must talk.'

'I can talk and sew, lass.'

'Leave it, Mother!'

Mrs Oldfield held out the yellowed christening gown at arm's length. 'Got it off the ragman for nowt,' she said. 'Told him it'd make a good duster, but I'm fixing this up for that old doll of yours. It'll make a fine dress. You can't have the poor mite sitting around forever with no clothes on.'

'Mother! I said leave it!'

Placing her sewing on the cushion and balancing the thimble on top, Mrs Oldfield folded her arms across her chest and leaned back in the chair.

'You have to stop encouraging Arthur from visiting.'

'But I thought you liked him, dear. He's so polite and helpful. And he has done such a lot for us.'

'A lot for you maybe!' Lucy sat down. 'There's just something about him which I don't like. And he's here every Sunday. Never misses.'

'And isn't it nice that we all go to chapel together? The ladies think he's such a lovely young man.'

'I don't care what the ladies think. I don't like it that he comes home after service and sits down like he owns the place and stays till after dark. Even then it's hard to get rid of him.'

'Lucy love, you're not being fair.'

'Mum, it's not a case of being fair. I'm *twenty-two* already and I'm not married and I would like to find a nice gentleman to walk me out, but I want to choose my own and not be rushed into anything.'

'Well, Arthur has been calling round for three months now. I hardly call that rushing things.'

Lucy shook her head. 'I'm wasting my breath, Mum, aren't I?'

'Just settle down, lass. Everything'll work out for the best. Now be a good girl and hand me that doll. Let me try this dress on her, then you can tell me how you think she looks.'

'Sorry I'm late,' Arthur shouted, as he threw his cap on to the sofa. 'I had a bit of extra work to do for me Dad. I'll put the kettle on.'

Lucy stepped down from the stairs. 'Mum's not well.'

'What's matter?'

'Doctor's not sure. He said she has a big lump in the side of her belly that shouldn't be there. He thinks it could be the cancer.'

'Can he do anything?'

'No,' Lucy said quietly. 'She's too old and besides we can't afford hospitals and doctors.'

Arthur picked up his hat and placed it on the hook behind the door. 'I'll go up and see her then? Might be able to cheer her up.'

'Yes, she'll probably like that.' Lucy dried two cups and saucers.

When Arthur returned Lucy noticed a change in his tone.

'She don't look too good, does she?'

'No, she doesn't.'

'She's a good old lass,' he said hesitantly. 'I suppose I took a liking to her because she reminded me of my old mum. Not that I can remember her much. She died when I was young. But she was a bright spark. Never a bad word for anyone. Just like your mum.'

Lucy sighed and let herself sink back into the sofa.

Arthur sat down beside her. 'I know I ruffle your feathers sometimes, but we could be good friends, you and me, if you know what I mean.'

As Lucy gazed into the fire he put his hand on hers.

'If there's anything I can do, just let me know.'

She thought about his words. 'But where can I find you if I need you?'

'Don't you worry, I'll come around during the week. If you want I can stay with her in the daytime.'

'But what about work?'

'Don't worry about that. I'll fix it with my Dad. It'll be all right.'

'No you mustn't do that. We've got good neighbours who'll give an eye to her. And if she's really sick I'll ask Mr Camrass to let me have some days off.'

'Suit yourself.'

She felt ungrateful. 'I'm sorry, Arthur. I know I sound abrupt sometimes, but it's just my way and I do appreciate what you have done for Mum.'

Leaning across he planted a peck on Lucy's cheek. 'There,' he said. 'That wasn't too bad was it?'

Lucy smiled through the tears and let him put his arm around her.

'There's something about a house when someone's sick,' she said. 'You can smell it, can't you?'

Arthur shrugged.

On Sunday 13 April, Mrs Oldfield died. The following day Lucy went to work but took Wednesday off for the funeral.

Arthur stayed for the whole week.

Chapter 3

Arthur Mellor

L ucy felt guilty asking for a day off especially when she had to lie to
her employers, telling them she needed the time in connection with
her mother's financial affairs. But having spent all his life involved with
the antique business, old Mr Camrass was well acquainted with the problems relating to deceased estates. Unfortunately, his sympathetic attitude
made Lucy feel even worse. She had not wanted to deceive the two gentlemen, but she could think of no alternative.

It took nearly an hour to walk to the station. It was still dark when
she left the house, but by the time she got to the city it was daylight. The
platform was cold but the gas fire burning in the waiting-room took
some of the chill off the air. As she sat on the wooden bench facing the
other travellers, she wondered if she was being foolish, behaving like a
child. If she had any sense at all, she would turn around and go home
and put the silly thoughts out of her head. But some of the things
Arthur said did not ring true. His conversations echoed in her head.
Something about him nagged at her, compelling her to go to Skipton to
search for an answer.

With a ticket in her hand and the engine belching steam across the platform, Lucy climbed into the end compartment. A gentleman got in after
her and chose the seat in the opposite corner, his back to the engine. As
the train pulled away he took a periodical from his coat pocket and did not

look up for the rest of the journey.

With her eyes fixed on the window beside her, Lucy absorbed the changing scenery as it flashed by: from the factories backing on to the canal, to the grimy buildings, tall chimneys belching smoke, and the rows of houses, not unlike her mother's, running parallel up the hills, like furrows in a field. Then, when the houses disappeared, they were replaced by woods and meadows. She saw sheep and cattle grazing and other sights she had not seen since the day she left the Hall. As opportunities such as this did not occur often, Lucy resolved to enjoy the outing, no matter what the outcome.

'Skipton! Skipton!' The station-master's voice rang like a tolling bell along the short platform. The train shuddered to a halt.

'Allow me, miss,' the gentleman said, as he opened the door.

Lucy thanked him. He had a kindly face. Fatherly. 'Excuse me,' she said, 'could you tell me the way to the post office?'

'You'll find it on the main road, directly opposite the police station. I suggest you follow the crowd; I think most folk will be going in that direction. Wednesday is market day.'

Lucy thanked him and stepped down to the platform. As the smoke and steam drifted away she was able to see how many passengers had got off the train. She was surprised. More than she had expected. But it had stopped at all the small stations along the way.

After joining the queue, Lucy filed past the ticket collector and mingled with the crowd heading for the high street.

It was ten o'clock and market stalls lined both sides of the road. Some spilled into the side lanes and alleyways. The busiest area was round the town's square where the crowds wandered leisurely down the road much to the chagrin of the carters and travellers who were passing through.

The stalls varied greatly in size and construction, from planks resting on empty barrels to large tables, handcarts and dray wagons each laden with all manner of goods – pots, pans and brushes, knitted socks, felt waistcoats, jars of preserves, fresh garlic, spices, smelling salts, soaps and candles. Each stall had its own distinctive sound and smell.

'Toffee! Bag of toffee, love!'

'Lavender! Dried lavender!'

'Best price, lady! Tuppence a pound!'

'Brand new cure-all! Dr Watts' special formula!'

Lucy walked on, mostly smiling but sometimes choosing to ignore the vendor. It was only her second visit to Skipton and she liked the atmosphere. Country markets were always far friendlier than those in the city.

Gazing at the wares made her forget what she was looking for and she had to retrace her steps. The red pillar box outside the post office was almost hidden between two stalls.

'I am looking for a family by the name of Mellor,' Lucy said to the clerk behind the counter. 'Mr Mellor and his son, Arthur. I understand they have a farm near here.'

'Mellor?' said the clerk scratching his head. 'Name don't ring a bell.'

'I believe they have some sheep.'

The man laughed. 'There's lots of smallholdings round these parts and lots of people got sheep.' He shouted to the back of the shop. 'Ivy, do you know anyone by the name of Mellor?'

'Not round these parts!'

'Try the police station. It's over the road,' the clerk said. 'They might know if they've had dealings with them.'

'I hope not,' said Lucy, imagining the worst. 'Thank you anyway.'

The result in the police station was the same. No Mellors in this area. As Lucy wandered out she felt confused. Had she misheard Arthur? Perhaps it wasn't Skipton he came from. And if that was the case, she had come on a wild goose chase and it had cost her dearly.

'I'm so sorry!' the gentleman said, as Lucy walked into him. He leaned down and picked up her basket.

'No, it was my fault. I wasn't looking where I was going. I'm afraid my mind was on other things.'

'I trust you found what you were looking for?'

Surprised by his comment, Lucy hadn't recognized the quiet passenger who had shared the train journey with her. She smiled politley, unsure of what to answer. 'Not exactly, but thank you anyway.'

Doffing his hat, the man bade her good day and continued along the street.

Lucy stood for a moment wondering what to do next. She knew the afternoon train to Leeds was not leaving until 3.30, that meant she had several hours to wait. She hadn't considered idling in the village for the whole day. She had expected to discover where Arthur lived and visit the place even if he wasn't home.

Now she must find something to occupy her time. A cup of tea appealed to her. It would be nice to be waited on, just for once. There was a little tea shop near the station. She could spend an hour over a pot of tea and before that she would waste a little time browsing through the stalls. No one would think it unusual for a young woman to be ambling about Skipton alone on market day.

Lucy would never have ventured down the narrow side street if it had not been for the horse and cart on the high street which was causing problems. It appeared that one of the wagon's shafts had broken, dragging the leather harness down with it. As the horse fought to untangle itself, it became increasingly agitated, forcing its load backwards into a group of stalls. Women screamed. Men shouted. Had she not seen what the commotion was about, she might have feared for her safety. The best thing, she thought, was to keep herself out of harm's way, so she turned down a narrow alley.

There was only one vendor in this side street. His makeshift stall consisted of a wooden table with two wheels attached at the front. It was cluttered with bric-a-brac and everything looked dowdy. There were vases, glassware, and oddments of china, timepieces, cheap beads and old jewellery. The stall holder, a grubby-looking man, was leaning against the table cleaning his finger nails with the prongs of a tarnished table fork. Beside him, an assortment of men's jackets hung like wet washing over an old wooden clothes-horse.

As Lucy drew closer, she wasn't sure if it was the clothes which smelled or the man himself. Nor was she certain which item on the stall caught her eye first, the crockery or the silver locket.

'Excuse me,' she said pointing to a cup and saucer. 'Can you tell me where that came from?'

The man tossed the fork back into the box of cutlery. 'No idea, miss. I get stuff from all over the place. Tell me what you like and I'll give you a good price.'

'May I look?'

'Help yourself,' he said, as he attempted to tidy the display. 'No charge for looking – so long as you don't break anything!'

Lucy picked up the cup and turned it over in her hand. It looked the same, but she could not be sure it had been her mother's. Replacing it on the saucer she reached for the locket. It was heavy. Obviously solid silver, but it had not been polished in a long time. The chain was almost black. As she examined it she remembered the clasp had been hard to open. It needed strong fingernails.

She prised it open carefully. The lock of her hair was still inside!

'I would like to buy this, Mr. . . ?'

'Entwhistle, Harry Entwhistle at your service.'

'How much is it?'

'Well, seeing I've done all right this morning, I'll let you have it for a bargain. Five bob to you lady!'

'Five shillings! I can't afford five shillings.'

'How much have you got then.'

Lucy loosened the string on her purse. There were a few shilling pieces in the bottom and a florin. 'I can give you two shillings,' she said. 'No more.'

'All right,' he said reluctantly. 'Two bob it be.'

'Thank you,' she said, as she slid both purse and locket into her pocket. It had been an expensive day. She had already forfeited a day's earnings. Then there was the cost of the ticket. And now this. She could not afford to spend any more. 'Excuse me, Mr Entwhistle,' she said. 'Do you happen to know a friendly young man from around these parts by the name of Arthur?'

The man grinned like a Cheshire cat. 'You mean, Arty?'

Lucy nodded. 'Yes, that's the name.'

'Aye,' he said. 'Arty's my lad!'

Lucy was shocked. Puzzled. She turned her head and looked about, as if expecting Arthur to be standing behind her, watching her. 'Could you tell me where I might find him?'

'You won't find him here, miss. He lives in Leeds. Only visits me once in a blue moon when he wants something. Got his own family, you see.'

'His own family, you say?'

'Aye,' he said proudly. 'A right pretty wife and two bairns already, and another on the way. Shall I tell him you was looking for him next time I see him.'

'No, thank you, Mr Entwhistle, that won't be necessary.'

Lucy sat by the fire cradling the doll in her arms. Rocking backwards and forwards, she was thinking of her mother, of Heaton Hall and Miss Beatrice. How she wished Lord Farnley had not decided to sell the house. How she wished she was still employed there – even with Mrs Gresham to answer to. Not in her wildest thoughts could she have imagined getting herself into the mess she was in now. In a way she was glad her mother had not lived to see it.

Her visit to Skipton during the week was now a blur in her mind. She could hardly remember the journey home. Could only vaguely remember the conversation she had with the gentleman in the train, though she knew she had talked too much. She could not understand why she had agreed to accept a lift with him in a carriage. The only thing she remembered clearly was him leaving her on the doorstep and his concern that she would be all right when he left. She had no idea why he had helped her, did not know his name and could not remember if she had thanked him. Her thoughts were addled. If only she could think clearly.

'Anyone home?' It was Arthur.

Lucy didn't answer.

'Well, what's going on in here? Not much of a welcome for your fella on a Saturday night, is it? No light on. No fire lit. Don't tell me there's no supper ready for me either!'

Lucy gazed into the empty grate.

'Did someone die or something?' he said jokingly.

'No,' she said quietly. 'I went to Skipton.'

'Oh, yes?' he said, sticking his hands in his pockets. 'And what may I ask took you there?'

'I was looking for you.'

'Well,' he said, as he stepped directly in front of her. 'You didn't find me, did you?'

'No, I didn't,' she said, gazing at his boots. 'But I found your father.'

He turned, spread his legs, and leaned his hands on the mantelshelf. 'You went right out to our place, did you?'

'No. He was at the markets.'

'Ah! What a coincidence,' he said cynically. 'You just happened to bump into him at the markets! And I suppose you spoke to him did you?'

'Yes.'

'And what did he say?'

'He said you lived in Leeds and you had a family.'

He laughed forcefully, turned and faced her. 'And you believed him?'

Lucy nodded and tightened her grip around the doll.

'Are you sure it was my father? Mr Mellor, Joshua Mellor?'

'No,' said Lucy hesitantly. 'He said his name was Entwhistle. Harry Entwhistle. But he said you were his son.'

'Huh! There you are, see. You got the wrong bloke!' he said, throwing out his chest and swaying back and forth on his heels. 'What am I going to do with you, girl? You are getting yourself in a real muddle these days. Better not tell any of your neighbours about this, they'll think you're going barmy.'

'But. . . .'

'No buts, come and give us a kiss, I've been out working all week while you've been running around the countryside playing detective.'

He pulled the doll from her hands and tossed it on to the sofa, but as he drew Lucy towards him she turned her face away. His jacket had a musty smell.

'Not in the mood tonight, aren't you, love?'

She didn't appreciate his tone and ignored his remark.

Neither of them spoke as she put paper and sticks in the grate and lit the fire. She let it burn for a while before adding the coal.

'The kettle won't take long,' she said flatly.

'I know what would warm us up,' he said. 'A nice drop of sherry. Your old mum always used to keep a bottle at the back of the pantry. Wouldn't be any left, would there?'

'Probably. Have a look if you like.' Lucy's voice was expressionless. She picked up the doll, straightened the long christening dress hanging loosely from its narrow shoulders, and rested it in her lap. From the pantry she could hear the sound of jars and bottles being pushed aside.

'Are you staying tonight, Arthur?' she said pointedly.

'Of course I am. Just like every Saturday night!'

'But how will you get home tomorrow?'

'On the train, of course,' he said, as he emptied the remains of the bottle into two small glasses. 'Like I always do.'

'But the ticket collector said there was no train on a Sunday.'

'No train?' he drawled. 'You must have got it wrong. Getting yourself confused again. I can see you need looking after.' He handed her a glass. 'I know what women are like. They go a bit funny in the head at certain times of the month.' He lifted the glass. 'Your good health,' he said, before running the contents of the glass into his mouth.

'Arthur,' she said, gazing into the fire. 'Will you marry me?'

A spray of sherry spurted across the room. 'What has come over you, woman?'

'I am serious, Arthur. If I stopped working would you support me?'

'What makes you ask a daft question like that?'

'Because I'm pregnant, Arthur. I'm going to have your baby!'

When Arthur left that night, on the pretext that he was going to the pub to get another bottle of sherry, Lucy never expected him to come back. She wasn't even sorry to part with the few shillings she loaned him. She considered it money well spent.

After that, she never saw Arthur Mellor or Arty Entwhistle again.

A few months later, on a foggy morning early in November, Lucy gave her notice to old Mr Camrass. For the second time she lied to her employer saying that she was going back into service for a while. And for the second time she felt terribly guilty about it.

During her last week at the antique shop, whenever Mr Camrass peered at her over his spectacles, she knew it was not to check her work. It was impossible for her to disguise her rapidly expanding figure.

'You realize that we will have to advertise your position, Miss Oldfield,' he said before she left.

'Yes, of course, Mr Camrass.'

'But you are welcome to call into the shop if you should ever decide to come back to Leeds.'

Lucy thanked him and said she would keep his offer in mind.

*

James Harrington Oldfield, a healthy six pound baby, was born on the 20 December, 1897. Lucy named him James after her father. Harrington was her mother's maiden name.

The following April, when James was almost four months old, she visited the antique shop. Having left her son with a neighbour, Lucy went alone.

It seemed strange entering the shop from the front entrance. The door bell was much louder than she had remembered, its ring vibrating along the row of silver cups, through the stacks of polished bowls to the elegant collection of candelabra.

When young Mr Camrass shuffled out from the back room, Lucy felt nervous, at first, not knowing what to say to him. The old gentleman, as always, was extremely polite, enquiring how she was and what she was doing. When she said that she was back in Leeds and looking for suitable employment, he asked her to wait, excused himself and shuffled back into the house. After a while he reappeared followed by his father.

Old Mr Camrass cleared his throat. 'We believe we will be parting with our current employee next week which means the situation which you filled will be vacant again.' He dipped his chin and looked at Lucy over his spectacles. 'Naturally, the hours and pay will be the same as before, but if you are interested, it would save us not only the necessity of advertising the position but of suffering the services of another new employee.'

Young Mr Camrass nodded in agreement. 'So hard to get competent workers these days. Today's young people have no appreciation of fine things.'

Lucy was relieved and delighted. Though it would not be easy for her to work full time, run a house and cope with a baby, having been in service meant the prospect of long hours did not daunt her. She found the job at the antique shop easy and knew exactly what was required. Though both Mr Camrasses liked to inspect her work on a regular basis, Lucy never minded that. Nor did she mind being kept busy. With new consignments arriving almost daily, the days and weeks passed quickly. And with the regular wage, she could manage to pay the rent, support herself and James, and have a few pennies left over each week, to put away.

Sally Swales, the young mother who lived across the street, was also happy to earn a few shillings each month by looking after Lucy's boy. With six children of her own, one more didn't make much difference.

Chapter 4

November 1905 – The Guy

'Don't you miss not having a man?' Sally said, one evening when Lucy called in to collect James.

'In what way?'

'You know what I mean?' she said, with a wry smile.

'I can't say I do, but why do you ask?'

Sally shrugged. 'It don't seem natural, good-looking woman like you, working every day and coming home to an empty house. Not to mention an empty bed.'

'You get used to it,' Lucy said.

Sally looked at her quizzically. 'Are you sure you're not kidding me? That you ain't got a man tucked away in the city somewhere? Maybe he calls into that shop you work at.'

'Goodness! What on earth makes you think that?'

'Well, I hear there was a dapper gentleman came down the street this morning asking after you.'

Lucy was puzzled.

'Knocked on several doors. Said he was looking for, "Miss Lucy Oldfield". He knew your name all right and said he'd been to the house before but he couldn't remember the number.'

Lucy's thoughts immediately jumped to Arthur Mellor. Was he back? Had his wife thrown him out? Was he hoping to take up where he left off? Surely, it couldn't be him. Granted, he usually looked smart, even though his clothes probably came from the market, but she would have hardly

43

called him a gentleman. The idea of him turning up out of the blue made Lucy shudder. No, she thought, even after all these years, Arthur could have found his way to the house with a blindfold on. 'Did the man leave a name?'

'I didn't speak to him. Her at number 38 did. But I gather he said he'd be back. And she said he sounded quite well-to-do.' Sally peered at Lucy eager for more information. 'That's why I wondered if you'd found yourself a gentleman at last.'

Lucy shook her head. 'Sorry to disappoint you, Sally, but I've no idea who the man is.'

'Penny for the guy?' the cry from a young voice interrupted them. It carried from the top of the street. With the nights already drawing in and no street lights, it was too dark to see who was calling.

'Penny for the guy?' This time it was Sam Swales.

'Penny for the guy?' echoed James.

The two women waited, listening. They could hear children giggling and the rumble of wooden cartwheels over cobbles. The voices carried down the row of terraced houses, like sound down a tunnel.

'What are they up to?' Lucy asked.

'It's Guy Fawkes' Day on Sunday. Didn't James say anything? The lads have been busy these last two weeks collecting stuff to burn. They've built a bonfire on the spare ground at the top of the street. You should see it, it's much bigger than last year's. They're very proud of their efforts. I thought James would have told you.'

Lucy shook her head. No, he hadn't told her. Perhaps because he knew she didn't like him playing on the rubble where the old mill used to stand.

The cries were louder as the group of children came into sight.

'Penny for the guy!' yelled James.

Lucy smiled tolerantly. Her son's hands and knees were filthy. He was wearing his cap cocked on the side of his head. The old muffler, wrapped around his neck, was tied under his chin and tucked into the front of his shirt, but he was wearing no jacket. He looked like a waif.

'Aren't you cold?' she asked.

'Not me!' he said, beaming proudly at the group of smaller children circled around him. 'Penny for the guy?' he crowed.

Lucy looked down at the cart and exploded. 'What do you think you are doing with that?'

'With what?'

'With that doll!'

James looked from his mother to the guy perched on the pile of sticks, its head poking from the neck of a child's threadbare overcoat, its legs buried in a pair of short trousers. 'That's Guy Fawkes!' he announced scornfully.

'No it is not!' Lucy yelled, grabbing the doll in one hand and her son in the other. 'Inside this minute, James Oldfield! That is not yours and you had no right to take it!'

'But, Mum. . . .'

'Inside!' she yelled.

'But it's just an old doll,' he whined. 'Look at it. It's got hardly any hair and it looks like a boy. It makes a great guy.'

The gentleman standing on the doorstep had a healthy colour in his cheeks. He spoke with a refined accent, was smartly dressed and carried a walking cane with a silver collet.

'You are Miss Lucy Oldfield, are you not?'

'Yes,' she said, cautiously wondering who the man was and the purpose of his visit. 'Is there anything wrong?'

He smiled. 'No, on the contrary,' he said. 'But I see you do not recognize me, though I remember you quite clearly.'

'I am sorry but . . .' As she studied his features she had some recollection of the face. But from where?

'Edward Carrington,' he said, holding out his hand. 'It is several years since we met. You were travelling to Skipton. We shared the same compartment on the train.'

Lucy inclined her head as she tried to gather the scant memories of that day, a day she had often wished to forget.

The man continued, 'You may think this very presumptuous of me, but may I come in and speak with you for a moment.'

Lucy glanced up and down the street. A woman standing at the washing line with a peg poised in her hand, looked away quickly.

'Please do,' she said smiling. 'It will give the neighbours something to talk about.'

After taking Mr Carrington's coat, she cleared a pile of linen from the sofa and invited the gentleman to sit down. Drawing up a straight chair for herself, Lucy asked him if he would care for some tea.

'No, thank you.' He paused and cleared his throat. 'I find this a little embarrassing as I feel you do not remember what we spoke of on the return journey. Thinking back, it was probably a little unfair of me to speak to you at the time. I recollect you were grieving the loss of your mother.'

Lucy nodded. 'It was not a good day for me. You will have to remind me of our conversation.'

The man spoke quietly, his eyes fixed on Lucy. 'You told me your mother had died and that you were on your own. You said you were unhappy and wanted to get away from here. You also said you had been in service at an estate in North Yorkshire.'

Lucy felt embarrassed having to admit she could not remember telling him all those things. 'Please continue.'

'Because you were so forthright, I found it easy to talk to you and relate the problems which were confronting me at the time. I explained that I was looking for a suitable companion for my wife, who had suffered an accident and was bedridden.' He leaned back in the chair. 'Although we had only met that very day, I took the liberty of asking you if you would consider the position. Do you remember?'

'I am sorry, Mr Carrington, my memory of our conversation is very vague. However, I do recall that you escorted me home and appeared concerned about my welfare. But one thing puzzles me,' she said, 'it is eight years since I took that train journey. Why have you waited all this time?'

He sighed deeply. 'My wife deteriorated rapidly and died a few weeks later. I found myself at a loss and decided to return to India where I had spent most of my early life. My father was a colonel in the army, you see.'

Lucy listened with interest as he became more relaxed.

'Having recently returned to England, I again find myself in need of assistance, but this time it is I who need someone to look after me.' He was quick to clarify what he was saying. 'A housekeeper. Not a companion. I have tried to obtain the services of a suitable woman through the usual channels but I find most of the applicants are too officious and I do not want to be subjected to a regimented lifestyle in my own home. You, however, appear to have an understanding nature and I don't doubt, with your years in service, you could contend with one quiet English gentleman.'

Lucy spoke as she moved the kettle on to the heat. 'I am sure your offer is very complimentary but I have a secure job, and,' she added, 'since we met on the train my circumstances have changed. I have a son to care for.'

'Ah, you must pardon me.' He stood up as if to leave. 'I did not realize that you were married. Your title. . . ?'

'No, I'm not married, though some folk call me Mrs out of politeness.'

He hesitated for a moment. 'Then please hear what I have to say. You do not have to answer immediately. I own three small cottages in the village of Horsforth just outside Leeds. You may know it.'

Lucy shook her head.

'On the day we met, I was travelling to Skipton to collect the title deeds from my solicitor. But that is not important. Currently I am living in one of the cottages while the other two remain vacant. My proposition is, if you are interested in keeping house for me, cleaning and preparing some meals, I can offer you one of the cottages rent free. And I will pay you a small wage beside.' He appeared embarrassed. 'Though they are quite old, the cottages are pleasant with a small garden at the front and a larger one at the back, where you could grow vegetables. And there is a school in the village.'

Lucy thought for a moment before replying. 'Mr Carrington, your offer sounds very appealing, but as a mother with the sole responsibility for my son, I must be practical. Presently I have a job which I have been in for eight years, a fair wage, and though the living conditions in this street are not always ideal, it suits me, and my son. I believe your offer is honest and genuine but I would hate to jeopardize what I have at the moment.'

'Then I shall press you no further. You must excuse me for taking up so much of your valuable time. But if for any reason you should change your mind . . .' As he got up, he pulled a piece of paper from his waistcoat pocket and handed it to Lucy. 'Here is the address should you wish to contact me. Now if you will excuse me.'

From the doorstep, Lucy watched as her visitor strolled down the street, his cane tapping on the pavement. Behind her in the kitchen, the kettle was spluttering.

*

The flames from the bonfire lit up the night and the guy, stuffed with straw and rags, burned bravely. When his wooden chair finally toppled it shot a shower of sparks high into the black November sky and the children cheered. Lucy watched from a distance, listening to the shrieks, mostly of laughter but occasionally of pain, as bubbling sap from a fallen twig burnt a child's finger.

Almost a hundred people were congregated on the site where the old mill had previously stood. There were folks from the rows of houses Lucy had never seen before. Neighbours who emerged on May Day, or New Year's Eve, or occasions like this to mingle and chatter like old friends, but for the rest of the year kept themselves strictly to themselves. Lucy wandered amongst them, exchanging pleasantries, but by eight o'clock was weary.

'Don't be too late,' she said to James who was helping to distribute the hot potatoes, roasted almost black in the bonfire ash. 'Come home with Mrs Swales.'

Walking home alone down the dark street, Lucy thought about Mr Carrington, the man who had visited her that morning. He appeared well mannered, pleasant and polite, but at first Arthur Mellor had seemed to be all those things too. She was conscious of her responsibilities, and though she liked the gentleman's offer she felt it sounded too good to be true.

Sliding the large key into the door lock she glanced over to the window sill and the wooden box where her mother used to grow daffodils. It was warped and empty.

It would be nice to have a garden, she thought.

Chapter 5

Horsforth

It was the burglary at the antique shop which upset Lucy and brought about her change of mind. It wasn't because the shop was broken into or that a constable was sent to the house to question her about her acquaintances, her family and her financial situation. That was disturbing enough, even though the officer assured her it was just a formality. What was far worse was that three weeks after the break-in, old Mr Camrass suffered a heart attack and died. Some said it was due to the stress he had suffered, others blamed January's bitter chill. No one mentioned the fact that he was in his ninety-second year.

After the funeral, it was obvious young Mr Camrass was lost without his father. He found it hard to cope in the shop and it was not long before his own health began to deteriorate. Lucy had not known there was yet another Mr Camrass, Mr Jacob Camrass, a great-nephew of the deceased. He arrived a few weeks later in mid-February to take over the business, supposedly on a temporary basis. Lucy found him knowledgeable about antiques, and efficient, but aloof and unapproachable, very different in nature from the two elderly gentlemen who had been her employers for the past eight years. Under the new management, the atmosphere in the shop was entirely different, and the work, which Lucy had enjoyed and taken pride in, became a chore. But, despite the change in her feelings and the nature of the proposition Mr Carrington had made, Lucy valued the position she held and was not prepared to give her notice until she had taken a train ride to Horsforth.

It was a fair walk from the station and uphill most of the way. By the time Lucy reached the outskirts of the village, the country road was skirted by fields and farms, but the dry-stone walls on either side of the lane blocked Lucy's view. With no sign of the cottages, she wondered if perhaps she was going in the wrong direction. Feeling weary, and on the point of turning back, she heard the clip-clop of horse's hoofs and the rumble of a wagon coming up the hill. As the farmer drew closer, he slowed his horse, tipped his cap and enquired where she was heading.

'Mr Carrington's cottages?' he replied. 'Just round the next bend and up the rise. No more than fifty yards. You can't miss 'em.'

Relieved, she thanked him. As the horse walked on, with the row of empty milk churns rattling on the back of the wagon, Lucy followed in the same direction.

When she rounded the bend, she caught her first glimpse of Honeysuckle Cottages and felt elated. The three adjoining cottages, set back only a few yards from the lane, had been freshly painted. The plum-coloured doors and windows contrasted warmly with the whitewashed stone walls. The low-pitched shingle roof appeared blue-grey. The building looked very old, but it was quaint and cosy.

The three small front gardens were enclosed behind a low stone wall. Tangled branches of climbing roses spilled across it into the lane.

How lovely they would look in full bloom, Lucy thought. How sweet the scent would be as it drifted through an open window.

A short pathway of crazy-paving led from each paling gate to the three front doors. The cottages were identical apart from the porch at the first one. A twisted old vine covering it cascaded down in a profusion of new leaves and early flowers. Lucy could smell the honeysuckle from the lane.

At the far end, the third cottage appeared nestled beneath the arms of an old horse-chestnut tree. As she watched, a flock of starlings burst from its boughs. For a while, they circled noisily above the branches, before flying away.

Lucy wasn't sure what she had expected, but the sight of the cottages made her pray that the gentleman's offer was still open. The thought of returning to the row of smoke-blackened brick terraces made her shudder.

Standing beneath the scented vine, Lucy knocked on the door of the first cottage. No answer. She checked the other two cottages. They appeared empty. Wandering around to the back of the building, she wondered if she would find the gentleman there.

The back gardens were bigger than those facing the lane. Another dry-stone wall enclosed them, separating them from a broad meadow. It was evident someone had been working outside. A fork was angled in a patch of freshly turned soil, a rake resting on a pile of leaves, a pair of Wellington boots standing on a worn mat outside the door.

From the back gate, Lucy gazed across the field to a row of trees and a small copse perched on the rise. The meadow was lush, rich with spring flowers. She could hear bees working busily, birds twittering. Why had she waited so long?

Beneath the twining branches of the honeysuckle, Lucy reread the letter she had written that morning. Satisfied with its wording, she slipped it back into the envelope, slid it through the letter box and heard it drop in the hallway. If Mr Carrington's offer was still valid, she would give her notice at the antique shop and move to Horsforth, but not before.

'I am not going!' the boy said defiantly.

'James! It's all organized!'

'I don't care! I'm not going with you!'

'You are being silly and I don't like to hear you talking like that.' Lucy lowered her voice. 'You will like the new house. There is a garden and a meadow.'

'What do I want a garden for? I want to stay here with Sam and the girls. I want to stay at Mill Lane School. You can go to Horsforth if you must and I'll stay here with Mrs Swales.'

'James! You do not live with Mrs Swales.'

'But I spend more time with her than I do with you.'

Lucy bristled though she knew what he had said was true. 'I've had to go out to work to keep us, but at Horsforth I'll have time to spend with you. Anyway,' she said, 'the arrangements are made and I do not intend to go back on them. I've finished at the antique shop and I start my new job next week. I've paid the last rent on this horrid house, and another family is moving in on Monday. The wagon will be here in the morning to collect our things and I will need your help. What's more, I do not want to hear any more of your foolish talk!'

James did not move.

Lucy picked up the doll from the sofa and fastened the button at the back of the neck. She dusted out the gown and pulled the fraying threads from its hem.

'Take the damn doll if you want someone to go with you,' he yelled. 'You think more of that doll than you do of me.'

'That is not true!'

'Stupid doll!' he shouted. 'You are always nursing it. Just like it was a baby. Mrs Swales says you nurse it because you can't have another baby.'

Lucy's face drained. 'James! That is a terrible thing to say! How dare you speak to me like that?'

'Well, it's true, isn't it? I ain't got no brothers and sisters, have I? And I don't have a father either.'

'And what does that have to do with us moving to Horsforth?'

'It's not fair,' he yelled. 'It's not damn fair!'

'James! Stop being daft! It doesn't matter what you think, we're going and that's final! And do not let me hear you swearing in this house again.'

'You won't! I'm leaving and I'm not coming back!'

The ornaments on the dresser rattled as he slammed the door. Lucy listened as he ran past the window and down the street. Anger and frustration were boiling inside her as she started after him, but she stopped herself before she reached the door. She knew she would never catch him, he was too quick, and if she shouted he would probably ignore her. He had never behaved like this before.

Lucy looked at the clock. It was five. Almost tea time. He would come in when he was hungry, she was sure of it. And later when he settled down she would talk to him calmly and make him understand.

Before doing anything else, she stuffed the doll to the bottom of a bag packed with linen. Best out of the way, she thought. She had no idea what had caused his sudden outburst. He hadn't objected to the move when she had first mentioned it. So why now? And what had caused his sudden outburst about the old doll? It had been in the house since before he was born. For Lucy, it was something which belonged there, like an ornament or piece of furniture, an object she took for granted, but missed if it wasn't there. He'd never complained about it before. Or had he?

Suddenly her thoughts flashed back to 5 November, the day he had taken the doll without her permission to use it as a guy. Had he really wanted to destroy it? To watch it burn on the bonfire? But why? Surely he wasn't jealous of the silly doll! It wasn't even pretty.

Putting the problem to the back of her mind, Lucy tried to think positively about the cottage in Horsforth, about moving, and the packing and cleaning she still had to do. But James's words kept nagging at her. And he had never run off before.

By 7.30 her concern turned to worry. A hurried visit across the street confirmed that he was not at Sally Swales' house. She tried two other neighbours but he wasn't there either. With the tea gone cold on the stove, she sat anxiously at the table listening to the clock ticking. By ten o'clock she was desperate.

James had run past the window and headed down the street. Pulling the shawl across her chest, Lucy set off in the same direction. Outside, the night air was cold and damp. Dimmed lamps glowed from behind curtains in upstairs windows. Most kitchens were in darkness. Most folk were in bed. She had to find him, and quickly.

'Have you seen a lad?' she said to man sitting on his doorstep polishing his boots. 'He's eight years old. He's not wearing a coat.'

The man shook his head.

She hurried to the main road at the bottom of the street.

A circle of yellow light reflected around the base of all the street lamps. It had been raining. Standing between the tramlines in the centre of the empty street Lucy spun around in all direction. Which way had he gone? What if he had begged a lift? He could be miles away. Behind her were the rows of houses; in front, the Leeds-Liverpool canal. Not more than fifty yards to the right was a set of locks. The area looked dark and forbidding.

'You 'right, luv?'

Lucy jumped. She hadn't noticed the man lying beside the path, propped on one elbow and nursing a bottle in his other hand.

'I'm looking for my son,' she said.

'Mind your step,' he drawled. 'A lot of rubbish gets thrown around here. Don't want to fall in!'

Lucy glanced at the murky water, coal black and still. It smelled foul.

Her stomach churned at the thought of James running along the bank, slipping over and sliding silently in.

'James!' she shouted. Her voice broke the night's silence. A dog barked. Barked again then stopped. Lucy picked her way along the bank, stumbling at times over obstacles she didn't see, never thinking of her own safety. Then she saw a dark silhouette sitting astride one of the lock gates. Her voice faltered. 'James!' she cried.

The boy looked up and raised his hand.

'Thank God!'

Mr Carrington helped James carry Lucy's furniture into the middle cottage. It was not an easy job as the passages were narrow and the heavy beams which ran across the ceiling meant there was little headroom. He had said the cottages were old but Lucy had not realized how old.

Individually, the rooms were smaller than at Loftholme Street, but each cottage had two separate rooms downstairs and a tiny kitchen. Upstairs there were two bedrooms. The windows were quite small but from the back of the house there was a view across the field to the patch of trees in the distance. From the kitchen door a path of broken slate led through the garden to the old iron gate which opened directly on to the meadow.

At Mr Carrington's suggestion, Lucy moved into the middle cottage. He explained that it would be more convenient for her if she had to run between the two on wet days. Furthermore, he said, the old chestnut tree kept the sun off the end cottage, and its back bedroom had a smell of dampness about it. It needed a good airing.

Despite having the front door wide open while they moved Lucy's possessions in, the new house was warm. Mr Carrington had lit the fire in both rooms early that morning.

As the empty wagon rumbled away, he turned to James. 'Have you ever ridden a horse, lad?'

'No, sir.'

'Then it's about time you learnt.'

James looked across to his mother.

'I like to ride and I enjoy riding with company. The countryside round here is ideal so I have arranged with the local farmer to lease the meadow at the back. Now all that remains is to purchase a couple of suitable horses. Every boy should be able to ride,' he said. 'I think I learned to ride before I learned to walk.'

Over the next few years James's education came on by leaps and bounds. Apart from his regular schooling, he learned how to ride and fish. He learned how to trap rabbits, shoot, and cure skins. How to chop wood, dig potatoes and grow beans from seeds. He learned to recognize the song of a willow warbler from a whitethroat and know the difference between a thrush's egg and that of a chaffinch. He learned how to identify a peacock butterfly from a painted lady, and learned the names of all the wild flowers which grew in the meadow. Mr Carrington was a walking encyclopaedia. The stories he told, of life in India and of his travels across the world, mesmerized James.

'When I am old enough I will join the horse guards and go to India,' James often said. Lucy would sit back with her knitting and listen to the pair talking late into the evenings.

From the day she moved into the cottage, when first he insisted she call him Edward, Mr Carrington was not like an employer. Though she prepared his meals and cleaned his cottage, and received a wage in return, for Lucy it was not like a job. She treated Edward as if he were an older relative who needed a little special care.

The more she came to know him and understand his ways, the harder it was for her to believe he had come from a disciplined army family. He was the most undemanding and patient man she had ever known, and despite their growing companionship he was always the perfect gentleman. He never forced himself on Lucy and James when he felt they did not need his company. Nor did he outstay his welcome when he was invited to share a meal or an evening with them.

James on the other hand was forever running to Edward's cottage, never knocking but bursting through the front door full of excitement, behaving as though the house was his own. Though Lucy reprimanded him, Edward assured her he was no trouble. And one morning when they were alone, he admitted how much he enjoyed having the boy around. He said, for him, James was the son he never had. From the first day, the pair thrived on each other's company.

A telegram delivered one afternoon upset Edward. It was dated 10 August 1910 and read:

Sorry to advise – Lydia very ill – Come immediately if possible Wainwright – Bombay

Chapter 6

The Accident

'Sit down for a moment, would you?' Edward's tone was serious. Lucy put down her duster. 'What is it, Edward? Are you worried about your sister?'

'Yes,' he said. 'But not only that.'

Lucy waited for him to speak.

'You have been good to me, Lucy,' he said slowly. 'It is strange how one changes as one gets older.' He paused. 'I love my sister Lydia, but we have lived apart for many years, and though she is my own flesh and blood, over the last five years I have come to regard you and James as my family.' He continued before she could interrupt, 'It is my duty to go to India. And I will be obliged to stay for however long is necessary. The problem is I do not want to leave here, or leave you and James.'

'But we will be here when you get back. You must not worry.'

'But I do worry. I worry about the journey – it is long and can be hazardous. I worry about the situation in India. The country has changed since I was a boy. I worry about the growing unrest in Europe, and the riots in the Home Counties with the suffragette movement. And I worry about leaving you alone.'

'James will care for me,' Lucy said. 'You have taught him so much and he is capable and strong.'

'You are a good woman, Lucy, and a good mother.' He paused. 'I remember the first time I saw you, on the Skipton train, how attractive I thought you looked. But you also looked a little lost, which was the way I

57

was also feeling then.'

'Edward, you've never told me that before.'

He smiled. 'It's true.' He leaned forward in his chair. 'Before I go there are things we must speak of.' He took out his pocket book and flipped though the pages. 'Firstly,' he said. 'I will arrange for your wages to be paid into a bank account. Do you already have one?'

'No, but I have a little money put away in a tin.'

'Then I suggest you secure it in the bank. If you will accompany me to Leeds next week I will assist you in opening an account in your name.'

'But I will not be working for you while you are away.'

'No, buts, please. Let me continue. Secondly, I intend to set aside some money to help with James's education. He is progressing well and I hope eventually he will go to the university. He has the brain for it.'

'But that is several years away!' The colour drained from Lucy's cheeks. 'Edward, you are speaking as though you have no intention of coming back.'

He touched her hand. 'I like to be prepared for all eventualities. Don't worry, Lucy, the booking I have is for a return journey even though I can't be certain when I will be returning.

'Now, another matter which I want you to consider. You don't have to answer immediately.' He looked directly at her as he spoke. 'Would you like to sail to India and visit me when I am there? If the answer is yes, I will arrange tickets for you both. It would be a wonderful experience for the boy.'

'Edward, that is very generous, but it is too much to offer. You are going because you are duty bound, but at this time I feel we should stay here. James has school and I have the cottages and gardens to care for.'

He stared down at the book in his hands.

'Perhaps,' she suggested, 'if you go again, then we could accompany you. I would not like to travel alone.'

'Yes! A splendid idea. We will do that.' He folded his pocket book and laid it on the chair arm. 'There is one more thing. How old are you, Lucy?'

It was a strange question.

'I was thirty-five on my last birthday.'

'As I thought. And I will be sixty while I am away. A considerable difference, is it not?' he said. 'After caring for me for five years, I think you know me as well as anyone has ever done. But what I ask is that while I am away you consider the idea of becoming my wife.'

'Edward?'

'I will say no more about it and I do not want your answer until I return. Now,' he said. 'I shall need help with my clothes for the tropics. They are packed away and will require airing. Until I get news of the sailing date I can't be sure when I will be leaving, but I would like to be prepared. Will you see to that for me?'

Lucy squeezed his hand. 'Of course, Edward.'

Less than two weeks later, Lucy and James waved Edward goodbye from Leeds station. As the guard waved his flag, Edward lowered the compartment window and leaned out.

'A safe journey,' Lucy shouted, as the train jerked forward.

James trotted alongside the compartment until he reached the end of the platform. As the engine clattered across the points and the train slowly turned away, the hand waving the white handkerchief was lost from view.

The station was smoky and cold. Outside in the middle of the square, the sun glinted on the huge bronze statue of a black-clad knight mounted on his prancing steed.

'The Black Prince,' said Lucy. 'His name was Edward also.'

'Was he a king?'

'No, but he was a great horseman and leader.'

'One day I will be like him,' James said.

Lucy did not reply.

It had been pouring for more than three hours. At times the rain, pelting against the kitchen window, sounded like tiny stones. The lane had become a river and a tributary was pouring under the gate into the front garden. A large pool had formed outside the front door and water was beginning to seep into the hallway.

Lucy was worried. James often rode for several hours on Sunday mornings, but he was always back well before it was time to sit down for dinner. It was over an hour since she had taken the roast out of the oven and now it was almost cold.

The sound she heard was his boot thumping against the kitchen door.

'Mum! Quick! I need help!'

Lucy opened the door. James was standing in the rain, shivering violently. His hair was stuck to his face and neck, his shirt sopping wet. In his arms he was cradling a child. She was wrapped in his overcoat.

'Goodness, James. What happened?'

Carrying the young girl into the living-room, he set her down on the sofa. 'Take care of her, Mum. I must get some help.'

'But what happened? Where did you find her?'

'On the moors. A wagon had gone over. Lost its wheel. The driver was dead – crushed underneath it. I didn't see her at first. She was cowering in the heather, wet through and freezing cold. At first I couldn't make her understand me. I don't think she is injured but she wouldn't speak.' He turned to the door. 'I must get some help and go back. There may be someone else stuck out there. I'll take Edward's horse.'

'But you're soaked to the skin! At least dry yourself.'

'I'll be all right. But I'll take my coat.'

Lucy slid it gently from around the child. Her eyes were open but she was staring blankly ahead.

'Be careful,' Lucy said, as she helped James into his wet coat.

'I will.'

As soon as he left, Lucy dried the girl's face and hair. But her clothes were soaking wet. After wrapping her in a blanket, she filled the hot water bottle and laid it carefully between the covers. Pushing the sofa closer to the fire, she added some wood.

With difficulty Lucy coaxed the girl to drink a little of the sweet tea she had brewed. 'What's your name?' she whispered, but the girl did not answer. Her hands were clasped tightly together, the knuckles squeezed hard against her cheeks. Sitting on the edge of the sofa, Lucy stroked her wet hair and hummed the nursery rhymes she used to sing to James. It was not many minutes before the drooping eyes closed and Lucy felt confident to leave her alone. She hurried up the stairs to find something suitable to dress her in.

She remembered the calico bag in the bottom of the wardrobe. It was full of linen and old clothes, including the nightshirts James had grown out of. One of the smaller ones would fit the child. Reaching in, she found an old cardigan. It had shrunk and no longer fitted her. There were socks too which were also too small.

Humming softly and without waking her, Lucy slipped off the girls' wet clothes and pulled the nightshirt over her head. The cardigan sleeves were far too long so she rolled them over several times. The girl was the size of one of Sally Swales' daughters – about nine years old.

It was after six when Lucy heard sounds from the lane. From the front door she could see her son and at least four other men with horses. The rain had stopped, but water was still streaming into the garden. James invited one of the men into the living room. 'Mum, this is Sergeant Wilkey.'

The man tipped his hand to his wet hair and leaned over the little girl. 'How is she, missus?'

'She's sleeping,' Lucy whispered. 'She drank a little tea and warm milk, but she won't eat anything.'

'Has she said anything to you? We have to know where she came from.'

'She hasn't spoken.'

He turned to James. 'And you say she didn't speak to you either?'

'Never uttered a sound.'

'Can you keep her here tonight, missus? Just until we find who she belongs to?'

'Of course.' Lucy turned to James. 'Did you say her father was dead?'

The sergeant answered. 'There was a man's body at the wagon. But we can't be sure it's the little lass's dad. Even if he is, they must have other folks somewhere and before long they should be out looking for them. Until that happens I shall have to notify the authorities and the girl may have to be taken into care.'

'She can stay here,' Lucy said defensively, recalling stories she had heard of the orphans' asylums. 'You can't move her now. I'll look after her.'

The sergeant sounded relieved. 'Right then! We'll leave her where she is till the morning. Let her have a good sleep. As for myself, it's been a long day and I've got to get that body down to the morgue.' As he turned to go, he took James's hand and shook it. 'You did a good job, young fella. If you hadn't come across them when you did, I reckon we'd have had two bodies by the morning.'

Lucy followed them to the door.

'If you have any problems with the lass, your son knows where to find me.'

James watched the men ride away before walking his horse around to the back of the cottages and the stable he had helped Edward build. By the time he came in he was tired but had no appetite for food. At Lucy's insistence, he swallowed one slice of meat, ate a cold potato, and drank a cup of cocoa, before going to bed.

The little girl asleep on the sofa looked pale and delicate. Seeing her lying there reminded Lucy of Miss Beatrice, the delicate child in the four-poster bed at Heaton Hall. Reminded her of the doll which had once rested in the crook of her arm. The doll she had stolen. The same doll she had forgotten about since she moved to Horsforth. It had been hidden away for more than five years. It was about time it was brought out and put to good use.

Chapter 7

Constance

Working by the window in the dim light of early dawn, Lucy stitched the pieces of cloth. She had cut the under-blouse from a scrap of white cotton put aside for a dusting rag and the tiny tunic from an old twill skirt. The cloth was coarse, rusty brown in colour and faded in parts. It was not exactly the material she would have wished to make a doll's school dress from, but it would suffice. After cutting a length of yellow ribbon to serve as a sash, Lucy was satisfied with the result. All that remained was to gather the stiches around the cuffs and sew a hem to the level of the ankles. The doll's lacy socks and buckled shoes were the ones it had been wearing when she had taken it from the Hall. They were still satisfactory.

As Lucy threaded another length of cotton, she realized the girl had woken and was watching her work. 'Would you help me?' she asked.

When the girl sat up and held out her hands, Lucy kneeled beside her and placed the doll on to her lap. 'There,' she said, as she carefully slipped the school dress over its head. Then she tied the sash into a neat bow at the back, and after gathering the cottons around the doll's wrists, pulled them tight and fastened them off neatly.

James stopped at the bottom of the steps. 'I see you have a helper.'

'Indeed,' said Lucy. 'We will be finished in a moment.'

The girl watched intently as Lucy ran a line of stitches along the hem. When she finished she cut off the ends of cotton and the doll's school tunic was complete.

'Now I will make some breakfast,' she said.

Crouching down beside the sofa, James took hold of the doll's hand. 'And what is your name?' he said addressing the wistful smile on the porcelain face.

The girl replied in a whisper, 'Constance.'

Glancing across to his mother, James winked. 'I'm pleased to meet you, Constance,' he said shaking the doll's hand. Then he turned his eyes to the little girl. 'And what is your name?'

'Alice,' she whispered.

'Hello, Alice. My name is James.'

'James,' she repeated.

Lucy smiled as she laid the cloth across the table. 'I didn't know you had a way with children.'

'And I didn't know you still had that old doll. I remember it vaguely from the old house. I seem to recollect you were fond of it.'

'Yes! And you and Sam Swales were going to use it for Guy Fawkes.'

'Was I really going to do that?'

Lucy laughed as she stirred the porridge.

'After breakfast I'll ride down to the police station,' James said. 'Sergeant Wilkey may have some news.'

'Good news, I hope.'

Alice wasn't listening, she was brushing her hand across the tufts of brown hair bristling from the doll's crown.

'When I come back, I will find something to fix that,' James said.

She looked up at him expectantly, her large brown eyes following his every movement. When he put his coat and hat on, she slid off the sofa. 'Can I come with you, James?' she said, her tone faintly anxious.

'Stay here and look after Constance,' he said. 'I won't be long.'

'Sergeant Wilkey said there have been no reports of missing persons. But he thought, because the accident happened on the moors' road, it's possible the pair were not from round these parts.'

Lucy sighed. 'So what will happen to Alice?'

'The sergeant asked if she could stay with us a little longer. He said we might get a visit from the Welfare Board, but it's just routine and you're not to worry.' James looked at his mother. 'Are you all right?'

'Yes,' she said. 'Just a little tired. I suppose I am missing Edward. I wish he was here now.'

'Cheer up. Let me show you what I have.' He pulled a small animal skin from his pocket. 'It's goat skin. From a kid,' he said.

Lucy turned it over in her hands. It was smooth and pliable, one surface rough, the other covered in tight black curls.

'Mohair,' he said. 'I'll cut a piece to fit the doll's crown. I have some glue,' he said. 'It will make a fine head of hair, don't you think?'

When Alice woke the following morning the doll she had named Constance was lying beside her. The sight of its new wig sent her running outside to find James. But James had left for school already.

Though Lucy spent the whole day talking with Alice and playing games, the girl was not content until James returned home. After dinner that evening, Lucy watched from the garden, as James led one of the horses around the meadow with Alice mounted on its back. She sat boldly astride the big mare, a hunk of mane grasped in one hand and Constance gripped securely in the other.

It was Thursday afternoon when the knock came at the door. Sergeant Wilkey was on the doorstep with a primly dressed lady of middle age.

'Mrs Oldfield,' the sergeant said. 'This is Alice's great-aunt, Miss Pugh.'

Lucy knew the call was inevitable. As she ushered the visitors into the living-room, she tried to smile.

'Miss Pugh is from Ilkley,' Sergeant Wilkey said. 'She is the aunt of Alice's father, the man who died on the moors.'

Lucy expressed her sympathy and listened as the woman explained she had been caring for Alice's mother who was heavily pregnant and poorly too.

'Yellow skin and swelled ankles,' said Miss Pugh, the stern expression on her face never faltering as she spoke. 'Not well at all. Doctor recommended bed rest until the baby's born. Least I could do for my nephew was to look after his wife. I knew he couldn't manage to see to her, what with work and the little one to mind, and her not being well and all.'

She said her nephew had a rented house in Horsforth, not far from Lucy. She said she knew he'd planned to drive to Ilkley the weekend of the accident, but when he'd failed to arrive, she blamed it on the rain. Knowing he only had the open wagon, she presumed he'd decided to postpone the visit until the following week.

'Never gave it a thought anything might be wrong,' the woman said.

The sergeant added that when he spoke to Mr Pugh's neighbours, they also didn't think anything was amiss. They'd seen him leave in the wagon, but when he never got home that night, they thought he'd decided to stay with his sick wife.

'Don't know what would have become of the little lass if your boy hadn't found her when he was out riding that afternoon,' the sergeant said.

The only good news from the whole wretched affair was that Miss Pugh had helped deliver a baby boy on the previous Tuesday. The infant was small and frail but the doctor thought he would survive. Unfortunately, Pansy, her niece was still far from well and the loss of her husband had been a setback to her recovery. Miss Pugh insisted the young mother and baby should stay with her in Ilkely until they were fit enough to return home. Now she was here with Sergeant Wilkey to collect her great-niece and take her back to Ilkley.

Saying goodbye was not only difficult for Lucy, it was confusing for Alice. The little girl was fearful of the sergeant who spoke in a gruff voice and was extremely tall, even without his helmet. She was also wary of her great-aunt who carried herself stiffly, never smiled, and had a strange vacant look in her eyes.

Not understanding what was happening or where she was to be taken, Alice clung to Lucy's skirt. Her plaintive pleas upset Lucy. She had enjoyed having the little girl in the house but it was obvious that Alice must now return to her mother. 'Take Constance with you,' Lucy said kindly. 'You can look after her now.'

Miss Pugh declined. 'You've done enough already.'

But Alice had the doll firmly secured in her arms and was not going to be parted from it.

'Take it!' Lucy insisted. 'The doll is yours now.' Bobbing down beside Alice, Lucy whispered in her ear. 'When you are back home and your mother is well, I will come and visit you.'

'Can James come too?' Alice asked.

'Of course.'

Sergeant Wilkey helped Miss Pugh into the trap and lifted Alice on to the seat beside her. As the rig rolled away, the little girl looked back and waved. The doll was perched on her lap, her arm was tightly clasped around its waist.

The house was quiet when James came home and for two days he said very little. In the evenings he would go riding for two or three hours, not returning until after dark. Though he never said it, Lucy knew he was missing Alice. But she was missing Alice also. And Edward. And now James, too.

Edward's letter was postmarked Bombay, India, 17 July 1911. It had taken two months to arrive.

James sat down and read it aloud:

My dear Lucy and James
By the time this letter reaches you I hope to be at sea. Wainwright and Lydia have decided to return to England and I will be travelling with them. Currently I am attending to the legal matters regarding the sale of their Bombay house. As I know from experience it is not easy to sell property in India as fewer Britons are investing in substantial houses in this region.

However, the house will be sold and as soon as soon as everything is settled we will book our passage.

Although Lydia is slightly improved from when I first arrived, her general condition is poor and I feel her health is continuing to decline. She shakes constantly and is unable to hold her head or hands still and is now finding it difficult to eat.

Wainwright is hoping to find a physician in England who will be able to help her and although the passage will be a strain, he feels it best to bring her home. Though I have not spoken at great length of my fears, his decision to leave India concerns me. They have lived in the tropics most of their lives and I fear my brother-in-law has forgotten how cold English winters can be. However, he has taken my advice to live in the south. When we return I will endeavour to find a house for them in Tunbridge Wells or on the coast. By that means they will be relatively close to the London hospitals and, I hope, far from the worst of the English weather.

I will contact you again briefly to advise the date of sailing but the next time you will hear from me proper will be when we disembark in Southampton. Do not expect me back in Yorkshire immediately. I feel it is my duty to assist Wainwright and Lydia in purchasing a house and in attending to the legal matters for them. Wainwright was a fine soldier, but I'm afraid he lacks a business brain. They have been good to me in the past and it is the least I can do.

I miss the cottage and the countryside of England and, of course, I miss you, Lucy and James. I was intrigued to hear about the girl Alice, and the way she entered your lives. I hope a friendship will blossom between the two families.

I hope Lydia and Wainwright will be settled by December but in any event, I intend, God willing, to be home in Horsforth to share Christmas with you.

My good wishes to you both

Your dear friend
Edward Carrington

Chapter 8

Pansy

When Lucy first visited Pansy at the old house she rented in the village, she was appalled. It was a cold, damp and dingy place backing on to the railway line. Pansy was still far from well and, in Lucy's opinion, she had returned from Ilkley and Miss Pugh's care far too soon.

Pansy was an anaemic-looking woman at the best of times, fine-boned with a sallow complexion and lank mouse-brown hair. She was softly spoken and sensitive, and the loss of her husband in the accident had deeply affected her. Apart from being emotionally vulnerable, she was also very gullible, believing whatever stories were told to her. But despite the traumas she had suffered, she was a devoted mother with infinite patience with her two children. The Pughs were not locals and though they had lived in Horsforth for some years, it appeared to Lucy that the young family had few friends.

Lucy visited every day for six weeks, helping with the chores and minding Alice and the baby when Pansy needed to sleep. When Pansy's health eventually improved, Lucy invited her to visit Honeysuckle Cottages, insisting that not only would the fresh air and exercise be good for her, but that the Sunday roast would ensure they all ate a good wholesome meal.

After the first visit, the weekend outing became a regular event.

Pansy would arrive at ten, exhausted after walking up the hill pushing the baby cart. Ten-year-old, Alice, however, was always full of life, excited to see James and looking forward to being taken for a ride on the horse.

If the sun was out, while the pair was riding in the meadow, Pansy would perch on the back wall and gaze across to the far trees decked in autumn gold, or wander beneath the broad boughs of the chestnut tree to slide her feet through the piles of fallen leaves. Sometimes she would walk to the woods searching for mushrooms and Alice would race up the hill after her. When she caught up to her mother she would take her by the hand and lead her back to the cottage.

Sinking exhausted into a chair, Pansy would quickly fall asleep, a contented smile curled across her face.

James looked forward to the Pughs' weekly visits. By November he didn't ride during the week as it was too dark by the time he got home from school. But on Sundays he would enjoy leading the horses around the meadow with Alice astride one of them. And when it was time for the family to leave, he would walk beside Pansy, carrying the baby in one arm and leading Goldie, with Alice perched proudly in the saddle. After seeing them safely home, he would ride back up the hill and out to the moors and not return until after the sun had gone down.

Never once did Alice visit the cottages without the doll hooked tightly in the crook of her arm. Pansy said she could never fathom why her daughter had called it Constance, as the family knew no one of that name. She also told Lucy that Alice and the doll had become inseparable.

'She won't let it out of her sight,' she said. 'She loved her father very much and used to go everywhere with him, but since the accident she has never mentioned him once. Now it's the doll she clings to.'

It promised to be a real family Christmas. Edward was coming home and Pansy and the two children had accepted the invitation to stay at the cottages until New Year's Day. Getting everything ready for Christmas reminded Lucy of the preparations at Heaton Hall. Decorations to be made, cooking to be done, and everything cleaned and polished until it shone. She remembered the sounds of the carriages, the chatter of house guests, children's parties and sumptuous banquets. Those were the good times before Miss Beatrice became sick.

It was at the Hall that Lucy had learnt how to weave holly into wreaths and now every year she collected a bundle of branches to make three wreaths, one for each of the cottage doors. This year had been a good season and the plump ripe berries glowed warmly against the waxy green foliage. The fruits on the mistletoe looked dull in comparison, but Lucy was happy, the sprig fastened over the front door would serve its purpose.

James and Alice spent the Sunday before Christmas sitting on the floor amidst pages of Edward's old newspapers, cutting lengths and gluing the pieces into paper chains. With Alice's direction, James strung them around the walls, and hung them from one corner of the room to the other. Lucy picked fresh ivy and laid it in swirls on the mantelshelf. Despite the frosts it had fresh shoots and green leaves. James potted a small fir tree in a square tin and stood it near the window. Lucy trimmed it with small ornaments and paper decorations.

It was an exciting week. Edward arrived back in Leeds on the Monday. The piano arrived the following day. It was an upright, made in Germany, which had belonged to his sister Lydia. As her health had worsened and she had realized she would never play again, she had given it to Edward. It had travelled a long distance, from India to Southampton then on to Tunbridge Wells. From there it went by goods train to Leeds where Edward met it and transported it home on the wagon he borrowed from Mr Fothergill, the local dairy farmer. When it eventually arrived at Honeysuckle Cottages, Edward announced the piano was to be installed in Lucy's front room. Though she argued against it, he insisted. The piano was soon to become the centre of attraction.

Edward proved he could play a little but his repertoire was limited. But whenever he played, Alice would stand beside him following his fingers. It was Edward's hope that James would take lessons and with that in mind presented him with a box of sheet music which he had bought for sixpence at a market stall in Tunbridge Wells.

It was after he had been playing on Christmas Eve that Edward asked Alice to address him as Uncle Edward. He also insisted James call him, Edward or Ted, saying he had always hated being called Mr Carrington.

Perhaps, Lucy thought, it made him feel old. When she looked at him closely she could see he had aged visibly in the twelve months he had been away. There were lines on his brow which had not been there before, and though he appeared relaxed and happy, he seemed constantly tired. Occasionally she noticed him looking pensive and attributed it to the worry over his sister's health. She hoped his wearied look would pass when he had been home for a while.

Apart from the joy Edward derived from watching the children, he also enjoyed the company of the two women. He teased them about the latest events happening in London telling them what damage 'those wild independent women', were causing. He spoke of speeches and protest rallies and placard-waving suffragettes marching through the streets. Lucy found his conversation exciting but Pansy appeared embarrassed by the actions of the women, preferring to talk about the seeds she had planted, or the lavender bags which she had been making to sell at a local shop. Though she had only earned a few shillings from her enterprise, she was proud of her efforts and said the extra money helped.

Squeezing everyone around the table for Christmas dinner was not easy. Edward carved the turkey and opened a bottle of wine which he had brought with him from the south. After lunch there were presents; a copy of *The Hound of the Baskervilles* for James, and for Lucy an embossed leather volume with blank pages to use as a diary. There was a teddy bear for little Timothy, a bar of scented soap for Pansy and an Indian doll dressed in a silk sari for Alice. The costume was exquisite; the threads running though the material glistened like gold. It made the brown tunic which Lucy had made for Constance, look decidedly dull. Alice was delighted with Edward's gift, but the old doll retained its pride of place.

After the presents had been passed around, the two families played charades, excusing Edward when he fell asleep. In the evening, they sang carols and no one noticed that the piano was slightly out of tune. It was one of the best Christmases Lucy could remember.

The next morning, Alice asked Edward to play the piano for her and show her a few simple exercises. Her attentiveness surprised him. James, however, was less enthusiastic to learn. He was content merely to sit and watch. When he eventually became bored, he suggested they give the horses some exercise. Edward agreed it was a splendid idea.

The weather was fine when they left the cottages, even a little sunshine filtering between the clouds, but before they returned home an icy wind, peppered with sleet, had blown up. Despite being warmly dressed, Edward suffered from the cold and when they got home he was stiff and sore. That was the last time James and Edward rode together.

Because Pansy and the two children were staying with Lucy, Edward never broached his question about marriage. At times Lucy wondered if she should say something about it, but decided it could wait until later.

A telegram, delivered on the afternoon of New Year's Eve, put a damper on what would have otherwise been a happy evening. A freak storm had deposited a blanket of snow across the south of England. Edward's brother-in-law, Wainwright, had slipped on the step and broken his hip, and Lydia was suffering bouts of severe depression. They needed his help urgently. Edward tried to hide his concern but Lucy knew he would not refuse their request for help. He regarded it as his duty.

'Is there anything I can do?' Lucy asked.

'Nothing.'

'How long will you be gone?'

'I cannot say.'

Edward packed one bag and left on the midweek night train to London. He said he had business to conduct in the City and intended to travel on to Tunbridge Wells two days later.

Lucy didn't go down to see him off. She bade him farewell from the house. As they stood in the doorway, beneath the sprig of mistletoe which they had joked about on Christmas Day, she could see the tears in his old eyes. He was happy at Honeysuckle Cottages and it was a wrench for him to leave the friends he had come to love. Lucy feared he was not strong enough to cope with the situation he was going into. When he had left for India she had expected him to return: this time she was not sure.

*

Lucy was pleased to receive a letter from Edward a few weeks later. He wrote saying he had bought a small flat close to his sister's house. He had also arranged for a resident housekeeper, and engaged a nurse to visit on a daily basis. By those means the physical and practical needs of both Lydia and Wainwright were largely taken care of. Wainwright was improving week by week, with the probability he would eventually walk again, albeit with a pair of sticks, but Lydia's mental condition was unchanged.

Being in the flat allowed him time to read or write or take walks in the nearby park. It also allowed him time to think. He said he had been doing a lot of thinking and that Pansy's situation had been of concern to him. After observing how well both families got on together, he said he had been considering offering Pansy a lease on the end cottage. He thought a peppercorn rental of one shilling a year would be appropriate, but would not go ahead with any agreement without Lucy and James's approval. He assured her, if any problems should arise, he would terminate the arrangement immediately.

After reading the letter, James had no second thoughts. He wanted to tell Pansy straight away. Lucy agreed, and wrote back to Edward advising him to go ahead.

The following week, when Pansy opened her door and found Lucy and James standing on her doorstep with serious expressions on their faces, she feared something dreadful had happened. But when they told her of Edward's offer, she almost collapsed into James's arms. She was overjoyed. Never again would she have to worry about finding money for the rent. Alice was thrilled at the prospect of living next door to James, and Lucy, though she tried to hide it, was delighted about having Pansy, Alice and little Timmy as neighbours.

Because Pansy had been forced to sell off some of her furnishings to support herself and the children, she had few possessions. What furnishings remained in the house were solid but basic. Her husband had been a good craftsman.

When Miss Pugh heard about the move, she made one trip from Ilkley to Horsforth to deliver a suitcase of linen which had belonged to her mother. When they were alone, the spinster confided in Lucy that she had worried about Pansy's future, with no man to support her. Though Lucy never enquired, Miss Pugh made a special point of explaining that she managed adequately on her own because she lived frugally. She said she owned her house, which had been bequeathed to her and received a small income from a trust. Unfortunately it was insufficient for her to provide any financial help to her niece. The spinster told Lucy she considered Edward Carrington's offer to Pansy exceedingly generous, then her mind wandered to unrelated matters and she never spoke of it again.

Edward returned to Horsforth for a short visit in the August of 1912 and again in May of 1913. Lucy felt that since he had slipped back into a bachelor existence, a gap had opened between them and that he was ageing rapidly. His pace had slowed and his back, once straight, curved markedly from the neck. His cheeks, which had glowed with the warmth of India, were now sallow and sunken. The children, too, seemed to sense a change, and though they enjoyed his visits, quickly became bored with his repetitive conversations.

Alice, however, was always anxious to play something for him.

Apart from providing the piano, Edward had engaged a lady to give James lessons. Every Saturday morning, Alice would sit in the front room and observe, and when the music teacher left, she would practise James's lesson repeatedly until she mastered all the notes. While James hardly ever practised, Alice was determined to learn to play and it was not long before she became quite accomplished.

The late spring of 1914 was near perfect. Alice celebrated her fourteenth birthday and, though James didn't seem to notice, was already blossoming into a woman. Timmy was no longer a baby and as Lucy minded him three days a week, Pansy was able to earn some money in the village working as a domestic maid.

Lucy enjoyed reading Edward's weekly letters in which he wrote of trips he took to the seaside or the City, and of the walks he enjoyed in the town's parks and gardens. She enjoyed her own garden, cultivating a variety of vegetables, pottering outdoors in the lengthening daylight hours. In the evening she would sit and spin, or sew, while James went out riding. Nineteen-fourteen was James's final year at school and his application to attend the University in Leeds had been accepted. He was planning to start his course in September.

One warm August afternoon, Lucy was enjoying the scents of the garden, when she was surprised by the sight of James running up the lane. He was shouting and waving his arms, but until he got close she could not make out what he was saying.

'War has been declared!' he yelled. 'The country needs men! I'm going to join the army.'

'But, James, you're just a boy.'

'No, I'm not! I'm old enough. I'm going to fight for England. It's my duty!'

Chapter 9

War Effort

James was infuriated. The first recruitment drive was for men eighteen to thirty which meant waiting four months until his birthday. He envied his friends who had already enlisted and were now in training. Some had already sailed to Europe. Joining the army was all he wanted to do: university was no longer an option. He would occupy himself until the 20 December – then he would enlist.

'But why are you so determined to go to war?' Lucy asked. 'You may be maimed or killed.'

'You don't understand, Mum. I have to! And if Edward were younger, he would go too. It's the right thing to do. It's up to every man who is fit to fight for the country and if he doesn't enlist he's a coward.'

Nothing Lucy could say would change his mind. She pinned her hope on the rumour that the war would be over by Christmas and the troops would be sent home. Maybe he would not have to go.

Alice gave little thought to the war or the future. She cared only for the present and was pleased to have James home everyday. That August holiday, she had more time with him than ever before. They went out walking, or riding together. They talked for hours about nothing in particular and in the evenings James listened as Alice played.

After seriously considering that James was using the war as an excuse not to study, Lucy dismissed the idea, but as Edward had provided the money for his on-going education, she felt obliged to write to him for advice. She did not expect him to discourage James from enlisting. She knew Edward's views on doing one's duty, but she felt that her son would listen to Edward's advice.

Two weeks after she had written, a reply came back. It was not addressed to Lucy but to Mr James Oldfield. It bore the Tunbridge Wells postmark and was dated 15 October, 1914. After reading it James passed it to his mother.

My dear James
Let me offer you my hearty congratulations!

Your mother tells me you intend to enlist on your eighteenth birthday. I admire you, and envy you. I think it will be the best decision you have made in your life.

Men who have served in the military are revered and admired. I am thinking here of my father and Wainwright, my brother-in-law, who served in the army in India and South Africa respectively. I know from my upbringing, that discipline builds character, and active service builds courage. I am also keenly aware past service is a passport into all walks of life. It is a path I never followed and because of this I shall go to my grave with regrets; regrets that I never made the effort, disappointment in my younger years when I was bypassed for promotion, and regret I never experienced the satisfaction of being the victor.

Being in my 62nd year, I am now too old for active service but I am pleased to say I find myself in demand to serve England in other ways. It is rumoured that if the war is prolonged (I hear talk in the City that the war will NOT be over as quickly as originally thought), England will suffer from not only a shortage of food, but also a shortage of workers to do the common jobs.

Thousands of men are being sent to fight on the Continent and, as you know, there will soon be another wave of enlistments. These soldiers will not return to England's shores until the war is over. Because of this there is a growing demand, at home, for those who are too old to fight on the front.

Naturally, I have volunteered my services and have been offered various positions, from munitions factory overseer to correspondence scribe. I declined these and other offers because they are in London. I have, however, accepted a job here in Kent, based in Tunbridge Wells. This means I can travel daily from my flat and will never be too far from my sister and Wainwright.

As I am neither farmer nor teacher, the role I have accepted may sound a little unusual. I am to organize the enlistment of young women to work on the land doing the jobs usually done by the menfolk. These young ladies will be taught how to cultivate the soil, plough the fields and plant and harvest crops. If the project is successful and the war continues, this type of activity will become widespread throughout Britain. I will write and tell you how the work progresses.

In the meantime, I gather from your mother you are currently looking for something to occupy yourself. Perhaps I can suggest a few things. These will not only help Lucy and Pansy but will allow them to contribute to the war effort in a similar manner to my own.

Here is a list:

1) Increase the number of sheep (ewes) you have and buy a ram. Speak with John Fothergill, the farmer who leases the meadow to me.

2) Acquire one or two hand ploughs (again speak with Mr Fothergill) and train both riding horses to work in the shafts. It is essential you take on this chore. It would be too difficult for the ladies.

3) If time permits and the ground is not too hard, plough the field in preparation for spring. Dig up the back gardens and grow vegetables.

4) Use some of the money set aside for your schooling to stock up on preserves. Fill the pantry, and if you run out of space, store them in the attic – it is dry and clean.

If the conflict in Europe is resolved by the New Year nothing will be lost. You will have a bountiful supply of provisions.

Dear James, you may think these words are the rambling of an old man but do not take them in vain. The coming years may be leaner than we have ever known. Think of your mother and Pansy. How will they manage when you are away?

I suggest you make provision for them now. On that note I will close. Give my fondest love to your mother, and pass my good wishes to Pansy, Alice and Timothy.

Write to me when you are abroad.

Regards as always,

Your dear friend
Edward Carrington

*

'I'm not strong enough,' Pansy argued, when first confronted with the hand plough. 'It's too heavy! I'll never push it!'

'You don't have to push,' James said. 'Just keep the blade half covered and follow Goldie. The horse will do the work.'

Wearing a pair of James's old boots and with her skirt tucked up at the waist Pansy was determined not to be beaten. 'If Lucy and Alice can do it, then I will do it too,' she said, as each morning she persevered until she mastered the implement. James realized Pansy's frail appearance was deceptive. She was both fit and strong. Living in the country had done her good.

The Indian summer of 1914 lasted well into October and with the bout of steady rain the soil was soft. As Edward's horse trudged across the field, the simple plough turned a furrow of earth behind it. At first the ruts drew zigzag patterns across the meadow, but slowly, as James showed the women how to work with the plough rather than against it, the lines became straight and parallel. As Pansy learned to control the horse, the satisfaction became etched in her smile.

Using both horses and two ploughs, it took the women less than three days to turn the whole of the meadow. James watched from the stable roof where he was working. When Alice lost control of the plough and slid sideways into the soil, he almost fell off the ladder. The horse stopped, turned and snorted at her lying in the furrow, her hands and face streaked in soil. Alice was sure it was laughing at her, too.

James bought timber and netting and erected a new hen house in Pansy's back garden. In the past, the chickens had been allowed to range freely but slowly they had disappeared – victims of the local foxes. He made sure the vermin would not get into the new run.

There was quite a commotion the day he arrived home with two sacks of live pullets. Timothy delighted in running through the hen house, making the birds squawk and sending birds and feathers flying. After being scolded, the three-year-old watched anxiously as James clipped their wings.

'Will it hurt them?' he asked.

'Of course not.'

On those late autumn evenings, with the smell of jam bubbling on the stove, the two families busied themselves preparing for Christmas. There was plenty to do. Fruit for the cakes and puddings to be washed and dried, flour to be sieved as fine as dust, apples to be wrapped and put away, jars to be boiled, filled and labelled.

Late in the evenings, Alice would play the piano and even though there was no fire in the front room, James would take his paper and sit with her until they were both called for supper.

By late December the pantries in all three cottages were stocked fuller than they had ever been. Apart from the bags of flour, salt and sugar, the shelves were stacked with pots of preserves, jars of sweet chutney and pots of pickled eggs.

James's eighteenth birthday fell on a Sunday. The following morning he presented himself at the barracks in Leeds. After being declared fit, he swore the oath with a group of six other men, but much to his frustration, he was told he must wait until mid-January to join his regiment.

Lucy and Alice were quietly pleased. Christmas Day would not be the same without him, especially as Edward could not join them. Lucy wanted to make sure it was a Christmas they would all remember.

The two families had agreed that this year they would have Christmas dinner in Pansy's cottage. With Timmy's help, Alice made the yards of paper chains to decorate her living-room. James found a small fir tree in the woods which he potted and placed next to the piano and, as usual, Lucy made three holly wreaths, one for each cottage.

As Pansy hammered a nail into her front door on which to hang the decoration, a man called to her from the lane, 'That looks right pretty, luv.'

'It does, doesn't it?' Pansy said, smiling. She didn't know the fellow, but with half-a-dozen dead rabbits hanging from his shoulder, thought he must be local.

'What about a nice hare or rabbit for dinner on Boxing Day?' he said.

Pansy thought for a moment. She could make a rabbit stew. She was sure James and Lucy would enjoy it. 'Are they fresh?'

'Fresh this morning. Shot 'em clean through the head. No damage to the flesh. Have a look if you like.'

'How much?'

'A shilling apiece. Three for half a crown.'

'Can you wait a minute?'

'I've got all the time in the world for you, luv!'

Pansy didn't notice the sly wink as she hurried inside. She returned with the shilling piece. 'I haven't seen you in the village. Do you come from these parts?'

'I get around,' the man said, as he unhooked one of his carcasses. 'How long you been here?'

'Almost four years,' she said.

'And you got kids?'

'Yes, a boy and a girl.'

'Nice family,' the man said, adjusting the load on his shoulder. 'I'll be back in a few days to collect the skin. Happy Christmas!'

'Happy Christmas to you!' Pansy echoed.

The man was whistling as he wandered down the hill towards the village.

That evening, the smell of mince tarts wafted into Lucy's front room where James and Alice were singing out the final verse of 'Good King Wenceslas'. Sitting in the armchair by the kitchen fire, Lucy was dozing when a noise woke her. It was a strange sound and it was coming from next door. Thinking it might be a chicken squawking with a fox at its tail, she grabbed the broom and ran into the back garden. Only when she was outside did she realize it was Pansy's cry. Her neighbour was screaming and black smoke was billowing from her kitchen door.

'James! Alice!' she yelled. 'Quick! The house is on fire!'

Chapter 10

Stanley Crowther

Within seconds of the candle toppling, the Chinese lantern ignited in a ball of fire and flames leapt to the paper decorations. With hardly a sound the fire ran right and left, consuming the chains, link by link, and at the same time, scattering burning fragments on the floor and furniture. Pansy had swung at the flames with a towel but her efforts had succeeded only in fanning the blaze. By the time the others arrived, the curtains were alight.

'Water!' shouted James. 'Buckets! Bowls!'

The thick smoke swirling overhead suffocated some of the blaze but when the running flame reached the corner of the room, the fire flared again. The longest chain hanging diagonally across the room seared from the wall and like a fiery dragon's tail curled and twisted before drifting down.

'Alice! Get out of the way!' James screamed. Too late. The length of burning paper settled on her shoulder and slithered down her back. Within seconds her hair was alight and the back of her skirt burning like a torch.

Too shocked to scream, she dashed at the flames with her hands.

James grabbed the rag rug and rolled her to the ground in it. Lucy fought the fire, desperately hitting the other trimmings from the wall while Pansy ran back and forth with buckets and James directed the water at the burning woodwork.

Only when the fire was finally out did the three sink to the floor, blackened, coughing and exhausted. For a while no one spoke. They had beaten the blaze before it had really got hold. The acrid smoke, the smell of singed hair and scorched cloth would fade in a few days. The ceiling beams, though charred and steaming, were strong and thick. The damage to the cottage could have been much worse. They had been lucky.

But Alice was not so fortunate. Since James had laid her on the floor she had not moved. Her hands were burned black. One side of her head was bald, her scalp red and raw. Where the fire had burned through her skirt, it had charred the skin from the back of her legs. As she lay on the floor, James knew it was serious.

'I'm going for the doctor!' he said.

After spending two weeks in Leeds Infirmary, Alice hobbled up the path from the taxicab. James had wanted to carry her but she wouldn't let him. Feeling helpless, he tried to chide her playfully for being independent but her forced smile couldn't hide the pain she was suffering. Unable to bend her legs, she swung them stiffly and leaned heavily on his arm.

As she lowered herself down on the bed, he could see tears shining in her dark eyes. At times her face bore the same desolate expression he had seen on that unforgettable day when he had found her on the moors.

'I can't go away and leave you like this,' James said, gently covering her with a cotton sheet.

Her voice was little more than a whisper. 'It's your duty, James. I will be all right.'

He wanted to hold her in his arms. He wanted to touch her hands but they were swathed in bandages. He wanted to sit beside her on the bed and stroke her hair but he dare not in case he hurt her.

'I love you, Alice,' he said, realizing for the first time how much she meant to him. 'Damn the army! Damn the war!' he yelled.

Alice smiled. 'You'd better not let your mother hear you swearing like that!'

'Promise you won't tell?'

'I promise.'

When James climbed the stairs to Alice's bedroom the following morning his feet felt heavy. He had come to say goodbye. His waiting was over.

Now he was going to join his regiment. But his burning desire to go had waned. Now he was angry with himself for being selfish. He regretted his eagerness to enlist more than he had regretted anything else before. It was as if the fire which had burned Alice's hands and hair had consumed his energy to fight. If only he could wait six months until she recovered, then he could leave and not feel as guilty.

Though he tried to sound positive, he knew his voice lacked conviction.

Alice listened but had little to say. She realized it was unlikely he would come home again before his company was sent to Europe. James knew it too. He would not see her until he came back from the war and neither of them knew when that would be.

Leaning down he kissed her cheek.

'Take care,' she called, as he turned away.

James wasn't able to reply.

Alice listened to his footfall on the stairs. Heard the front door creak open. Heard her mother's muffled voice. The words, 'Good luck!' echoed by Timmy's high pitched cry. Heard the front door close. Lying alone on the bed, listening to the silence, Alice knew that James had gone.

On the chair beside the bed Alice's old doll sat upright, her luminous blue eyes fixed on the window across the room. The porcelain face was dirty, streaked with smoke from the fire, the tunic smeared with ash. Alice reached out her bandaged hands. She wanted something to hold. But as she touched the doll it wavered on the chair and almost fell.

Pushing her face deep into the pillow, Alice closed her eyes and wept.

Pansy heard the cry from the lane: 'Skins! Rabbit and hare!'

'Just a minute,' she replied, as she collected the dried skin and took it to the man at the front gate. As he opened his sack, Pansy dropped it in.

'Have you got any more rabbits,' she asked. 'My daughter likes the stew. She's been sick and it's helping her get better, so I don't mind paying.'

'I'll bring a couple next week. And seeing your daughter's sick, I'll only charge you for one.'

'That's very kind of you, Mr. . . ?'

He winked. 'Stan Crowther's the name, but you can call me Stan.'

She hesitated for a moment. 'Do you do odd jobs, Stan?'

'Depends on what you have in mind?'

'The tree out the back of the cottages lost a big bough in the wind last week. It landed on the garden wall. It needs chopping up, and the wall needs rebuilding otherwise the horses will get out.'

'You got horses, eh?'

'They're my neighbours.'

'Where's your man? Gone to war, has he?'

'I'm a widow,' Pansy said.

'Sorry to hear that. What about the missus next door?'

'She's on her own too. Her lad went off a few weeks ago.'

'So you've got no men around. How do you manage?'

'We're not useless! We manage all right with most stuff. But that limb's too heavy to shift.'

'Heavy, you say?'

'If you can't do it, my neighbour says she'll get someone from the village to do the job.'

Rubbing the stubble on his chin, Stanley Crowther glanced up to the dense canopy of bare branches extending over the roof of the cottage. 'I'll think about it,' he said. 'Perhaps I'll take a look next week.'

Pansy smiled. 'Next week then.'

'What did you say his name was?' Lucy asked.

'Stanley Crowther. He's the man who brings the rabbits. I got two more this morning. Alice likes the stew.'

Lucy stood at Pansy's kitchen window regarding the man working in the meadow just beyond the back wall. As she watched, he leaned the axe handle against his thigh, arched his back and glanced up at the tree. In the chill of the morning Lucy wasn't sure if it was moist breath or tobacco smoke blowing from his mouth.

'He's not doing enough to warm himself up!' she said cynically. As she spoke, Crowther spat on his palm, grasped the axe handle and swung it above his head bringing it down hard on the bough. After a dozen strokes he stopped, lifted his cap and wiped his sleeve across his brow.

'And where does this Stanley come from?'

'The other side of the moors.'

'How does he get here? Surely not on that old bicycle?'

'I don't know,' Pansy said, not lifting her head from her ironing. 'He's doing a good job, don't you think?'

Lucy frowned. 'How much did he say he would charge?'

'He didn't, but he said it wouldn't be much.'

Shaking her head, Lucy wandered out into the back garden. The chickens, expecting some scraps, squawked. On hearing the noise, the sheep trotted towards the gate. Lucy looked at the small flock. Last season's lambs had grown well, they were almost the size of the old ewes.

The man had heard the hens and was looking Lucy's way but he didn't acknowledge her. Leaning down he swung the axe again. This time she heard the timber crack.

What was it about this man which irritated her? There was something about him she did not like. It was a feeling she'd experienced before. She shivered. It was cold outside.

The trees on the far hill were bare but in a few weeks it would be spring and their branches would meld in a haze of fresh green. She thought of James. Wondered if his regiment had reached the Continent. Wondered where he was and if Europe was already warmer and greener than England? She wondered what the countryside of France was like. If the flowers were out in the meadows. It was hard to comprehend a war fought on fields bursting with the fragrance of spring.

'Aunt Lucy!' Alice's voice startled her. 'You look worried, Aunty.'

'I was thinking of James.'

'I think of him all the time,' Alice murmured.

Lucy smiled sadly. 'Let's go inside, dear. The wind is cold.'

'Will you help me with my bandages? Ma says you're a good nurse.'

Lucy nodded and followed Alice inside.

The weak morning light fell across the girl's hands as she rested them on the table. Lucy unwrapped the lengths of cloth with care. When the final turn was unwound, Alice held out her hands and screwed her face. 'They look like a pair of hen's feet! Don't they?'

Turning them over Lucy sighed. 'They need fresh air and exercise!'

Alice's laugh was half-hearted.

'I'm serious, girl!' she said, running her fingers across the coils of twisted skin puckering the once soft palms. 'I'm no expert but I think you must leave the bandages off. If you don't start using your fingers soon you'll never use them again.'

Alice looked at her claw-like hands. They were stiff as dried clay. The yellow-brown scars across her palms which reached right around her wrists looked as ugly as the one running down her neck, only partly covered by her short hair.

'I want to be a nurse,' Alice announced suddenly. 'I want to help the men who've been burned in the war.' She looked into Lucy's eyes. 'I won't be able to do it if I can't use my hands, will I?'

Lucy brushed the hair from the girl's face and smiled sympathetically.

'Will I, Aunty? Tell me honestly.'

'I believe nursing isn't easy.' She paused. 'The girls who do it have strong hands and agile fingers.'

'But it's what I want to do!'

Lucy rolled up the strips of cloth. 'No more bandages! I've some white gloves upstairs, you can wear those. But you must keep away from the rose bushes and out of the hen house. You don't want them to get infected and go bad.'

'But what can I do to make my fingers work again?'

Lucy thought for a moment. 'Stretch your hands and wiggle your fingers, and when they start to work, play the piano for me. I have missed hearing your tunes.'

That evening Lucy sat beside the fire and reread the first three letters James had written to her some time ago. All three had been posted in England within a period of six weeks. She smiled as she opened the first one. It was etched with youthful enthusiasm.

James wrote how proud he was to wear his uniform despite the coarse cloth making his neck itch and the boots rubbing skin from his heels and ankle bones. He said he was pleased he had learned to shoot long and straight and had Edward to thank for teaching him that. He said the training was tough, but he was revelling in the company of other boys who, like himself, shared a sense of freedom at being away from home for the first time. He was counting the days when his regiment would sail for the Continent. It was obvious to Lucy, the thrill of going to war excited him.

The second letter was shorter and though it still bore an air of elation, it was tinged with frustration. He was tired of basic training, PE and more

PE, drill and more drill, and a sergeant who seemed to dislike every new recruit, particularly the young lads like himself. But he said he was not alone.

The third letter had been posted in Dover the day before he sailed. Never had a boy sounded more proud to be going to fight for his country.

As Lucy gazed into the fire, she was pleased for him and proud of him too. Every mother should be proud to see her son go to war, to fight for England – the posters on the streets and in the daily papers reminded her of that fact. But it didn't stop her worrying. Every night she prayed for James. Prayed that he would survive the war and one day return home safely. But she was aware the predicted early end to the conflict had never happened and that the war in Europe was worsening. The army needed more men and rumours that the government was considering conscription were strengthening. Lucy knew it was every woman's duty to encourage her husband, son or brother to enlist. Enthusiasm for the war was infectious and throughout the country men were responding in their thousands. The fact that on the battlefields hundreds were dying, and the injured soldiers were being shipped home to fill hospital beds, seemed completely irrelevant.

Every morning and afternoon over the following months, Alice wandered into Lucy's front room, sat down at the piano and attempted to play.

From the kitchen, Lucy could sense her frustration as she reverted to the first few simple exercises Edward had taught her. Despite her previous accomplishment, her efforts were crude and childlike. At times her perseverance gave way to exasperation and she thumped her fists down on the keys or slammed the piano lid shut.

From outside the door, Lucy would sometimes hear Alice sobbing but resisted the temptation to sympathize or interrupt her. Then after a short break the notes would ring out again, chords or five finger exercises, repeated over and over again.

'Your girl taking lessons?' said Stan Crowther, as he stood at the cottage door one Saturday dinnertime. Pansy listened to the sounds drifting from next door.

'No,' she said.

'What's all the piano playing for then?'

'To make her fingers work again.'

'Good idea,' the man said. 'How old is she? Fourteen? Fifteen?'

Pansy nodded. 'Are you coming in?' she asked.

Crowther kicked off his boots on the front step and followed Pansy into the living-room. 'Can't have her sitting around all day when you're out working. Plenty of jobs for girls in munitions. Time she brought a wage in, isn't it? Helped you with the rent money.'

'She's set her heart on nursing,' Pansy said proudly. 'And besides, I'm fortunate, I don't have to pay any rent.'

'Well, who's the lucky one then?' Crowther's eyes scanned the neat room. 'Nice little place you've got here.'

'Thanks,' she said, a little guiltily. She didn't intend hiding the truth or deceiving the man, but she hardly considered the peppercorn rent of a shilling a year worth mentioning.

'You know they're paying girls two pounds ten shillings a week in the munitions factories, and they're looking for women to work as conductors on the buses, because there's no men to do the job. Don't you fancy giving that a try?'

'I've got my job, thank you very much. Four days suits me and I don't mind house cleaning. It keeps us in food and I've only got to go as far as the village.'

'Suit yourself. Just thought a bit of extra would be nice to line your pocket.'

Pansy looked at the man sitting opposite her. 'Why don't you get a regular job, if there are so many around?'

'I got plenty to occupy myself during the week. I don't only come here for odd jobs, for you. There's plenty of work to be had.'

'Tell me something,' Pansy said inquisitively. 'You're a fit fella, why haven't you volunteered like the rest of the menfolk? I heard the army needed every able-bodied man.'

Crowther laughed. 'Don't be daft, woman! I'm not going to no bloody war to get my block knocked off for no one.'

Pansy's eyes narrowed.

'But I tried,' he added quickly. 'Failed the eye test. They won't have you if you can't pass the medical.' He laughed. 'I'm classed as unfit.'

Timothy was watching him from the doorway.

'Lad a bit shy is he? Different from his sister, eh?'

Pansy turned to her son. 'Go get Alice from next door, then come and wash your hands!'

The boy ran off without saying a word.

'And what about her next door?' Crowther continued. 'I don't think she likes me. How does she manage?'

'What do you mean?'

'With food money and rent and the likes? I ain't never seen her going out to work.'

'That's none of your business, Stanley. She manages all right, thank you very much! Now before I get cross, do you want a plate of stew and dumplings or aren't you stopping?'

'Don't mind if I do,' he said, letting out a long satisfied sigh.

As Pansy set the table, he stood up and stretched, unfastened the buttons on his waistcoat and knocked the ash from his pipe on the inside of the chimney. Sliding the bowl into his breast pocket, he sat down and waited to be served.

'Why do you invite him in every time he comes around?' asked Alice. 'I don't like him, Mum. He looks at me kind of funny. Always makes me feel creepy.'

'Because I quite like him, that's why! And it's a long time since I had a man around the place. And he's handy.'

'Yes, Mum, but he only does the jobs because you pay him. And you have to go out to work for your bit of money!'

'Well he works for his and he'll do anything.'

'I'm sure he will, given half a chance.'

'Alice! Hold your tongue!'

'But I see the way he looks at you. I wouldn't trust him if I was you.'

'That's quite enough, girl! Anyway, talking about money, I think it's time you got yourself a job so you can bring some money into the house. All you do is sit around all day fiddling on that damn piano. I reckon if your fingers are strong enough to push them keys, then they're strong enough to work on a production line.'

The words made Alice boil. She knew what her mother was saying was true. She knew she had done almost nothing lately either inside the house or out, and she felt guilty. But it wasn't her fault. She hadn't burnt her hands on purpose. She didn't set the room on fire. She only tried to put it out.

'If that's what you want,' Alice yelled, 'I'll go out and get a job. And I'll save up and go and live somewhere else, then you can have your fancy man calling on you every day and I won't have to get out of the house, and you can do what you do with him, whenever you want!'

Alice ran from kitchen, through the cottage and out on to the lane, slamming the door behind her.

From the next cottage Lucy could hear Pansy calling after her, begging her not to go. From the window she saw Timothy running down the hill after his sister, shouting her name.

But Alice didn't look around. She kept on running, her gait stiff and ungainly as the knurled skin at the back of her legs was stretched to the limit.

Chapter 11

Bad News

It was a long and tedious winter, cold and bleak in more ways than one. Lucy missed the warmth which had previously existed between the two families living at the cottages. With Edward and James away, the atmosphere was not what it used to be and the rift widening between Lucy and Pansy was gradually pulling the two friends apart.

December 1915 was not an easy month, but for the sake of Alice and little Tim, Lucy made a special effort. She wrapped presents and made cakes, even helped the children with the decorations. But the sight of the paper chains dangling from the ceiling rekindled memories of the previous Christmas, and when it was time to take the trimmings down Lucy was relieved to pull them from the walls. After screwing the chains into tight balls she pushed them deep into the ashes. The decorations smoked before the flames appeared, but it wasn't the smoke which made Lucy's eyes water.

Alice never mentioned last year's fire or complained about her burns, even on the days she had to struggle down muddy tracks or through deep snow to get to work. She liked her job at the munitions factory and liked the girls she worked with. Even wearing trousers instead of a skirt was a novelty to her. Wearing the factory uniform made her proud to be contributing to the war effort. But her desire to become a nurse never wavered. It was a matter of waiting until she was old enough to begin her training.

Lucy missed seeing Alice. Missed the times they had spent together and the closeness of the conversations they had shared when they had talked as if mother and daughter. Because Alice left for work before dawn and was not home until after dark, lately, Lucy hardly ever saw her.

On the days Pansy was working, Lucy minded Timmy. Though he was only four, he was a bright boy and ready for school, but in size he hardly looked it. He was small, delicate and fine-boned like Pansy, but unlike Alice as a child, he never demanded Lucy's attention and was content to amuse himself.

When she sat alone at night Lucy would think about James and reread all his letters. Though she looked forward to getting news from him, she found his tone had changed. They were becoming increasingly depressing. Gazing into the fire, with the bundle of letters on her knee, she tried to picture the scenes he described, imagine what the battlefields were really like. The bullet-riddled houses pockmarked and cracked like lumps of coke. Charred piles of rubble, villages reduced to ash and cinders. The smell, not of wood smoke and warmth, but of bodies rotting in trenches. And the fields so bombed and burned not even a single blade of grass could grow.

Lucy shuddered. It was a horrible war and it was showing no signs of stopping. It didn't end in 1914 as predicted. And 1915 had come and gone and nothing had changed. Now older men were being conscripted to replace the young ones who were being sent home on stretchers, or in boxes, or merely identified as a name on a War Office telegram:

His Majesty regrets . . . killed in action . . . deepest sympathy.

How could James possibly live through it? Survive to the end – whenever that might be? If only he could come home. If only he could be injured – not badly – just enough to be withdrawn from the front line. Not merely sent to the field hospital but returned to England. But there were stories of men brought back, who, once recovered from their injuries, were sent back to fight on the front line. Lucy's heart ached for them. For their mothers. For James.

She couldn't write back. Not immediately. There was nothing positive to write about. She had not heard from Edward and was worried about him, hoping he was all right. She was worried about the trouble Stan Crowther had stirred up between herself and Pansy, and between Alice and her mother. Ever since her father's death on the moors, Alice had been close to her mother. Now Stanley was demanding all of Pansy's attention.

Maybe her thoughts were negative, unfounded. Perhaps Alice's job in the munitions factory would change her outlook. For the first time she had a little money of her own and she enjoyed mixing with other girls her own age. Occasionally her mother had allowed her to go out dancing and she had met a few nice boys. But they were all very young and none of the boys were interested in courting girls. They were merely biding their time, waiting till they were old enough to enlist.

On the positive side, Lucy was amazed how much movement and strength Alice had regained in her fingers during the past year. Handling ammunition all week had proved good therapy for her fingers. Lucy was only sorry Sunday afternoon was her only chance to play the piano. She looked forward to that as Alice's tunes were always bright and the music managed to cheer them both.

Alice still limped a little on her right leg, but as the months had passed it had become less noticeable. Her hair had grown sufficiently to cover the keloid scarring running from behind her ear. Alice was thankful her face was not marked and pitied the poor soldiers burned on the battlefields.

Lucy cut the red cross from two snippets of satin ribbon. It was very striking on the tiny white bodice. She made the cape from a remnant of red velvet and the dress from a piece of bleached cotton sheeting. The skirt was a little too long, falling almost to the doll's feet, but the miniature nurse's veil was perfect. Lucy stuck it to the doll's coarse hair so it wouldn't fall off. Heavily starched, it stood out perfectly.

'I thought it was time Constance had a change from that old school tunic,' said Lucy, as she handed the doll to Alice. 'Do you like her uniform?'

'You're so clever,' Alice said, wrapping her arms around it and leaning forward to peck Lucy on the cheek.

'It won't be long before you have your own uniform,' Lucy said, with a sigh.

Alice's eyes glowed with excitement. 'Only a few months now.'

'I'm going to miss you, but I know you will make a good nurse.'

'And I'll miss you too. Will you write to James and tell him what I am doing? And to Uncle Edward too?'

Lucy nodded.

'And when I am away, will you take care of Constance for me? After all she was yours in the first place.'

'Of course,' said Lucy, indicating the empty chair near the window. She can sit there, and when you are gone, when I look at her uniform, I will think of you.'

Alice smiled. 'And will you look after Mum too? She's not as strong as you and I'm afraid she will get hurt if she's not careful.'

Lucy hugged the girl she loved. 'I promise I will do my best.'

Stanley Crowther visited Pansy every Saturday and Sunday. He always arrived mid morning and stayed until after tea. He was also on her doorstep early on the mornings she did not work. Occasionally Lucy saw him outside with Timothy but she hardly ever saw him working. It was hard for her to say nothing, but she made a point of never asking Pansy what Stan was doing there. Pansy in turn never mentioned him. Though they lived in adjoining cottages, the two women, who were once close friends, saw little of each other.

Sometimes Lucy wondered if she was jealous. Not of Pansy's relationship with Stan, but of her having a man around the house. It was years since she had enjoyed a man's company, and her experiences had been both brief and disastrous. She had never considered her friendship with Edward in that regard. He'd always been kind and considerate. Like a father. Never a lover.

As the months passed, Lucy tried to be polite to Stanley, but something about him still rankled her. If they passed on the lane, his tone was brash and cocky, his friendliness affected. Whenever she saw him, he reminded her of Arthur Mellor. His swagger. The way he turned his head. His false smile. Reminded her how gullible she had been, vulnerable to his smooth talking and suave mannerisms. Reminded her how she had been used. She hoped Pansy would not suffer a similar fate.

'Can you lend me a few shillings?' Pansy begged. Her eyes were bloodshot, her cheeks streaked where she had rubbed them with smutty fingers.

'Whatever is the matter?' Lucy asked.

'I owe Stan some money and he says he wants it. He's coming back on Saturday and he says if I don't have it he'll find some other way of getting it. Lucy, I know I shouldn't ask but you're the only one who can help me.'

'Come in. Sit down. Now tell me, how much do you owe him?'

'He says I owe him fifteen pounds.'

'How much!'

'Fifteen pounds,' she said meekly.

'My goodness, Pansy! How on earth can it be so much?'

'I don't know,' she sobbed. 'I thought he visited because he liked me but it seems he's been keeping a book. He's written down all the times he's been here, right from the start, and all the odd jobs he says he never got paid for. Now he tells me I must have been barmy if I thought he was doing it all for nothing. He says I can afford to pay him 'cause I ain't got no rent to pay, and I got my own wages, and the money Alice has brought home since she's been on the munitions.'

'Have you got any money put aside?'

'He's had it all. Every last penny. Always nice-talking me and bringing us rabbits and things. I thought he liked me, Lucy, honest I did.'

Lucy shook her head. 'Pansy, I wish you had listened.'

'I knew you would say that.' She screwed her hands together. 'What do I do, Lucy?'

'Well, you don't pay him another penny! And next time he comes, tell him you don't want him stepping over your doorstep ever again.'

'But how can I tell him that. He's always so nice.'

'Don't open the door. Keep it shut!'

'But I can't'

'It's up to you, Pansy Pugh, stop right now or he'll be the death of you!'

Lucy trudged slowly back from the village. It was all uphill and the bag of shopping was heavy. As she turned the corner of the lane she saw Crowther's old bicycle leaning on the limestone wall by Pansy's gate. With no signs of the man it was obvious he had wheeled his way back into the house. Lucy shook her head. There was nothing she could do about it. Pansy had made her bed and now she must lie on it. And, Lucy thought, quite likely Stan Crowther was on it with her at that very moment.

Before she reached the gate she heard the rumble of a motor bike driving up the hill. Apart from the milk wagon, few vehicles ventured up the lane. As the engine rattled to a stop Lucy turned. The driver was wearing a postal worker's uniform. When he pulled an envelope from the small leather pouch around his waist, Lucy's heart dropped. She knew it was a telegram and a telegram could only mean bad news.

Chapter 12

The Legacy

Without waiting for a reply, the rider touched his cap, smiled sympathetically and pulled the goggles over his eyes. After kicking the machine back into life, he twisted the throttle. The engine revved and backfired blasting black smoke from the exhaust pipe. As he drove off, the back wheel spun in the dirt sending a shower of grit over Lucy's feet. Within a few seconds, bike and rider had disappeared from view.

Lucy's hands were trembling as she walked inside. She didn't wait to take off her hat and coat before opening the envelope.

The sheet of paper bore only three lines:

Sorry to advise Edward Carrington died Thursday
Funeral Monday
Wainwright

As she caught her breath, Lucy's eyes filled with tears. Fully expecting to read that James had been killed, she felt relieved, almost elated. But at the same time she was confused. Her dearest friend Edward was dead – but how and why? She realized she hadn't heard from him lately. Nor had she written. That made her feel guilty. Perhaps he had been ill for some time and she'd not known about it.

She wondered if she should attend the funeral but decided against it. It was too late to organize the journey to Tunbridge Wells and besides she had heard the trains were packed with soldiers. After making a drink, she sat down and wrote a long letter to Wainwright expressing her sympathy, telling him how attached she had been to Edward and how much she would miss him. Though she had never met Wainwright, she felt an empathy with him and concluded the letter by asking after his wife, Lydia. She did not expect to get a reply.

It was not until the following morning Lucy realized the full consequences of Edward's death. Not only had her source of income come to an end, but her rent-free tenancy at Honeysuckle Cottages was over. She hoped she would be allowed to stay on until the cottages were sold and perhaps even continue as a tenant with the new owner, whoever that may be. If that wasn't possible, then both she and Pansy would need to find new accommodation, and she would have to get work so she could afford to pay rent for a small house or rooms elsewhere.

'What!' Stan Crowther yelled. 'When you said you didn't pay rent, I thought you owned this house. You never told me some old bloke from the south let you live here for nowt. I'd like to know what you did for him to get that sort of arrangement.'

Pansy was hurt. 'It's not what you think! Edward Carrington was a dear kind man and he was good to Lucy and me.'

'So he had the pair of you, did he?'

'Get out, Stan! Get out of here!'

'I'll get out if you pay me the money you owe me.'

'I don't have any money and if I did, I'd not give you a farthing of it!'

'Bugger you!' he yelled, before banging the door. 'And bugger you too!' he shouted towards Lucy's cottage. 'I'll be back!' he yelled from the gate. 'And I'll get what you owe me one way or the other. That's a promise!'

'What did you say his name was?' the constable asked.

'Crowther, Stanley Crowther.'

'Not Stanley Green or Stan Blenkinsop? Are you sure it wasn't either of those names?'

Lucy and Pansy both shook their heads.

'Well, from your description I'm certain it's the same fella. Bit of no good, he is. Been known for quite some time. Preys on women who live on their own. And with so many menfolk away at the war, right now he's having a birthday.'

'Where does he come from?' Pansy asked.

The old constable shrugged his shoulders. 'Gypsy-type I gather. Has an old caravan somewhere on the moors though he spends most of his time hanging around the towns. Once he gets a women's sympathy, he weedles his way into her life. Sometimes works two or three different houses at the same time. Hangs around one area for a while, usually till he gets found out, then moves on. He's done the rounds in Halifax and Knaresborough and, before he came here, he was over in Ilkley. I reckon his moral values are lower than a snake's belly!'

'Is there anything we can do if he comes back?'

'Apart from kicking him out, I don't know. I can tell you ladies, we'd love to get our hands on him but somehow he manages to keep himself clean. He sweet-talks his way into free food and lodgings, and somehow picks up enough money to pay for his bets and whisky. What we need is something criminal to pin on him, like if he stole something. Then we'd come down on him like a ton of bricks. Trouble is he's as slippery as an eel. But don't worry, ladies, we'll get him one of these days.'

'What if he lied at his army medical so he wouldn't have to be conscripted? Is that criminal?'

Surprised by her question, Lucy and the constable both looked at Pansy.

'What are you getting at, luv?'

Pansy spoke cautiously. 'Well, he told me he failed the army medical.'

'So?'

'He told the medical board he couldn't see, but I know he can hit a rabbit between the eyes across the meadow. And he's threaded many a needle for me. I'd say Stan Crowther has better eyesight than all of us put together.'

The constable wrote her words in his notepad then flipped it shut.

'Leave it with me, ladies. The right words in the right ears can work wonders. Don't hold your breath though. Nothing'll happen immediately, but I'll guarantee you this, if the army gets their teeth into him, they won't let go in a hurry!' The constable winked at the two women. 'Mr Crowther, cum Green, cum Blenkinsopp, could be in for a rude awakening.'

*

The two envelopes in Lucy's hand looked almost identical. The stationery was the same, as was the handwriting. Both were stamped with the Skipton postmark, but while one was addressed to her, the other bore the title, James Harrington Oldfield Esq. Lucy was puzzled as she examined them. The only two people she knew from the Wharfedale town were Arthur Mellor and the man called Harry Entwhistle whom she had presumed was Arthur's father. Surely after twenty-one years neither of those men would be renewing acquaintance with her, especially as in all those years Arthur had never once enquired after his child.

Taking a deep breath, she sliced the knife blade along the envelope addressed to her. The gold letters, embossed along the top of the page, shone in the light from the window. It read: Proctor and Armitage, Solicitors and Barristers, Main Street, Skipton, West Riding of Yorkshire. She knew the letter must be important.

Dear Mrs Oldfield

It is our sad duty to inform you of the death of our client, Mr Edward Carrington of Tunbridge Wells. As executors of his estate we advise that under the terms of his last will and testament you are a beneficiary.

As this matter is fairly comprehensive and there are certain conditional clauses, we feel it would be in your best interests to visit our offices to discuss the matter further.

We look forward to hearing from you in the near future.

Yours sincerely

J. Cranford Proctor

For Proctor and Armitage.

In James's absence, Lucy opened the letter addressed to him. As she expected, apart from the addressee's name, the wording was identical.

Lucy was confused. 'What does all that mean?' she asked the two rather elderly gentlemen sitting at the opposite side of the heavy walnut desk.

'What it means,' said Mr Armitage slowly, 'is that under the terms of Mr Carrington's will, two of the cottages, commonly known as Honeysuckle Cottages, have been left to you. The third cottage, the one which our client occupied until he took up residence in the south, has been left to your son, Mr James Oldfield.'

'But regarding the conditional clauses?'

Mr Proctor answered. 'When the two cottages are transferred into your name, the lease agreement, held over the property currently occupied by Mrs Pansy Pugh, will come to an end. However, when we last spoke to Mr Carrington, which was some two years before his death, he made certain requests which he asked us, as his executors, to outline to you.'

Mr Proctor took off his spectacles and laid them on the desk. 'Mr Carrington, I may say, held you in high regard.'

Lucy acknowledged him with a nervous smile.

'He also had great faith in your judgement and felt you would handle the lease of that cottage in a fair and proper manner. He did however express the hope that you would continue the current lease arrangement with Mrs Pugh. But, naturally, as the new owner, you are at liberty to demand a reasonable rent on the cottage and by this means you could provide yourself with a weekly income.' The solicitor paused, giving Lucy the opportunity to pass comment.

'Please continue,' she said.

'The other matter our client asked us to convey to you was his wish that you, and your son, continue living in the cottages rather than selling them. I must point out this is not a stipulation, merely a request. He also requested that in the event of your death the title to your two cottages is passed to your son, James. Again this at your discretion. Once the titles are transferred, you are at liberty to dispose of the two cottages as you see fit.' He leaned forward and rested on his forearms. 'Mr Carrington was aware that you are, if I may say, an eligible woman who may choose to marry. It was our duty to advise him of this at the time he made his will.'

Lucy pondered on what the lawyer was saying 'Perhaps I should make a will right now, Mr Proctor?'

'It may be a little premature as the deeds are not yet in your name.'

'Then if I tell you what I wish, can you have one drawn up for me when everything has been settled?'

'It will be our pleasure.'

'There is just one other matter,' Mr Armitage added. 'The residue of Mr Carrington's estate has not yet been determined, but it is likely both you and your son will be beneficiaries to the terms of several thousand pounds.'

'Goodness,' said Lucy. 'I never knew Edward was such a wealthy man.'

'And an astute man, I would say. We will be in touch when the matter is finalized.'

Once the remainder of the business was concluded Lucy shook hands with the two solicitors. 'Thank you. Good afternoon.'

Outside on Main Street the air was fresh. Market-day was in full swing and Lucy had two hours to wait for the train. With memories of Arthur Mellor and his father rekindled in her mind, she had no intention of visiting the stalls. Instead she chose a small teashop where she waited, considering her situation. She wished James had been with her and deeply regretted that her new-found fortune was at the expense of Edward's life.

Pansy looked distraught. 'I know you'll say I am stupid, Lucy, but I have told Stan that he can live here.'

'You must be daft in the head, girl! Weren't you listening when we were in the police station? Wasn't it you who said Crowther tricked the army medical board?'

'Yes, but I got it wrong, and now I feel guilty because I said what I did.'

Lucy shook her head in disbelief.

'Stan told me he does have trouble with his eyes but it comes and goes. It was his flat feet which made him fail the medical. And he said the constable had got him mixed up with some other man called Stan, and that it wasn't the first time people had got the two of them mixed up.'

'But what about the money he wanted from you? Can't you see he's taking advantage?'

'He said he was a bit short at the time and it was wrong of him to ask. He told me he was really sorry. He meant it, Lucy, I could tell he did.'

'So what happens now? And what happens the next time he's short?'

'He's promised me faithfully it won't happen again, and when he moves in he says he'll get a regular job, so I won't have to go out cleaning.'

'And you believe him?'

'Lucy, you don't know him like I do. Stan's good at heart, and he gets on well with Timmy and I enjoy his company.' She heaved a sigh. 'And he said that although you and him have never really hit it off, he'd like to get better acquainted with you, especially as the property now belongs to you.'

'Huh!' exclaimed Lucy. 'Is that so? Well, all I can say is, I think you're crazy for listening to him. You don't know what you are letting yourself in for!'

Pansy turned away.

'Imagine what Edward would have said. He'd have had Stan locked up by now.'

'Lucy, don't say that. It's all lies. Stan said so. You'll see!'

'Yes I will, won't I?'

Lucy could hear Crowther yelling, but it was the tinkle of falling glass that brought her running into the front room. Through the broken window she could see him standing in the lane, facing her cottage.

'I ain't signing no bloody lease!' he screamed. 'And I ain't paying you no two quid a week. You're a thieving greedy bitch, Lucy Oldfield, that's what you are. Got your hands on a bit of property and now you want to squeeze a few lousy bob out of every other poor sod. Well, you won't get a penny out of me. You can stick your lease and your cottage!'

Lucy could hear Pansy's plaintive cry coming from her garden and watched as he turned back to her.

'And you know what you can do, Pansy bloody Pugh! Expect me to work for you so I can pay your bloody rent! Bloody women! You're all the bloody same! Waste of bloody time the lot of you!'

'Don't say that Stan!' Pansy begged. 'I'll work something out with Lucy. I promise.'

'Bloody promises! That's all I get, bloody promises!'

'Stan!' she cried. 'Don't be like that.'

'I got better things to do with me time than get tangled up with your sort. What you got to offer anyway? You think if you feed me a bit of stew I'm going work my balls off for you. Well you're bloody well wrong!'

Lucy jumped back as the second rock came hurtling through her window, showering shards of glass across the carpet. By the time she dared peer out again, Stanley Crowther had gone.

Chapter 13

Night

That night Lucy could not sleep. She felt ill at ease. It was pitch black outside. No moon and the wind blowing across from the moors was strengthening. The board nailed across the broken window rattled as if someone was pestering it, trying to get in, while the tree branches, rubbing on Pansy's roof, sent an eery scratching sound along the length of the eaves. For no apparent reason, the hens squawked occasionally, their haunting cries acknowledged by the anxious bleating of the sheep. It was obvious the animals could not sleep either.

Pulling the blanket to her ear, Lucy turned over. She couldn't get Stanley Crowther out of her mind. She hoped that after tonight's incident she would not see him again. In a way she felt sorry for Pansy but at the same time she was angry with her for allowing the situation to get out of hand. If James had been home, she was sure it would not have happened.

In the morning she would speak with Pansy, tell her what she had done and why. Explain that her threat to increase the rent had merely been a ploy to get rid of Crowther and that the peppercorn lease would remain unchanged once the man had gone. The ruse had certainly achieved its desired effect and had worked far quicker than Lucy had expected.

As she drifted to sleep she questioned what Pansy had told her. Had Stan really failed the medical because of his flat feet? Could there possibly be two men with the same name taking advantage of women in the village? In the morning she would speak with the constable, report what had happened and ask if anything had been done about the man from the moors.

The constable reread his notes. 'What you are telling me, is that last night one of your sheep went missing and the night before four chickens disappeared?'

'That's right,' said Lucy.

'And you think Stanley Crowther's the culprit?'

Lucy nodded. 'The first night we thought the wind had pushed the hen house door open. That's why I didn't mention it yesterday. But now one of the best ewes has gone, I think someone took it and I'd bet all I have it was that man.'

'And you don't think the sheep could have strayed.'

'She's was a pet. We raised her on a bottle. She wouldn't have strayed.'

The policeman shook his head. 'Not a lot we can do, I'm afraid. It's hard to prove someone's taken something unless you can catch them with it. Best advice I can give you is to keep a good eye out and make sure you lock everything up, including your front door.'

'Don't worry I will.' Lucy paused at the door. 'By the way, Constable, did the army do anything about Crowther's medical?'

'Not to my knowledge. The information was passed on but I reckon they might be too busy with enlistments.'

'What will they do if they catch up with him?'

'If he's lied, they'd probably have him sworn in then send him straight to prison. A military prison. Not a civilian one. Once he's served his time – maybe six months, then they'd ship him off to the front line. That's what I think.'

'Thank you, Constable.'

The following morning Lucy noticed Goldie grazing alone in the meadow. Edward's horse had gone.

The constable sounded sympathetic but said there was little hope of getting the animal back. He said he would contact the local knackers' yards with a description. The only chance they had was if the old mare had been sold to a farmer in another district. He said with the war on there was a shortage of horses, especially ones trained to work in the shafts.

*

It was the bleating that awakened Lucy. She hadn't meant to fall asleep but had dozed off in the armchair. Edward's rifle was lying within arm's reach on the table, the box of ammunition was next to it. Lucy slipped the gun under her arm, dropped the box in her pocket and roused Pansy from the sofa.

The pair agreed not to go out through the kitchen. Instead they slipped out of the front door, hurried quietly past Pansy's cottage and stopped by the farm gate which led into the meadow.

They did not have to wait long. Silhouetted against the field was the black shadow of a man leading a horse. Crowther's swaggering gait was unmistakable.

'Leave the horse!' Lucy ordered.

The man kept walking towards them.

'Let go of the horse!' she yelled.

The horse whinnied and shook its mane.

'Well, what do we have here? Owooo!' he howled. 'A pair of witches out this fine dark night.'

'If you go any further I will shoot.'

The man stopped. He could see the rifle levelled at him.

'Let go of the horse!'

'You're not going to shoot me. You ain't got it in you.'

Lucy pulled the bolt back and fired in the air. The rifle cracked. The horse reared. Lucy quickly reloaded.

'Bloody stupid bitch, what did you do that for?'

'That was just a warning. Now let the horse go!'

'I was just going to,' he said, as he lifted the rope bridle. 'I was only going to borrow it for a couple of hours. I'd have had it back by the morning.'

'Step away from the horse!'

He didn't move.

'So what you going to do now?' Crowther said. It was the same smarmy tone which Lucy hated. 'You ain't going to shoot me, are you?'

'That's far enough!' she said.

He moved towards her.

'That's far enough!' A voice boomed out from behind him.

Surprised, Stan Crowther turned.

Outlined against the meadow were two men. The police helmets were unmistakable.

'Leave it to us now, Miss. We don't want you doing anything you'll regret later.'

Lucy's knees suddenly went weak. Her arm dropped and the barrel hit the ground. Her heart was thumping. Behind her she could hear Pansy sobbing. Her hands shook as she slowly released the bolt, turned the rifle over and let the live cartridge fall into the wet grass.

Would she have fired the second round? She did not know.

*

October, 1918

My dear Mum

Thank you for all the news. You do not know how good it is to get your letters.

I am pleased to hear you are well and this season's crop was good. Your description of the ricks of hay made me smile. 'Like Indian tepees' you wrote. I can imagine young Timmy dancing around them. I wonder if the lad will remember me when I get back. What a difference four years make.

I got a letter from Alice saying she had moved to Cookridge Hospital where all the burns victims were being taken. She said she was enjoying her nurse training though the hours were long and the night work made her very tired. She also said she has moved out of the cottage and was living at the nurses' home. You and Pansy must miss her.

I didn't want to worry you but I got injured and had to spend two weeks in the field hospital.

I was in a trench one night when a mortar bomb came over. It's the size of a rum cask and it seems to roll through the air in slow motion. Everyone just stands and watches to see where it's going to land. If it's close, you cover your ears. The explosion is loud enough to shatter your eardrums.

Well, I saw this one floating in my direction. It was too close for comfort, but when you are stuck in a trench there's nowhere to go. When it went off, I was knocked out. I found out later, I got a dent in my tin helmet. I also got a piece of shrapnel in my shoulder and one in my leg. I would have been all right but they couldn't get one bit out and it turned bad. It laid me up for three weeks.

Half the time I didn't know where I was. I remember it was cold in the tent, and every noise seemed so loud, even the flapping canvas sounded like thunder. Anyway I'm better now and apart from a couple of scars, there's no damage. I was lucky.

Though the men in my regiment laugh and joke, we all miss England. Sometimes I wonder if we will ever go home.

It was ironical to learn I am now a wealthy man. Fancy, a cottage of my own and over four thousand pounds in the bank. But that doesn't matter out here. How can I plan for the future when men around me are being killed every day?

On a more positive note, we have heard the fighting is drawing to a close and the war could be over before Christmas.

How I would love to be shovelling snow from the front door instead of shovelling muck from the bottom of this filthy rat hole.

I'm sorry to end on this note, but I can't write it any other way.

All my love to you,

Your son, James.

*

'He's coming!' Alice yelled. 'He's coming up the lane! Come quick, Aunt Lucy!'

Lucy's eyes filled with tears as she waited by the gate and watched her son striding up the lane. Pansy and Alice stood beside her, their arms around each other's waists.

'Go on,' said Pansy to Timmy, encouraging her son to run down the hill to greet him. But the boy was unsure of the slim man in the khaki uniform.

As James got closer, Alice left her mother and ran to meet him, flinging her arms around his neck.

The kit bag dropped from his shoulder as he hugged her. 'My, look at you!' he said. 'I can hardly believe my eyes. And look at you,' he said, as he ruffled Timothy's hair before sitting the dented helmet on the lad's head.

Alice led him by the hand to the gate and the two women waiting for him. James kissed Pansy on the cheek then took his mother in his arms and held her tightly.

She found it hard to mouth the words: 'Welcome home, son.'

Chapter 14

The Aftermath

'You have to go out and do something, James. You can't just sit around all day.'

'But I like it here. It's quiet.' His voice was weary. 'You don't know how many times I prayed I might sit here and do nothing.'

'I'm sorry,' Lucy said sighing. 'I don't understand what's got into you. I only want what's best for you, but seeing you moping about worries me. You must pull yourself together.'

She waited for James to answer but he seemed preoccupied. She knew he had heard her but he did not reply.

'I'm going down to the village,' she said. 'Can I get you anything?'

His eyes, fixed on the empty grate, never shifted. 'No, I'll be all right.'

Lucy closed the door quietly as she left.

James heard the click. Then the silence. He was alone and everything was still. He glanced right, then left. His eyes darted around the room. Everything was closing in – getting smaller. There was no space to move – no room to walk. On the chair the doll was eyeing him, gazing at him with a glassy stare. He looked away – glanced back. Yes, definitely watching him. From the framed picture on the mantelshelf, another pair of eyes was on him. A girl. A nurse. He knew the face. From the field hospital? He wasn't sure.

The fire was out. He was glad. It was always safer in the dark. But it was cold and the night would be bitter. He could see a light shining outside. Daylight? Through a hole. A window? No. A tunnel through the wall. A way to escape. Looking up, the heavy beams loomed threatening. What if the house crumbled? What if the roof timbers collapsed? He would be crushed. Killed. He must get out. Get away.

On the lane, James shook his head and gasped. Outside the air was clear and fresh. How strange! The sky was blue, flecked with fine wafts of white. A sparrow landed on the bird bath and splashed its wings. The gravel crunched beneath his feet. The sound of feet was familiar.

He had to walk. He knew he had to walk – but where? Just walk, he told himself, the usual way. He knew it well; knew every fence and drystone wall, knew every hollow tree which hid a squirrel, knew every patch of earth which stank of garlic, the tangled hedgerows where the blackberries grew, knew every rut where, after rain, a clear stream ran across the path. He knew the contours of the distant hills which offered sanctuary to the sun.

Inside the gate of Fothergill's farm, he slowed, his mind remembering. The smell. Decay. Deep litter. Dung. Warm steaming hay. The sound of cows. The spring of soft earth beneath his feet. Thick clover wet after rain. Daisies. Cowslips. Dandelions.

He stopped. How strange, he thought, to see flowers growing on this ground. He reached out his hand to touch.

Before his eyes the flowers faded – disappeared. The earth grew bare. The mud felt wet and warm, sticky like blood. He stopped, looked up and from the corner of his eye he saw it coming, rolling slowly through the sky straight at him.

'Mortar!' he screamed as he dropped to the ground, covered his ears and waited for the bang.

The crow landed on the fence and cawed.

Hunched on his hands and knees, James wept.

Lucy rubbed the loose flour from her hands. The dough was still stuck between her fingers as she opened the door.

Mr Fothergill was on the doorstep with James standing meekly beside him.

'I thought I'd better bring the lad home.'

'What's the matter?' she asked.

The farmer shook his head. There were tears in his eyes. 'Best get the doctor to have a look at him, Mrs Oldfield.'

Lucy took James's arm and led him into the house.

'Let me know if I can be of any help,' the man said.

'Thank you,' she said. 'I will.'

The morning of the eleventh had been misty. But at least it wasn't raining.

At eleven o'clock, Lucy thought of the soldiers marching to memorials throughout Britain. Gathering to commemorate the war. Standing in silence to remember. She had already decided not to remind her son what day it was.

As she sat reading, James fitted another piece into his jigsaw. She looked up from her book. How many puzzles was that? She had bought at least two dozen in the last few months – every jigsaw the local shop had in stock. The shopkeeper had ordered more but was still waiting for them to arrive. It didn't matter to James how many pieces each puzzle contained or what the pictures were; rose gardens, stately homes, boats lolling in quiet Cornish harbours, or waves crashing on angry seas. After completing each one he would mix a dish of flour and water paste, spread it thinly over the puzzle, then immediately start on another.

In the front room, Timmy tootled on the piano hammering out unrelated notes. Lucy hadn't heard the lad come in, but wasn't surprised. He often wandered into the room without saying anything, especially when Pansy was out at work.

As she turned the page, Lucy noticed James had stopped. Without saying a word, he got up from his puzzle and walked to the front room. Lucy was about to ask if there was anything he wanted, but she stopped herself.

As he stood in the doorway, Timothy looked up at him.

'Can I join you?' James asked.

'Yep,' said Timmy, his fingers still tapping out the notes as he slid along the piano stool, making room for James to sit beside him.

James hesitated for a moment, watched the boy, then lifted his hands and rested them gently on the keys. The ivory was cool.

'Can you play something?' Timothy asked.

'I don't know.'

'Play a Christmas carol and I will sing. We should practise,' the boy said enthusiastically. 'It'll be Christmas soon and you can come round the streets with me. I'm sure Mum will come.' He looked up. 'Will you come too, Aunt Lucy, when we go carolling?'

From the doorway Lucy smiled sadly. As James lifted his head and smiled back at her, she felt a tear trickle down her cheek. It was that single smile which told her his battle was over. Her son had finally come home.

Chapter 15

Alice

'Edward had so many interesting things,' Lucy said, as she dusted the ebony elephant and placed it back on the glass shelf in the cabinet.

From the floor, where he was sitting stacking his jigsaw pictures, James looked up. 'What am I going to do with these things?' he said. 'They can't be used again. I made sure of that, didn't I?'

Lucy grinned. 'Give them to the chapel for the fête or store them in the attic.'

James shrugged, tied them securely and leaned the bundle against a tea chest which bore a faded Bombay shipping mark. 'Is there anything in here you want to keep?'

Lucy shook her head. 'Nothing,' she said. 'I only wish I had a photograph of Edward. Perhaps Wainwright has one.' She sighed. 'Maybe I will write to him and ask.'

'Are you sure you don't mind me moving into Edward's cottage?'

'Of course not! It's what he intended. And it's yours now.'

James grinned. 'It's not like I'm moving far away, is it?'

'It will be nice for you and Alice when she comes to visit,' Lucy said.

The leather armchair sighed as he sat down on it. 'It's strange,' he said. 'When I was in France, I used to think of Alice a lot. Most of the men had girlfriends, but I didn't, so I suppose I thought of Alice as my girl.' He looked at his mother. 'But she wasn't, was she? While she was growing up, she was like my little sister and we were friends. Close friends. I never thought of her as anything more than that. But look at her now,' he said. 'She scares me a little. She's grown into a lovely woman. A nurse. Independent. And look at me. What can I offer her?'

Lucy scowled. 'James! You have money and the cottage. Compared with most men of twenty-three you are very lucky.'

'But is that enough?'

Lucy pushed the key into the clock and wound the spring. 'She'll be here very soon, why don't you ask her?'

After his mother left, James spent half an hour preparing for Alice's visit. He was excited. Nervous. It was an unusual feeling. He had known Alice since she was a little girl, from the day he had found her hiding on the moors, frozen and afraid. From that time they had played together, talked, confided in each other. Taken long walks and ridden for miles always comfortable in each other's company. But since the war, he had only seen her briefly on the afternoons she visited her mother, and his memory of the twelve months he was sick was vague.

Now things were different. He was fit and well and moving into Edward's cottage – his cottage – and he was about to entertain her alone. It was a daunting prospect. What would he say to her? What would they do?

For the umpteenth time he went to the door and checked the lane. At last she was there. Walking up the hill, pushing her bicycle.

'So, this is your new home,' she said as he took her coat and followed her into the front room. She stood for a moment looking around. 'Just as Edward left it.'

James felt guilty. 'Perhaps I should have bought new furniture. I can afford it.'

'No' she protested. 'It's very gentlemanly and hardly worn. And,' she added, 'it suits you.'

Standing by the fireplace, James watched as Alice wandered around looking at the ornaments, admiring some, examining others, asking about particular ones. A group of miniature soldiers assembled in the china cabinet attracted her attention.

'Ghurkhas!' he said.

Alice nodded. 'Can I make a cup of tea?'

James apologized. He should have thought of that.

She insisted. 'I'll do it,' she said.

After a few minutes, she returned with a tray. Edward's Royal Worcester teapot and crockery. James watched as she poured. Her hand was steady, but when she sat down, she looked weary. Pulling off her shoes, she leaned back in the chair.

'It's a long ride from the hospital. Are you tired?' James said.

'A little,' she said. 'Tell me what you have been doing.'

James couldn't think. What had he done lately? Nothing really. Just jobs around the cottages. Things that needed doing. Propped up the stable roof where it collapsed. Bought six new hens. Went to town. Wrote a few letters to the men he had served with – uncertain if the addresses were correct – uncertain he would get any replies. Pruned the crab apple tree. That was about it. 'Not much,' he said.

'Have you thought any more about university?'

'No.'

'Have you been riding?'

'No,' he said quickly, wanting to turn the conversation away from himself. 'Tell me about the hospital.'

Alice leaned back and talked at length about the hospital itself, the building, the wards, corridors, the other nurses and the shift work. She described the nurses' quarters and the strict rules and regulations which the girls had to adhere to, but she didn't speak about herself.

'When do you get a holiday?'

'Why do you ask?'

'Because I would like to go away for a holiday. Take my Mum and yours – and Timothy – and you.'

'Where to? And when?'

'Scarborough. By train,' he said. 'Have you ever been there?'

Alice shook her head.

'Neither have I, but I understand there are some nice hotels overlooking the sea. Imagine staying in a hotel and being waited on.'

'It would be terribly expensive.'

'I can afford it. And it's something I'd like to do.'

'Timmy would love it.'

'That means you will come?'

Alice thought for a moment. 'Yes, if I can arrange to get time off.'

*

'Does Alice Pugh live here?'

'No,' said Lucy, wondering who the man standing by the garden gate was. 'Her mother lives next door,' Lucy said. 'But no one's home today. Can I help?'

He looked disappointed. 'Just thought I'd call in. I was in the neighbourhood. First time I've been round these parts.'

'Alice doesn't actually live here,' Lucy explained. 'She lives-in at the hospital. She's a nurse.'

'Yes, I know. I work there as a porter. It's her day off today and she'd told me she usually goes home when she's got the time. I thought I'd find her here. I wanted to surprise her. Wanted to show her my new transport.'

As he spoke, he stepped back allowing Lucy full view of the new motor bike propped up on its stand. 'Never mind. Sorry to trouble you, missus.'

'When I see her shall I tell her who called?'

'Aye, say Bertie Bottomley was looking for her. On the other hand,' he said, pulling the goggles down to the bridge of his nose. 'Don't worry. I'll catch up with her on the ward tomorrow.'

'You haven't forgotten about Scarborough, have you?' James asked casually.

Alice shook her head as she continued reading the newspaper.

He had asked the same question every time she had visited during the past month, but on each occasion her answer was the same – it wasn't easy to organize time off but she was still trying.

'Do you have to work?' James asked bluntly.

Alice looked up.

'Wouldn't you prefer to stay at home?'

'But I've got to work! How would I live otherwise? I can't expect Mum to support me at my age.'

'But what if I supported you.' He paused. 'What if you and I were to get married? You wouldn't have to work again.'

Alice didn't answer.

'I can afford it. I've got plenty of money and you can buy whatever you want, clothes, furniture, even a radiogram or a wireless. You must know I would do anything for you, Alice.'

'I know you would. You're very kind, James. But Edward's money –

your money – won't last forever and I don't want all those things.'

He turned away, but not quickly enough. He knew she had read the disappointment clouding his face.

'You must give me time, to think about it,' she said. 'It is a very good offer.'

When Lucy opened the front door she found John Fothergill standing on the doorstep rolling his cap around in his hand. It was raining.

'Mornin',' he said, touching his knuckles to his forehead.

'Mr Fothergill, what can I do for you?'

'If you don't mind, I wanted to have a quick word about the field out the back.'

'Come in out of the drizzle. I'll make a nice cup of tea.'

The farmer looked down at his Wellington boots caked in farmyard muck.

'Take them off and come in.'

'Well if you don't mind,' he said, as he kicked them off and followed Lucy through to the living room. She offered him a seat at the kitchen table. As he sat down he crossed his feet and slid them under the chair, but not before Lucy had noticed the large holes in his socks.

'I see you've left the field fallow this year,' the farmer said.

'You mean we didn't plant it.'

'That's right. I took a walk over it yesterday. Some good feed growing!'

Lucy glanced out of the window. The meadow was thick and green, scattered with the tall stems of self-seeded barley. The slender stalks swayed in the still air, as a group of birds investigated the fresh green ears.

'Is it all right with you if I put a few cows out there? It's nice clean pasture. Shame to waste it.'

Lucy looked puzzled. 'But it's your field, isn't it?'

'That's right, but I'm still obliged by the lease. Mr Carrington paid me five years in advance.'

'But Edward has been dead for over two years.'

'I know. But he was an honest man and generous and, even though he's dead and buried, I have to honour my side of the bargain. Besides,' he said, 'you and Mrs Pugh did a wonderful job when things were scarce. I take me hat off to you. All that work you did for the war effort. I'd never begrudge you the use of it.'

'Everyone did what they could,' Lucy said.

'I should have done more,' the farmer said shaking his head. 'But I had enough on me plate at the time.'

As Lucy placed the mug of tea on the table, the farmer glanced at the dirt embedded deep beneath his fingernails. Sliding his hands to his lap he hid them beneath the table cloth. Lucy looked at the man. His face was leathery and weathered, his expression gaunt and drawn, his grey-green eyes half sunken in the sockets. He wasn't a tall man but he was wiry. His hair was wiry too, grey and sparse on top except for his sideburns which were ginger and matched the colour of his overlong moustache. Like his hair, it was in dire need of a trim.

'Well if it's all right with you, Mrs Oldfield, I'll bring a few heifers down tomorrow.'

'Should I get James to move the horse?'

'No, leave it. Cows won't mind a bit of company. Only interested in what's under their noses.' He sipped the tea and looked around the room.

Lucy watched him, following his gaze. First he glanced at the doll sitting on the straight-backed chair, then at the photo on the mantelpiece. Both subjects wore white uniforms bearing the distinctive red nursing cross.

'Is that young Alice from next door?'

Lucy smiled. 'It is,' she said as she took down the picture and handed it to him.

'Fine girl. Don't see much of her these days.'

'She works away. At Cookridge Hospital.'

'Ah!' he sighed and handed the photograph back to Lucy. 'Do you want a calf?'

Lucy was surprised at the question. 'Pardon?'

'A calf. Only a week old,' he said. 'On the bottle. I'll give you the milk. Much as you want. It's just we can't manage it.'

Lucy wasn't sure.

'If you don't want it, I'll kill it. Just thought I'd ask.'

'I've raised a lamb on a bottle, but never a calf. You say you can't manage. Is it a problem?'

'Calf's no trouble, it's just we can't spare the time messing about with it. There's only me and me daughter, Grace, these days.'

'But I remember Edward telling me you and your wife had two grown boys.'

The farmer rubbed his hand across his thinning hair. 'We lost both boys in Flanders in 1917. Not more than two months apart. That was when my wife took to her bed. Doctor said it was women's troubles but I think it was the shock and grief. Same ailment as got to your boy – only worse. She ain't never got over it.'

'I'm sorry,' said Lucy. 'I didn't know.'

'She wouldn't let me tell. Said she didn't want anyone knowing her business. Trouble is now at times she can hardly breathe and I think she's proper sick. That's what made me think about a nurse for her.'

'Shall I speak to Alice when I see her? Ask her if she can spare a bit of time?'

'I don't know what my missus will say. She only lets Grace tend to her these days. Doesn't even like me going into her room.'

He wiped the tea from his whiskers. 'It's hard on the lass, helping me with the milking and trying to look after her mother and the house as well. She's twenty years old and says she don't intend to be tied to the farm for the rest of her days. It was all right when she were young but now she says she's had enough of mucking out sheds. She wants to go to the city to work. What can I do?'

Lucy shook her head.

'Can't really blame her, can you? She's a good lass, but I worry. I don't know what she'll do if she leaves. She's got no learning. We paid for the boys to go to high school, but we couldn't afford it with her. Didn't seem necessary at the time. She left school at twelve to help the missus. Now I wish. . . .'

'I'd be happy to take the calf,' said Lucy.

'That's good. I didn't really want to knock it on the head. Nice little heifer calf. If she grows all right, we'll put her to the bull when she's big enough. You can start your own herd.'

Lucy laughed. She felt sorry for the farmer. He was a nice man.

James asked Alice to marry him three or four times during the summer of 1920. And both Lucy and Pansy tried to encourage her to accept James's proposal.

'You can get a job in the village,' said Pansy. 'Or work as a private nurse in one of them big houses if you really want to work.'

'Serving cups of tea and bathing some rich old biddy every time she wets herself! No thank you!' Alice was not going to be persuaded.

Even James's new car made no difference.

It was the latest model, a 1920 Morris Tourer – brand spanking new. The metal trim gleamed, even the leather upholstery shone. It seated four or five comfortably and had a concertina top which could be pulled up when it rained. It was one of the few cars in the Horsforth district and certainly the newest one for miles around. Lucy and Pansy felt like royalty when they travelled in the back. Timothy always took pride of place in the front passenger seat.

Much to James's chagrin and disappointment, Alice was indifferent to the motor car, almost averse to it. She complained about the petrol fumes. Said the car was noisy and cold to ride in. And when James suggested he drive her back to the hospital and carry her bike in the back seat, she objected saying she preferred to ride her bike. It was good exercise, she said, and asked him what people would think if they saw her being driven to the nurses' home by a toff in a fancy car.

James managed to hide his disappointment.

'I thought of taking Goldie for a walk,' he said casually, after lunch on one of her visits. 'Would you like to join me?'

He was surprised when she accepted, especially as she sounded enthusiastic. Perhaps she had spent too much time that morning talking with her mother and Lucy. Perhaps because it was a fine day she wanted to get out in the fresh air. James didn't care, he was just pleased she had agreed.

It was a long time since she had been in the saddle and a long time since Goldie had been ridden and at first both seemed a little nervous. Holding the bridle, James led the old horse out of the gate beside Pansy's cottage and into the lane. It was the way he had led her many times when she was a little girl. How could he forget those times? How happy she had been then, full of fun and excitement, chattering non-stop while riding confidently, one hand on the horse's mane, the other wrapped around Constance, her doll. Walking beside her, James looked up, but Alice was staring straight ahead and did not return his glance.

Skirting around the field via the back lane, he led Goldie along the narrow path into the pocket of woodland overlooking the meadow. Mr Fothergill's small herd was camped by the marshy ground at the far end of the field contentedly cudding. Honeysuckle Cottages, the only building in sight, was half hidden by the boughs of the old chestnut tree.

Alice sighed as she held out her arms for James to help her dismount. 'Being here reminds me of when I was a girl,' she said. As she slid from the saddle her body brushed against his, her hands slipped loosely around his neck.

James held her for a moment. 'Shall we sit for a while?'

With the horse blanket beneath them, the pair reminisced.

'I remember the thrush's nest,' Alice mused. 'I used to lie here and watch you climb, looking for eggs. And we used to catch butterflies and take them to Edward. But remember, if your mother called we would pretend we didn't hear her.'

He smiled.

'And sometimes we would fall asleep in the sun,' she said, laying her head back on to the rug. She closed her eyes as the sun filtering through the branches flickered across her face.

James lay down beside her. 'And you would look just as you do today. Lovely,' he sighed. 'You cannot imagine how many times I longed for a moment like this.' He closed his eyes and touched her. Her skin was soft and warm. His hands trembled.

A dragonfly hovering over the grass nearby ignored them. Above their heads the new season's acorns decorated the branches like candles on a Christmas tree. A bird flitted between the leaves. The old horse flicked flies from his tail and grazed amongst the wildflowers, whose seedpods, were firm and full and almost ready to burst and cast their crop on the late summer breeze. Goldie didn't wander far. The cows never stirred. The sun continued flickering and it was almost two hours before Alice decided it was time she should leave.

'Perhaps you'd reconsider what I've been asking,' James said, as he touched her cheek.

'Don't ask me now,' she said. 'Please, not now.'

Chapter 16

Bad Times

L ucy and Alice sat next to each other at the pine table in the farmhouse kitchen. Mr Fothergill, perched on a stool near the fireplace, spoke in a low voice.

'Her mother never made it easy for her,' he said. 'Always picking on the lass.' He sighed deeply. 'The two lads were always her favourites. And I suppose, if I was honest, I'd say Grace was always mine.'

From outside the window a dog barked. Grace Fothergill kicked off her boots before popping her head around the kitchen door. Plump and freckle-faced, she wore her long ginger hair wound into two plaits. Her impish grin belied her twenty-two years. Wearing dungarees, hand-knitted socks and an old jumper which had obviously belonged to her father, a look of embarrassment flashed across her face when she saw how smartly Alice was dressed, but it quickly disappeared. She smiled. 'Have you been to see Mam yet?'

'No,' said Lucy. 'We waited for you. Did you tell her I was bringing Alice?'

'I said you might call in just to say hello.' Grace turned to Alice, her expression serious. 'At first she said not to bother, then she asked if you was a real nurse. When I told her you were, I think she was pleased because she kept asking when you was coming.'

Mr Fothergill fed the fire from the pile of chopped wood heaped beside it. A kitten wandered over to Lucy and rubbed itself against her leg. Grace shooed it out of the door and then beckoned the two women to follow her down the passage which led through the house. The door to the end room was closed. Grace knocked on it gently before ushering the two ladies inside.

As she opened the bedroom door, Lucy was struck by the unsavoury smell of sickness. It was always the same – only this time it was worse.

Mrs Fothergill was propped up in the bed with a pile of cushions behind her. She was gripping a towel which was pulled up under her chin. Around her shoulders was a faded blue bedjacket. Loose skin drooped in folds from her forearms. The once silver hair was dull and matted. She looked much older than her fifty years.

'Hello, Mrs Fothergill, I'm Alice.'

The woman smiled weakly. 'I'd never have recognized you,' she said, fighting for breath with every word.

Grace offered Lucy the only chair in the room. 'Mam can't talk for long,' she said quietly. 'She gets tired easily.'

Lucy and Alice exchanged glances before Alice sat on the edge of the bed and took Mrs Fothergill's hand. 'How are you?' she said kindly, not expecting an answer. It was difficult for the sick woman to speak. Grace answered most of the questions for her.

'Is there anything you can do for her?'

'I'd like to help,' Alice said, 'but I think your mother needs a doctor.'

'No!' the woman breathed emphatically. She tried to repeat it but her voice was no more than a whisper. 'No! No doctor!'

Alice turned back to Grace.

'How long has she been like this?'

'A few months now,' said Grace tucking the sheet in at the side of the bed. She whispered to Alice. 'She's got this horrible boil on her chest and it's getting worse. I've tried poultices but they don't help. Trouble is she doesn't like me to touch it. Doesn't even like me to see it.' Leaning forward she said softly, 'Mam, let Alice have a look at your chest.'

The invalid murmured something to her daughter, but, as she was speaking Alice put her hand on the towel covering her. Instinctively the woman held it to her chin, but Alice pulled it gently from her fingers and peeled the cloth back.

Lucy had never seen anything like it. A purple ulcer had puckered the skin of her right breast. At the top edge a pale cauliflower-like growth was protruding from it. The exudate, weeping from it, smelled foul.

'That's a bit of a mess, Mrs Fothergill,' Alice said in a kind but pragmatic tone.

'No, doctors, luv,' the woman begged allowing a tear to slip sideways across her temple.

Alice squeezed her hand, talking quietly as she replaced the piece of towelling. 'Perhaps I can get something from the hospital to help you sleep,' she said.

Mrs Fothergill nodded. Her eyes closed and within seconds her breathing indicated she was asleep. The visitors left quietly without saying goodbye. Grace closed the door behind them.

The expression on Lucy's face answered the question Mr Fothergill was about to ask.

'Isn't there anything you can do for Mam?' said Grace.

Alice shook her head. 'You should call the doctor.'

'No point. She'll not let the doctor near her. I'm surprised she let you look.'

'I'm sorry, Mr Fothergill,' said Alice. 'There's nothing I can do. Sleep is probably the best thing for her. A little brandy might help, if she'll take it.'

'Teetotal, all her life. Even before the pledge. Won't allow a drop past her lips. Always been a stubborn woman.'

Lucy needed to get outside into the fresh air. She excused herself by asking Grace if she could look around the garden while she and her father spoke with Alice. Outside it was cold and damp. A black dog sniffed at her boots before flopping down in a makeshift kennel it was sharing with the family of kittens.

At the side of the farmhouse was an untended vegetable patch. The only evidence of recent digging had been done by the hens. She could hear cows and geese but was unable to see them from the side of the house. She was relieved when Alice emerged from the kitchen.

As they walked home, Alice was quiet.

'She's not long for this world, is she?'

'No, not long.'

Lucy visited the farm twice a week for the next three weeks. Alice only managed one more visit before Mrs Fothergill passed away. The funeral was a quiet affair. Lucy, Pansy and Alice went. Timothy wasn't feeling well and stayed home alone. James gave his apologies saying he would wait in the car outside the chapel.

'You must go!' Lucy said. 'People will think you are rude!'

'I don't care what they think,' he said. 'I'm not going.'

After the service Lucy and Pansy decided to walk home. As Alice wanted to catch the bus back to the hospital, James offered Mr Fothergill and his daughter a lift in the car. The farmer was grateful. He had found the service trying but when he sat in the car, he started to relax.

'Can I get your advice sometime, sir?' James said.

Mr Fothergill was surprised. 'Anytime lad. You know where we live. You're welcome to call in.'

In the back seat, Grace sat bolt upright. With her fingers gripping the seat in front, James thought, at first, she was nervous, until he realized her expression was one of sheer excitement. She never listened to the men's conversation, and as the car sped up she soaked up the new experience. The wind on her face. The sound of the engine. The vibrations thrumming through her body. The movement of the car twisting around the country lanes. For the farmer's daughter, the ride home was the most thrilling experience she had ever had.

'Would you let me take you out again sometime?' James said, as he opened the car door. 'If that's all right with you, Mr Fothergill,' he added.

Grace looked at her father, her eyes wide and smiling. 'Can I, Dad?'

'About time you had a bit of fun, lass,' he said. 'And that goes for you too, young man! Go out and enjoy yourself, the pair of you.'

Alice stopped playing, closed the piano lid and turned to James. 'I have something to tell you.'

James glanced up from his book. Through the window he could see it was still raining. He really must finish building the garage for the car.

'I'm going to have a baby.'

James turned around. 'What did you say?'

'Don't worry it's not yours.'

He shook his head. 'Whose then?'

'Someone from work.'

'Bertie Bottomley?'

'How do you know that?'

James shook his head. 'Have you told your mother?'

'No. And I don't want to tell her. Not yet anyway.'

'But what about the hospital? They will know soon enough.'

'I will have to leave,' she said, wringing her hands. 'I'm stupid, aren't I?'

James looked at her. She was verging on tears. He knew if he put his arms around her she would cry. He wanted to say he was sorry, say he wished it had not happened. He wanted to ask her why on earth she had allowed herself to get into such a situation. Ask her about Bottomley. He wondered how long she had been going out with him and why she hadn't mentioned him. Wondered what it was that made her love Bottomley and not love him. But James kept the questions to himself. Yes, you are stupid, he thought.

'Is Bottomley going to marry you?'

'Yes. We are getting married at the Register Office in three weeks.'

'And where will you live?'

'I don't know, James,' she sobbed. 'I really don't know.'

'Have you time to come in and rest your legs?' Lucy said.

The constable took off his helmet. 'Don't mind if I do, Mrs Oldfield. They won't miss me at the station.'

Lucy cleared a chair and invited the policeman to sit down. 'What can I do for you?'

'I don't like to worry you but I thought I better bring it to your attention. There's been a bit of funny business going on over the other side of the valley.'

Lucy listened as she offered him a cup of tea.

'Man by the name of Wilkinson, Stanley Wilkinson, been bothering one of the spinster ladies. I haven't seen him myself but from the description he sounds awfully like that Stan Crowther who was bothering your neighbour, Mrs Pugh.'

'I hope you are wrong, Constable.'

'I hope so too, because this man has a nasty streak. Poor woman was found wandering the streets. Didn't know who she was or where she was. When they brought her into the station, I called the doctor and he took her to the hospital himself. I didn't get the man's description till yesterday.'

The policeman sipped his tea. 'I hope I'm wrong but I think Crowther's back. I wanted to warn you and Mrs Pugh to watch out. Will you pass the message on when she comes home?'

'Yes, I will. Thank you.'

Lucy wondered what Pansy would say when she told her. Wondered what would happen if Crowther started coming round again.

That night, though the front door was locked and bolted, Lucy checked it several times before going to bed. Unable to sleep, she was vigilant to the sounds of darkness; mice skittering in the ceiling, tree branches scraping along the eaves, the gate creaking on its rusty hinges. By closing her eyes, she could not shut out the image of the man which haunted her thoughts. She knew if he returned to seek revenge, it might be more than a rock which would come through the window next time.

Timmy's eyes were itchy, his throat sore. He was hot and felt miserable. Pansy told him not to complain. It was only a cold. It would soon pass. When the red rash appeared on his face and neck she took him to the surgery. She had never seen measles before. The doctor said to keep him inside away from other children. Though frail-looking, he was a fit lad and the infection should pass in a week.

But by the end of the week Timothy was confined to bed. The rash had spread all over his body, and the cough, which had developed suddenly, was exhausting him. For three nights neither he nor Pansy slept. Then, when he was too exhausted to clear his lungs, he drifted into sleep. A deep, deep sleep. Though Pansy begged with him to wake, at times shaking his limp body, he never stirred. He never ate or drank and only twice did his eyes open, but they were glazed and he saw nothing. The few sounds he made were incoherent. Hour after hour, Pansy sat beside him mopping his brow while the fever boiled inside him. She wished Alice were home and prayed for Sunday to arrive. Her daughter had promised to come home on her day off. Being a nurse, Alice would know what to do.

But Timothy Pugh couldn't wait for his sister's visit. He died in his mother's arms on the Saturday morning. He was nine years of age.

Chapter 17

The Attic

'Come on, luv, I thought you'd be pleased I made it through the war without a scratch,' he crowed. 'And the war changed me. You'll see!'

Pansy felt exasperated. She didn't want Stanley's attention. Or any other man's for that matter. What she wanted was to be left alone. But Crowther was not prepared to listen.

Whenever she went out, he followed her. She would catch glimpses of his reflection in shop windows trailing a few yards behind her, see him waiting on corners, or outside shop doorways, or loitering behind a post box. Sometimes he would launch himself at her, questioning her angrily, demanding to know what was in her basket, how much she had spent, how much money was left. Other times he appealed to her good nature, begging for a few shillings to tide him over.

Even in the evenings he gave her no respite, constantly tap-tapping on the kitchen window until she succumbed and looked out at his face pressed against the pane; tongue distorted, lips squashed, eyes staring. Afraid and desperate, Pansy would try to escape his taunts by running upstairs to hide, but he would lob tiny pebbles at the bedroom window, not hard enough to crack the glass but loud enough to remind her he was still there.

'I can't take any more,' she cried, as she stood shaking in Lucy's arms. 'He won't stop.'

'Goodness, Pansy, look at the state of you! Why didn't you tell what was happening before now?'

'Because last time you said I was encouraging him. Now I'm not. I keep telling him to go away but he takes no notice.' There was real anguish on her face. 'You must do something,' she begged. 'Help me. I'm worn out. I've lost my energy. I feel tired but I can't sleep. I used to like working but now I hate going outside. I avoid people. I don't want to talk. I don't even look forward to Alice's visits. Please help me.'

Lucy waited until the sobbing stopped. 'You remember Miss Pugh, your Aunt who lives in Ilkley?'

Pansy nodded.

'Could you stay with her for a week or two?'

'Probably. But what about my job?'

'Say you are sick or taking a holiday. If they stop you, there are plenty of other houses to clean.

'What will Alice think if I'm not here?'

'I'll talk to Alice. She'll understand. And I'll get James to take you in the car.' Lucy paused. 'As for Stanley Crowther, I'll speak with the constable again.'

Pansy tried to smile.

'I just wish you'd told me sooner, before getting yourself into this terrible state.'

Miss Pugh opened the door apprehensively. She did not recognize her niece, the small slim woman with the suitcase in her hand, or remember James who was standing behind her. Jogging the memory took a little explanation, but once the pieces were reassembled she was happy to invite Pansy to stay with her.

When they stepped inside, Pansy was both surprised and appalled by the state of the living-room. She wondered about the condition of the rest of the three-storey house. Miss Pugh had always been an extremely particular person. Everything had always had its rightful position. Everything was always spick and span, neat and tidy. Nothing was ever out of place.

But today the living-room was a shambles. A blackened saucepan sat in the armchair by the fire. A pile of dirty clothes was sitting in the coal scuttle. A slice of bread on top of the writing bureau was curled and dry, and a quarter-inch of dust covered all the furniture.

Seeing the worry on Pansy's face, James felt concerned. His instinct was to leave and take Pansy with him. He was afraid the responsibility of minding the elderly spinster would drain her even further and she was not strong enough for that.

'I want to stay.' Pansy said. 'Aunty needs me. Besides, it will give me something worthwhile to do and I want to repay a little of the kindness she showed me when I was ill with Timmy.'

Reluctantly, James conceded and by the time he left the two relatives were reminiscing happily. Noticing the soft smile which had returned to Pansy's face, he felt satisfied. It had been absent for some time.

As he drove back to Horsforth, James decided Pansy would be fine living with Miss Pugh, just so long as Crowther didn't know where she was. He would never find her there, James thought.

Lucy held the chair steady, as James swung himself through the hole in the bedroom ceiling and up into the attic. The candle she handed him flickered from lack of air in the roof cavity.

'Is there anything up there?' she called.

'Lots of cobwebs! My old jigsaws. Empty boxes. Tea chests.'

From below she could hear things being shifted about.

'James, be careful.'

For a while there was no answer then his head poked down through the hole. 'Smells like we've got rats in one of these boxes. Can you manage to take it?'

As he lowered the tea chest, flakes of dust floated down settling on Lucy's hair like grey snow. She sneezed.

Peering in the box she could see where the rats had their home. A felt tea-cosy lined with scraps of paper and cloth made an ideal nest. In the centre was a family of pink-skinned babies no bigger than Lucy's thumb. They squirmed like a collection of juicy caterpillars.

After transporting the chest to the back garden, James scattered the contents of the tea-cosy on the ground beside the back wall. Not having the heart to kill the rats himself, he was sure the crows who roosted in the chestnut tree would quickly make a meal of them.

With a small fire of dried leaves and twigs, James burned the nest and its lining. The felted cloth was damp and smoked before igniting, but the stained newspaper which had been underneath it, burned brightly. As the newsprint curled, James noticed the bold header: *The Bombay Chronicle*, and in smaller letters and brackets, the words: *English language edition.*

Beneath the rat's nest was a stack of similar papers which James fed to the fire. But, on delving beneath, he was surprised to discover a cache of unusual items; a long leather glove, its stitches rotted along the seams, a tarnished spur, a crested pendant, and a military jacket decorated with braided epaulettes and metal buttons. The uniform had obviously fostered generations of moths. As James lifted it out, he sneezed.

The only item, apparently not affected by the years, was a black wooden box. It was the size of a gentleman's toilet case and was wrapped in a length of canvas. Uncovering it, James realized it was an item of value. It was old and the workmanship was exquisite. The smooth lid was inlaid with shards of mother of pearl depicting an elephant drinking at a waterhole. The box's hinges were metal, blackened, but definitely silver.

James shook it gently. It didn't rattle. As he raised the lid he expected to see a moulded velvet lining housing an assortment of gentleman's toiletries. But the ebony box contained neither moulding nor lining. It was crammed with letters and papers and pieces of folded parchment. Beneath the papers were other items: a box suitable for a ring, a fob watch with chain, a wad of bank notes and two purses. Without opening it, James knew from the feel that the purse made from animal skin contained coins. The other purse interested him. It was handmade in black silk with an exotic dancer embroidered on it in gold thread. Inside was something hard. It felt like gravel or small river pebbles. Loosening the string, James tipped the contents into his palm.

'Mother!' he yelled.

Sitting across the table from Lucy, James rolled the stones over with his finger. They resembled tiny transparent marbles, glassy but chipped. The colour was a beautiful cornflower blue.

After examining the birth, death and marriage certificates, old school reports and personal letters, Lucy put them to one side. She was busy gazing at the other papers which had almost filled the box. The legal documents confused her. Title deeds. Leases. Stock certificates.

'It appears Edward's father had several holdings and Edward had shares in a sapphire mine in Kashmir.' Lucy looked at the stones on the table. 'Sapphires? Is that what they are?'

James shrugged his shoulders, amazed. 'Is there anything else?'

The coins in the purse included some sovereigns. The fob watch was gold. The wad of banknotes consisted of old notes, both English and foreign currency. There were cufflinks, a tiepin and a lady's brooch set with a large red gemstone.

'A garnet?' suggested Lucy.

'Or a ruby! This lot could be worth a small fortune! What do we do with it?'

'We pay a visit to Proctor and Armitage and let them sort it out. These things obviously belonged to Edward or his father.'

'But why did he leave them in the attic?' asked James. 'Had he forgotten about them?'

'I wouldn't think so. He probably hoped to come back and collect them one day. He didn't expect to die suddenly.'

'But he lived a very simple life.'

'That was his choice,' said Lucy.

'But if these are his, who do they belong to now?'

'The lawyers will know.'

'But didn't Edward leave the residue of his estate to you.'

Lucy nodded.

'Then they could all be yours!'

The content of Pansy's letter came as a surprise.

Dear Lucy

I am writing to let you know I have decided to stay in Ilkley indefinitely. My aunt needs someone to care for her. She is quite forgetful and prone to wandering. I found her the other morning on the road. She was wearing only her nightdress and it was bitterly cold. As I am her only relative, I feel it is my duty, but besides that, I like it here in Ilkley. It's peaceful and no one bothers me.

If it is not too much trouble, there are two favours I have to ask.

Could James please bring me the rest of my belongings?

The other thing, I beg to ask; can Alice and her husband, Bertie, move into my cottage? Alice says they can afford to pay a small rent. She says they have looked at rooms elsewhere but they are disgusting, and with the baby due in only

six weeks, Alice is getting desperate. She told me it would be impossible for them
to continue living with Bertie's parents as it is causing too much strife between
them.

I hope you will be able to help them out.

Your dear friend, Pansy.

After confirming her thoughts with James, Lucy sat down and wrote two letters. The first was addressed to Mrs Pansy Pugh. In it she told Pansy that she and James would deliver the rest of her personal possessions the following Saturday morning and that they would arrive in Ilkley about eleven.

The second letter was addressed to Mrs and Mrs Albert Bottomley. Wording it carefully, Lucy asked Alice and Bert to call in to see her to discuss a lease to be made out in their names. She suggested a rent of seven shillings and sixpence a week. If they could afford that, she wrote, they could move in immediately.

Chapter 18

The Cow and Calf

The sudden clucking of the hens alerted Alice. She knew it was Crowther or a fox, and, as it was broad daylight, she settled on the former. Peeping through the lace curtain she saw the man leaning over the hen house. When he walked towards the door she drew back. The handle rattled. Then she heard him shout her mother's name.

'Pansy, Pansy,' he called, his voice polite at first, but it soon rose in both pitch and urgency. Then the tapping began, first on the door, then on the window. From the room's shadows, Alice watched him as he pressed his face against the pane. Unable to see anyone inside the man stepped back and looked up towards the bedroom. Picking up a handful of soil, he lobbed it against the window. It showered back into his hair. Alice could see his exasperation festering.

The squawk of the chickens drew Alice back to the window. One of the birds was hanging limply from the man's hand. She didn't see him break its neck but saw the ball of warm red feathers as it disappeared inside his jacket. When he climbed over the wall and headed for the lane, she ran through the house to the front room.

Though Alice had not seen Crowther for many years, she recognized him as the man who hawked rabbits, the man who had wheedled his way into her mother's life, the man Lucy had warned her about. No doubt he had come back looking for Pansy, unaware she had moved to Ilkley. Standing in the hall, Alice watched the brass knob as it turned. She'd locked the door just in time. Outside, Crowther cursed and rattled the knob. Then there was silence. Alice held her breath not knowing what to expect. The gate creaked on its hinges. Venturing into the front room, she watched as Crowther mounted his bicycle and rode off down the hill. Alice was trembling. She felt sure he would be back, but didn't know when.

'Let me explain,' the solicitor said. 'Firstly, we are not certain of the viability of these title deeds. Though they appear authentic and indicate Mr Edward Carrington was the rightful owner, it is possible the properties have been disposed of. New deeds may have been drawn up if these originals were considered lost. Alternatively, if the rates and taxes were unpaid for many years, the properties may have been sold to offset any accrued debt.'

Mr Armitage continued, 'With regard to the various property leases, we must assume they all expired some years ago, unless we can find some record of the terms being renewed.' He turned to the next document in the file. 'Of course, with all these investments being located in India, the problem of tracing and verifying them is made doubly difficult.'

'The same applies to the stocks and bonds,' interrupted Proctor. 'I have to warn you, Mrs Oldfield, these documents may not be worth the paper they are written on.' He paused. 'On the other hand. . . .'

'The gemstones,' said Mr Armitage, 'could be worth a considerable amount because of their number and size. But I am not an expert. We should arrange to have these valued by a professional.'

Lucy nodded.

'I have no doubt they belonged to Mr Edward Carrington and from the colour would assume they came from Kashmir. I doubt there will be any contest over proof of ownership.'

'Then there are the coins, notes and other curios . . .' the old gentleman added. 'It may take some time to finalize this matter. Return mail to the Indian sub-continent can take several weeks.'

'Should I notify Captain Wainwright, Edward's brother-in-law of this discovery?' Lucy asked.

'For what purpose?' asked the solicitor.

'Wouldn't he be a beneficiary if this is part of Edward's estate?'

'Lydia Carrington was Edward's sister, but as she is dead and left no heirs, the residue of his estate, after his special bequests, goes to you. It will just be a matter of time before we can ascertain the value of the box's contents but as soon as we hear anything, we will let you know.'

'Open the door, Pansy!' The muffled shout came through the letterbox. The tone was intimidating.

'Come on Pansy! Why don't you let me in? I just want a bit of company. Five minutes' chat. Com on, luv. It's dark and cold out here. Don't be mean.'

Getting no response Crowther wandered round to the back of the house and rattled on the kitchen door. It was locked also. A few moments later he began tapping. As expected, his repertoire had not changed. When the stones hit the bedroom window Bertie Bottomley was ready to move.

After shouting abuse at the silent house, Crowther walked back towards the lane where he had left his bicycle.

Slipping quietly out of the kitchen door Bertie followed him. James was crouching in the shadows across the road, waiting.

When a light came on in the hallway, Stan Crowther grinned, swaggered up to the front door and waited until he heard the key turn in the lock.

'Now you are seeing sense at last,' he said, as Alice let the door swing open. She took one step forward and pointed James's rifle at Stan Crowther's stomach.

His chin dropped.

'Get away from here and don't come back!' Alice shouted.

'Wait a minute, luv,' he said, laughing nervously. 'Put the gun down. I just came to say hello to your mam. We used to be good friends.'

'You have no friends, here!' she said.

'Be fair,' he sneered, his eyes set on her enlarged belly. 'You on your own right now?'

Alice didn't answer.

'If you'd like a bit of company, your condition don't bother me.'

Before Alice had time to answer, Bert grabbed him by the shoulder. Spinning him around, he landed his fist square on Crowther's chin sending him reeling into the rose bushes. As he tried to get up, James swung at him hitting him in the stomach. Crowther rolled on the ground nursing his stomach and groaning.

'Go inside, Alice!' James shouted. After another punch from Bert, blood dripped from Crowther's lip. Alice quickly closed the door and listened. She heard more punches being thrown and then Crowther's whimpering cry.

'Come back again if you want more of the same!' James challenged, as he watched the man stumble down the lane, bent almost double, his arms wrapped around his belly.

Standing beside the garden gate, James and Bert rubbed their knuckles and then shook hands.

'I think that'll be the last we shall see of him,' James said.

'Certainly hope so,' said Bert. 'Fancy a wee drop to celebrate?'

'Don't mind if I do.'

Alice opened the door. It was the first time she had invited James into her own home. It was a nice feeling.

Though it was broad daylight outside, little light filtered into the Fothergills' farm shed. From the doorway, James could see Grace struggling to fix the cow's head in a wooden yoke. He called out to her, but his voice was drowned beneath the bellowing and when the cow began to thrash about, he felt anxious.

'Be careful,' he shouted.

Grace glanced up at him as she stepped from the stall and rubbed her hand along the animal's rump.

'Can I be of any help?' he asked.

'Yes,' she said, pushing her sleeves high above her elbows.

As she looped a piece of cord around her thumb and gently pushed her hand into the cow, James watched intently. And, when she rolled her arm around, the bellowing grew louder. Closing her eyes, Grace bit on her bottom lip and concentrated.

'Got it!' she announced, as slowly she withdrew her hand and handed the ends of the cord to James. 'Now pull slowly but firmly, when I tell you to.'

As the cow strained, James pulled, while Grace provided encouragement to them both. When the calf's head emerged, she ran her fingers through its mouth, then eased it into the world sliding it down on to the bed of hay. As if suddenly petrified, the cow was still and silent, but within minutes of Grace releasing its head from the yoke, it snorted, sniffed at its calf and started licking it.

James glanced at Grace as she wiped her bloodied hands on a length of rag. He could see she was pleased.

'Would I ever make a farmer?' he asked.

She laughed but did not commit herself to an answer. 'Want a cup of tea? I made some scones this morning.'

'I'd like that but I have to drive to Ilkley.'

'Is anything wrong?'

'No,' he said. 'It was a piece in the paper which said a woman had been found wandering near the Cow and Calf Rocks. Mum was concerned it might be Miss Pugh so I offered to go to Ilkley to make sure everything was all right. Would you like to come?'

'Of course,' she said. 'I wouldn't miss the chance of a drive.'

Standing side by side, they watched the calf struggle to its feet, searching for its first drink.

'I was talking to Mum the other day,' he said casually. 'She said you were fed up with the farm and wanted to move to the city.'

Grace laughed. 'What would I do in the city? I love the farm and the animals. I've got no plans to leave.'

Looking across at her, James was unable to stop the smile curling on his lips. 'Good,' he said. 'Shall we go?'

Chapter 19

Leaving

Six weeks after Rachel Bottomley was born, Alice invited a small group of friends and family to celebrate her daughter's christening. Lucy hosted the party in her cottage.

Unfortunately, Bert got very drunk. His voice was loud and his behaviour, at times, distasteful. Alice was relieved when Grace and James left to take John Fothergill home. The farmer excused himself saying he was anxious to get back to the farm to attend to the milking, but Alice knew he was just being polite.

Pansy never said a great deal to anyone, appearing content to sit beside the fireplace, in one room or the other. Lucy tried to entice her outside to take a walk across the meadow or wander in the garden but she insisted she was quite happy indoors. Pansy never admitted that the sound of the tree branches tapping on the window made her feel nervous.

When it was time to leave on Sunday afternoon and she climbed into James's car, it was obvious she was pleased to be returning to Ilkley and Miss Pugh.

Alice had enjoyed seeing her mother and cried a little when she left. She had wanted the visit to be special, had wanted to be able to talk to her mother, intimately, as one woman to another. She had been little more than a girl when she left home to take up nursing, but now she was married with her own baby and she thought things would be different. She was disappointed she didn't have the opportunity to find out.

From the window, Alice saw James bending over to crank the car's engine. As the motor burst into life, a puff of smoke rose from the exhaust and drifted through the tangled branches of the briar rose. Alice watched as he slid on to the front seat, beside Grace, and leaned his head towards her. His lips touched her cheek. Their eyes smiled, and as the car rolled away, Grace's arm glided across James's shoulders.

Shaking her head, Alice wandered back into Lucy's living-room. Why was I so stupid? she thought to herself.

Lucy was knitting while Rachel slept in the pram. From its seat on the straight-backed chair the doll's glass eyes appeared to be looking at Alice.

'Constance,' she said 'I had almost forgotten you.' Picking up the doll, she sat it on her knee and turned towards Lucy. 'Has she been sitting there all the time I've been away?'

Lucy nodded. 'She's part of the furniture. But she's yours to take whenever you want her.'

'May I have her? For the baby.'

'Of course. I'm sure when Rachel's older she will love her as much as you did.' Lucy put down her needles and looked at the doll perched on Alice's knee. 'It's about time I replaced that old nurse's uniform. It's old-fashioned, too long, and grubby. The haberdasher in Horsforth has some nice remnants. I'll buy some lace and make her a new dress. Modern. 1920s style.'

'Aunt Lucy, you were like a mother to me when I was growing up, and here I am back again, twenty-five years of age.'

Lucy retrieved the ball of wool which had rolled on to the floor. 'We don't get any younger, lass.'

'Tell me,' Alice asked tentatively. 'How did you manage with a baby? You were on your own, weren't you? Was it hard in your day?'

'Probably harder than today. Women who had a baby out of wedlock were thought of as loose, treated with contempt. But I managed. I had good neighbours. And James seems no worse for it.' Lucy took off her glasses and rubbed her eyes. 'Why do you ask? You and Bert having problems?'

Alice sighed. 'Maybe it's just me or my imagination but Bert seems uninterested in me these days. He's working longer hours but he never brings home any more money. He says he deserves to keep the extra. That's fine, but he complains all the time that he hasn't enough and has to borrow.'

'And do you give him a few extra bob?'

'Sometimes. Well, he knows exactly what I have in my savings. He made me draw out the money to buy his new motor bike. He said he had to have one with a bigger engine because we lived further away. Said it was my fault I got pregnant and had to stop work.' She straightened the red cross on the doll's uniform and placed it back on the chair. 'I had a good wage compared with Bert's, but now I can't work again till the baby grows up.'

'Does Bert know how much money you've got left?'

Alice nodded. 'I've seen him looking in my bank book. He said he wanted to buy a sidecar for the bike so he could take me and the baby out, but I spent the money on the pram and cot and told him I couldn't give him any more.' She looked at herself in the mirror. 'Since Rachel was born, I feel flat. It seems there's nothing left between us anymore. He never touches me. Never even kisses me.' She smiled sadly at the picture of herself on the mantelpiece. 'When I see James with Grace, I feel jealous. She's young, and pretty in a way, and they're always laughing and going out, driving or dancing or to the pictures. I wish I could do all those things.' She shook her head. 'How stupid I was! All I ever wanted was to be a nurse. I loved the job and I was good at it. But I made no time in my life for James. And when he wanted me, I never listened. And look where I am now.'

'Give Bert a chance, Alice. A man gets his nose pushed out of joint when a baby comes along. He'll come around. Just give him time.'

'But how long? There's talk about prices going up and men being put out of work. Bert's only a porter and to be quite honest he's not very popular at the hospital. I've even heard people say he's lucky to have a job because he's lazy. What happens to us if he loses his job? What will we do then?'

'You'll manage. Your mam and I managed in the Great War. And don't you worry about the rent if he's out of work.'

'But what about you, Aunt Lucy? How do you cope?'

'I'm fine. Edward left me a bit of money.' Lucy rolled the wool around the ball and pushed the needles through it. 'Come on,' she said cheerily. 'Let's go in the other room. I'd love to hear you play.'

Alice sat down at the piano and lifted the lid. Resting her hands on her knees she thought for a moment. Her fingers touched the keys lightly as she played, Beethoven's, *Für Elise.*

'Bert Bottomley! You're drunk again!'

'Too right I'm drunk. And I've spent all my pay on booze. Every penny! There's none left! And no more where that came from! No more money and no more work! It's all gone!'

'What are you talking about?' said Alice.

'I mean, Mrs Bottomley,' he drawled, 'I am out of work and from this week, unless you have a secret stash of money, we've got nothing.'

'Then you'll have to find another job.'

He laughed as he steadied himself against the sideboard. 'Me, find another job? Easier said than done. You should go down to Leeds and see the queues of men lined up for every job that's going.'

Alice resisted the temptation to ask what he had been doing in the city. 'Why not try the farms? Maybe you can get some work locally.'

'What! After the hospital. I'm not stomping around in no stinking cow shit.'

'Bertie!'

'Oh, shut up, woman. I'm sick of listening to you. If you want some money, you go out to work.'

'I can't go back yet. I have to feed the baby. Maybe in three or four months, but not now.'

Albert Bottomley had always lacked patience. He sloped around for only two weeks, constantly complaining to Alice about his lot in life. During that time, however, he somehow found enough money to visit the village pub, staggering home drunk every night. Alice wasn't sure if he had money put aside, or if he was getting it from someone else. She didn't think he had resorted to stealing.

When he left there was no final argument or fight. Bert was demanding but never violent. One morning, after eating his breakfast, he said he was off. He put on his leather helmet and gloves, kicked the motor bike into life, jumped on and rode away. Alice never saw him again.

Someone told her later he had gone to America, but Alice found that hard to believe. How could he have paid the passage? She thought she saw him once when she was on a tram in the city, but it went by too fast. For a while she felt sad. Sorry for herself. At times, lost and a little guilty. But after a while, as Rachel began to smile and coo, life took on a different aspect.

When Lucy agreed to mind the baby three days a week, Alice returned to work. Not at the hospital, but as a nurse in a private nursing home in Headingley. She didn't mind looking after the old gentlemen, but the young men, whose bodies had been broken in the Great War, were her favourites.

'The conservative value of your assets, taking into account the properties, and the sapphires, is around thirty thousand pounds.' The solicitor paused to allow Lucy to digest what he was saying. 'That is a considerable fortune, Mrs Oldfield.'

'Have you given any thought to what you would like to do with the other foreign investments?' Mr Proctor asked.

Lucy shook her head. 'I cannot imagine what these houses are like. You say they were once quite fashionable. But they are so far away.'

'May I make a suggestion?'

'Please do.'

'You have no commitments that I am aware of?'

'That is correct.'

'And you have never travelled?'

Lucy looked at him quizzically. 'Correct.'

'If I may suggest, in my estimation a voyage to India on one of the modern liners, travelling first class of course, would be a wonderful experience for you.' Mr Armitage peered over the rim of his glasses. 'If you embarked on such a journey, we would arrange for a representative to meet you in Bombay, someone able to show you round your various holdings. After seeing them, you will be in a better position regarding your decision as to what to do with them.' He cleared his throat before continuing. 'If you will excuse me for being forthright, Mrs Oldfield, but it would be best to embark on this sort of venture before you are too old.'

'But I wouldn't dare to travel alone.'

'Then take your son. Or advertise for a companion. You must remember, you are now in the very fortunate situation where money is no object.'

Lucy raised her eyebrows.

'Please give it some thought. From our point of view, if you decide to sell the properties, it would be easier for the business to be conducted in India while you are there. That will facilitate a saving in both time and money. Of course, Mr Proctor and I will attend to all your travel arrangements.' He paused. 'May I suggest winter would be a good time? I gather India gets rather hot in the summer!'

Chapter 20

Captain Wainwright

Winter arrived early and was bitterly cold. Blizzards blowing over the Pennines blocked the roads and brought the towns to a halt. On the country lanes, drifting snow banked to the height of the horses' withers. Lakes became skating rinks, hillsides, slopes for children's sledges. Water pipes froze solid, shops sold out of candles and folk with no food in the pantry went hungry. For the poor souls without firewood, the only chance to keep warm was to take to their beds. For the farmers, the job of keeping animals fed and watered was near impossible.

Despite his mother's pleas not to venture out, James was concerned about Grace and her father and decided he must go to the farm. Once he stepped outside, the soft snow swallowed his boots. It was worse than he had thought. Every step he took was an effort. When he eventually rounded the last turn in the lane and saw a wisp of smoke curling from one of the farm's tall chimney-pots, he felt some relief. He was looking forward to spending the afternoon with Grace. He would be home in time for tea.

When he arrived at the farm, James was surprised to find the fire almost dead and the house empty. A path had been dug in the snow. It led from the house door and headed towards the cow shed but it stopped half-way. Picking up the shovel, James dug the remainder of the distance. Expecting to find Grace and her father inside, he called out.

Two cows turned their heads and looked lazily at him from the stalls. James shouted again. No reply. Swishing their tails, the animals blew steam from their nostrils and returned, unconcerned, to their feed of hay.

Checking outside James found a trail leading away from the barn. The two sets of footprints indicated that Grace and her father had headed towards the far meadow. There were no tracks to show they had come back.

The far field, which completely crowned a hill, was the largest of Mr Fothergill's paddocks. Every summer it was ablaze with waving wheat and when the sun dropped behind it, it gleamed as if draped in a cloth of gold. Now buried beneath its winter mantle, the field, fences and clustered trees, formed the picture of a perfect Christmas card; vestal white, pure, untouched.

But the wind was biting cold and fine slivers of ice stung James's face like red-hot needles. Screwing his eyes against the sleet, he turned up his collar. 'Grace!' he yelled, as he followed the deep footprints which led towards a wooden stile. Seeing the snow knocked from the slats, he knew the pair had crossed.

'Mr Fothergill!' he yelled. 'Are you out there?'

'Over here!' The voice was faint. It was Grace.

James lumbered awkwardly through the drifts in the direction of the call but could see nothing but snow. 'Where are you?' he shouted.

In the corner of the field, sheltered only by the bare branches of a line of tall poplars, was a group of black and white beasts. Completely saddled in snow, they were huddled against the fence line. Not far from the cattle, an arm poked up from the snow and waved. Grace had burrowed a small alcove and was sitting in the snow with her father's head resting on her lap.

'Thank goodness you're here,' she said, as he dropped down beside her. 'I only found him a short while ago. He was worried about the cattle because they'd been here two days with nothing to eat. He said he tried to move them but they got confused and when he fell one trampled his leg. I think it's broken.' She looked up at James. 'I can't move him but we've got to get him out of here otherwise he's going to freeze.'

It took more than an hour to get the farmer back to the house. James supported him all the way, but with the extra weight his feet sank deep in the drifts, making every step extremely difficult. Grace went on ahead to build up the fire and warm some water and by the time James reached the farmhouse, he was exhausted.

'We can't get him to the doctor while the weather is like this. And I'd never make it to the village before dark.'

Grace looked to him for an answer. 'What do we do, James?'

'Wait till morning. I'll go down to the village at dawn and get the doctor to come here.' Though he did not want to leave the farm and didn't want to step back out into the cold, he had promised his mother he would be home. If he didn't return, he knew she would worry. 'Will you be all right if I leave you tonight?'

Thawing out slowly in the warmth of the log fire, Mr Fothergill was apologetic for the trouble he was causing. He had no alternative but to accept James's suggestion and was adamant he would manage until morning.

Wrapping his arms around Grace to say good night, James could feel her body warm against his. 'Take care of your dad,' he said, as he kissed her gently. 'I will see you tomorrow.'

As the time of their departure for India drew closer, James was less and less sure he was doing the right thing, but the arrangements had been made and he knew his mother was not confident to travel without him.

His main concern was Grace. He wondered how she could possibly manage the farm on her own while her father was incapacitated. When she told him that her father had hired a local man to help out in the dairy until his leg was healed, James felt a little better. To a lesser extent he was concerned about Alice and Rachel being left alone, as Alice was used to being independent. He wondered if she would visit Grace and her father while they were away, but doubted she would.

On the morning of their departure, Grace arrived very early, pleased to be able drive James and Lucy to the station. The morning air was heavy with mist. It was damp but there had been no frost. All the snow of the recent blizzards was gone. They all hoped the worst of winter was over.

Leeds Station was cold and dismal. It was filled with the familiar railway sounds and smells. When she saw the train waiting at the platform, Lucy became anxious. Doors were being slammed and steam was hissing from the engine. After ensuring they had the correct seats, James checked their trunks in the luggage van and after settling the smaller cases on the overhead rack in the compartment, he stepped down to the platform.

There was a host of things he wanted to say to Grace before they left. She must call the doctor if her father's leg didn't improve. She must check on Alice and the baby, if she had time. Must make sure the new calf was feeding. Check water in the car's radiator and drive carefully. In turn, he told her he would write from the ship and from India. He knew, above all, he would miss her, and told her so. Before Grace had chance to respond, the shrill sound of the guard's whistle blew along the platform. James closed the door as the train pulled away. From the window he could see tears in Grace's eyes.

'I'll bring you back an Indian elephant,' he shouted. Then a cloud of smoke engulfed her and she disappeared.

The SS *Oceanus* was not due to sail from Southampton until the following Tuesday. This gave Lucy and James time to pay a visit to Edward's brother-in-law in Tunbridge Wells. Despite Captain Wainwright extending an invitation for them to stay with him, they preferred to be independent and booked two rooms at the Grand Palace Hotel. Although Lucy and James had both corresponded with the captain before their journey, neither had ever met him, and both were uncertain what to expect when they did. Lucy had presumed Wainwright was older than Edward Carrington – probably around seventy years of age – but that was purely an assumption. She had not known how old Edward's sister, Lydia, had been when she died.

The Bower, Wainwright's house in Tunbridge Wells, was a substantial two-storey detached Victorian residence with the characteristic tall chimney stacks. The gardens at the front were neat and well tended and, like every other house in the street, boasted a variety of bare rose bushes. The house's stone walls, once clean and white, bore the grey shades of age. The front door was recessed between two Doric columns, its coloured leadlight glass adorned an otherwise austere façade.

James pulled on the brass bell.

The housekeeper, who introduced herself as Mrs Mac, took their coats and led them into the conservatory where Captain Wainwright was reading.

It was a delightful room, obviously a recent addition to the house, surrounded on three sides by glass walls which reached from floor to ceiling. The conservatory overlooked a lawn where veined leaves and stilled sycamore seeds littered the damp grass. Around the garden an old creeper grew rampant over the eight-foot fence. In the centre of the neatly trimmed lawn was an imitation wishing well, custom built in wrought iron and tied to the top-most swirl of metal was half a coconut. A family of blue tits were pecking at it hungrily.

Inside the room, the soft furnishings glowed with the warm shades of autumn. The high-back chairs woven from cane, were elaborately decorated with twisted swirls and rosettes. A large rug, which reflected the dull sheen of Indian silk, covered the slate floor.

On the small table beside Wainwright was a pile of journals and a magnifying glass. The captain had a shawl over his knees, as would an invalid, but he removed it when Lucy and James approached and got to his feet. He was not as old as Lucy had expected, probably several years younger than Edward. He was also taller than she had imagined, and his back was as straight as a book's spine.

After James had introduced himself and his mother, Mrs Mac offered them tea.

Lucy felt a little overawed at first, mainly because of Wainwright's colonial accent and behaviour. He was every inch an English gentleman and obviously a man of means. Some of his mannerisms reminded her of Edward Carrington, but Edward had never displayed the nuances which she associated with money, authority or the affectation of upper class. She soon realized, however, that Captain Wainwright was not trying to create an impression, he was merely being himself.

'Can I get you anything else?' the housekeeper asked.

'Thank you, Mrs Mac,' the captain said. 'I'm sure we will manage.'

He waited until his guests were settled before sitting down. 'Now,' he said. 'I am looking forward to hearing more about this trip. I do envy you. The passage is one I would love to repeat. The ports of call: Gibraltar, Port Said, Suez. Fascinating places.'

Lucy relaxed as they spoke of the voyage and as Wainwright spoke affectionately of his brother-in-law. 'Edward was an astute man, honest and loyal. He had intellect, integrity and selflessness and would have made a fine officer. That he did not enter the service was a great disappointment to his father, Colonel Carrington. The Colonel could not understand why he refused to pursue a career in the army. Of course,' Wainwright said, not meaning to sound boastful, 'I was completely accepted into the family. "An appropriate choice for my daughter", I once heard the old Colonel say.' He turned to James. 'And you, young man, I understand, served your country proud in France.' He lifted his tea cup. 'I salute you, sir.'

James acknowledged the gesture.

'But to other matters. I have taken the liberty of writing to one of my old colleagues in Bombay advising him and his wife of your intended journey. They live in the town of Nashik, one hundred miles from the coast. Nashik is a cool and pleasant place situated in the hills. You must contact them when you arrive and if time permits, I recommend a visit. You will not only enjoy their company but a visit to them will allow you to see something of the Indian countryside.'

Lucy thanked him and promised she would get in touch with them.

Wainwright was exuberant when talking about the country he had lived in for most of his life. He responded eagerly to all James's questions, offering advice on modes of transport, dealing with natives, making purchases, even dress code. He supplied a list of places they should visit and areas to be avoided. He advised James about tipping, about baggage in transit, even how to combat heat, scorpions, crowds and beggars.

By the time the captain had finished speaking, Lucy was a little apprehensive and confused, not sure whether she should forgo the whole venture and allow the firm of Proctor and Armitage to settle her affairs by post.

'It is a wonderful country,' Captain Wainwright said, gazing from the window as if staring into a giant crystal ball. 'You will find yourself treated like royalty. It is a shame that apart from my club, the same standards are not maintained in England! Which reminds me,' he said, taking a card from his waistcoat and passing it to James. 'Introduce yourself to this gentleman and mention my name. If there is anything which requires a little extra persuasion while you are in Bombay, Colonel Winters is the man to see.'

James thanked him. 'I hope that won't be necessary.'

The captain nodded and with a flamboyant flick of his moustache added, 'You are sailing on Tuesday evening, I believe.'

'That is so.'

'Then you must allow me to indulge myself. I intend to hire a car and driver to deliver you to the docks and to accompany you there. When you board you will invite me to join you as your guest, so I can savour, albeit for only a few hours, the opportunity of stepping inside one of the latest luxury steamers.' He held up his hand to continue. 'And if you will permit, I will order a bottle of the ship's best champagne to drink a toast to your safe journey.'

James and Lucy returned to The Bower the following day to have lunch with Captain Wainwright and invite him to join them for dinner at their hotel.

That evening, Lucy again enjoyed the captain's company, as he reminisced about his early life in India, about his late wife, Lydia, and about her brother, Edward Carrington. Though he related his adventures in a matter-of-fact manner, at times Lucy was overawed by his experiences.

James appeared totally relaxed in the captain's company and Lucy was proud of him. Any lack of breeding James suffered was compensated by his personality. He exuded charm and wit, traits he had learned from Edward. He dressed and carried himself well, and although lacking in tertiary education he was well read in both the classics and popular Press and could carry on a conversation on many subjects. His only downfall, Lucy considered, was his accent. Like hers it was not entirely broad Yorkshire, but it was a far cry from that of a cultured English gentleman like Captain Sebastopol Wainwright.

When they waved farewell to Wainwright from the ship's rail, Lucy could see the envy etched in his expression. In a way she wished they had invited him to travel to India with them, but she had business to attend to and was not sure when they would return. As the tugs pulled the ship from the wharf and the coloured streamers floated down to the oily harbour water, Lucy wondered if she would miss England, and if India would prove as intriguing as the captain had promised.

The SS *Oceanus* was everything Lucy could have dreamed of and more. For the first few days of the voyage she was apprehensive, not used to being treated as if she were an aristocrat.

The service on the ship was impeccable. The ship's décor sumptuous. The lavish ballroom with its sweeping staircase and chandeliers conjured images from a fairytale. The elegant dining-room with silver service brought back memories of her days as a maid. As dinner was served, she smiled at the waiter as he lifted the silver cloche. It reminded her of the hundreds she had polished for old Mr Camrass. But this was the first time she had eaten from a plate which had been covered by one.

Afternoon tea was also a splendid affair with the choice of over twenty different varieties and flavours. Tea was served in the finest china, with cucumber sandwiches and iced fancies presented on silver platters.

'I don't know why you are nervous,' James said. 'You are as elegant as the rest of the ladies here. And,' he added, admiring the blood-red brooch decorating the lace yoke on her frock, 'you are probably worth more money, too!'

She smiled. It was hard to believe.

With the fox fur draped around her shoulders, Lucy took James's arm as they stepped out on to the first-class promenade deck. The sea was calm. The port side sheltered from the breeze. From the bow they could see the promontory of Gibraltar looming in the distance but they were just too late to see the sun setting across the Rock.

A well dressed elderly gentleman was leaning against the forward rail gazing out towards the land. He was alone.

'Good evening,' James said politely, as they approached.

The man turned. 'Beautiful evening isn't it.'

'It certainly is.'

Both men reached out their hands simultaneously.

'Farnley,' the man said. 'Archibald Farnley.'

Lucy swayed backwards. James steadied her.

'James Oldfield,' he said. 'May I introduce my mother? Mrs Lucy Oldfield.'

'I am pleased to meet you, madam. Are you travelling through to Bombay?'

Lucy nodded.

'And planning to stay long in India.'

James answered. 'Perhaps a few months. My mother has business dealings to transact.'

The gentleman turned to Lucy, 'Would you excuse me for asking what may appear to be a strange question?'

Lucy nodded nervously wondering if the man had remembered the girl who had once worked in his household as a maid.

'When we were boarding I thought I recognized someone I used to know.'

Lucy felt a flush of heat colouring her face.

'An old friend of mine. I saw him at the gangway with you and I have been looking for him, unsuccessfully, ever since. After checking with the purser it appears he is not on the passenger manifest. I am puzzled.'

Lucy sighed as she relaxed a little. 'Would you be referring to Captain Wainwright?'

'Yes, that's the man. Sebastopol Wainwright. Polly Wainwright, we used to call him. Captain, eh! Would you happen to know his cabin number?'

'I'm sorry,' Lucy said. 'Captain Wainwright is not on board. He accompanied us to the docks and took afternoon tea with us in the cabin before we sailed.'

Archibald Farnley was obviously disappointed. 'Darn shame. Not seen him in forty years. We were gentlemen cadets together at the Royal Military Academy. Of course he was born to the service as you are probably aware. Unlike me. I soon discovered I was not cut out for the life.' He thought for a moment then added, 'I remember he married the colonel's daughter, Miss Lydia Carrington.'

'That is correct, but I'm afraid Lydia passed away recently.'

'I'm sorry to hear that. She was a fine girl; however I am pleased to hear they had many years together. I envy him.'

'And you, sir,' James said. 'May I ask the purpose of your journey?'

'Purely a pleasure cruise,' he said. 'Escape the worst of the English winter. Enjoy the sea air. I will be disembarking at Port Said. Visiting the Pyramids. I am indulging myself in my family for a short while. My son and his family are accompanying me.' He turned to Lucy. 'I have a granddaughter, her name is Felicity. She is two years old and has the face of an angel.'

Lucy smiled.

'You must excuse a doting old man. My daughter-in-law admonishes me every time I use that expression, but believe me, when you see her you will agree. Perhaps you will let me introduce you tomorrow.'

Archibald Farnley smiled. It was the same smile Lucy remembered from Heaton Hall, though the sadness he had carried in his eyes was now replaced with obvious pride. He was a little plumper than she remembered and he stooped slightly. His hair had thinned considerably and his hairline had receded several inches. His upper lip was shaved clean.

She must have changed too, possibly more then she realized. Certainly her wardrobe was now elegant and fashionable, a far cry from the serge dress and frilled pinafore she wore at the Hall. Her once dark hair was now seasoned with shades of salt and pepper. Her skin remained healthy, her colour good, but her mouth and eyes were etched with an assortment of lines.

Accepting his invitation, Lucy was careful not to address his lordship by his formal title. She looked forward to meeting his family, especially his son – one of the two boys, who had been sent away when Miss Beatrice became ill. She also wanted to meet the son's wife and the little girl with the face of an angel.

Lucy and James remained on deck as the ship steamed slowly through the Straits. As it entered the Mediterranean, Lucy gazed at the expanse of sea and marvelled at the waves each edged with a sliver of moonlight. From that moment, any reservations she had held about the voyage disappeared.

If only Edward was with her to share the experience. If only she had gone with him to India when he had invited her all those years ago.

Chapter 21

Trouble

L ucy was sorry when Lord Farnley and his family left the ship at Port Said. She had enjoyed their company, particularly that of Felicity, his lordship's granddaughter. With a mop of white blonde curls and pink cherub lips Lucy could hardly disagree with Lord Farnley's affectionate description of her.

James was also going to miss them. He and Freddie Farnley had shared a common interest in motor cars and birds. They often chatted together on deck or in the cigar room, taking the opportunity to escape from the ladies. It was during one of their conversations that James discovered that the family now lived in a modest mansion on the cliff-top near Bexhill-on-Sea, a distance of only twenty miles or so from Tunbridge Wells. As he told his mother later, he felt confident Lord Farnley would be paying Captain Wainwright a visit when he returned to England.

Before the ship sailed from Port Said, Lucy handed the purser three letters for posting: the first, addressed to Captain S. Wainwright, the second to Mrs Alice Bottomley at Honeysuckle Cottages, and the third, a letter from James to Miss Grace Fothergill.

Only one week after Lucy and James left for India, Stanley Crowther started making a nuisance of himself again. The first time Alice saw him, she was pushing the pram to the village. Not immediately realizing who he was, she smiled when he tipped his cap and bade her good morning. That was a mistake. She noticed him twice more that day: outside the greengrocer's shop, and at the post office. She wondered if it was just coincidence but when she saw him trailing behind her as she walked home up the hill, she knew that wasn't the case.

After unlocking the door and pushing the pram safely inside, she confronted him. Standing in the lane, arms folded across her chest, she waited until he was within in a few yards of her before she spoke. 'Are you following me?' she demanded.

His mouth dropped open. 'Who me?'

'Yes, you! I know what you're like, but you'll not bother me the way you did my mother. You can sling your hook, Stanley Crowther!'

'Now, that's not a very nice thing to say, is it?'

'Well if you don't go I'll get the police on to you.'

'Whatever for? I am just taking a stroll up a country lane.'

'You're a liar and a con-man and I'm not joking.'

'And what do you think the police are going to do?' He laughed. 'I'll tell them I was out walking when all of sudden you come out from the house, large as life and started shouting abuse at me. Not very ladylike, do you think?'

Alice knew if she argued till doomsday she could not win. Exasperated, she shook her head, turned her back on him and walked into the house. Once inside she slammed the door as hard as she could. The sudden bang startled the baby. As she lifted Rachel from the pram she heard Crowther calling.

'I'll be back tomorrow. You might be in a better mood then!'

The following morning Alice tried to ignore his plaintive cries but they went on and on. When at last she thought he had gone and it was safe to go outside, she wandered into the garden. Intending to scare her, he popped up from behind the wall.

'You're mad!' she shouted. 'Don't you ever give up?'

'Free country! No law says I can't sit out here and watch the birds.'

At first, though his constant visits were annoying, Alice tried to be philosophical. She told herself he was quite harmless. His actions were those of a child. Immature. Attention-seeking. She thought it a shame he had nothing better to do with his life, and a shame the spell he spent in the army had taught him nothing.

But it was not long before his nocturnal visits started affecting her.

Apart from being cold and lonely, the nights were long and darkness fell early – too early for Alice to go to bed – and it was impossible to sleep with all his taunts and noises. But darkness brought with it increased abuse. Drunken abuse. Foul language. And threats which would grow to a crescendo culminating in a shower of rocks thrown against the front door, or the clatter of the milk churn kicked around the garden.

Unfortunately, when he had disappeared and the taunts finally subsided, the slightest sound unsettled Alice. Her imagination began to play unkind tricks. The branches moving outside the window became hands, night clouds – faces; the chicken's squawk – a scream; shadows from the fire – ghostly figures creeping along the wall.

Alice knew from what she had been told, that Crowther's actions were a repeat performance of the treatment he had given her mother, and every morning she told herself she was stupid for allowing herself to be affected. But she also knew her defences were being worn down – and Crowther probably sensed it too. How much longer could she hang on? Not much, she thought. Certainly not until Lucy and James got back.

'Take your foot out of the damn door!' Alice screamed.

'Don't be like that. Let me in. I only want a chat and a cuppa.'

'I said get out! Go away! I don't want you here!'

'Strikes me you must be lonely. Left all alone!'

Alice wasn't going to let go of the door until it was shut and the bolt shot. She was angry with herself for opening it. Crowther had been cunning and had fooled her. This time he had approached the cottage silently, knocked quietly, like a child, making her think it was someone else. 'Damn you!' she cried.

He laughed and pushed his knee between the door and jamb breaking her grip on the handle. The door banged against the wall.

'It does open after all!' he sneered.

'Get out of my house! You bastard.'

'Such words in front of the baby. Tut-tut!' He put his forefinger to his lips. 'Shhh!'

Alice had had enough. As she flayed at him with both fists her knee came up hard and hit him in the crotch.

He dropped towards her, his weight pressing on her shoulders. 'You bitch,' he breathed.

'Get out!' she screamed as she fought to lift her knee again. This time she could not reach.

'Bitch!' he yelled, grabbing her neck with one hand and throwing a punch with the other. She could feel the moisture running down her cheek. It was not tears.

'Get out!' she cried, her voice weak and trembling.

As Crowther let her go, she slid down the wall to the floor. She had no energy left.

'Bloody bitch!' he said. 'I'll get you!'

Bombay was a bustling city, far busier than Lucy could ever have imagined. The dusty thoroughfares were crammed with all manner of people and vehicles, all competing in a cacophony of curses, cries and car horns.

The hotel, which the firm of solicitors had booked for Lucy and her son, was just the opposite. It was spotlessly clean, spacious and the atmosphere was relaxing. The only sounds in the reception areas, the echo of footsteps across the marble floor and the gentle murmur of quiet conversations.

The letter, handed to Lucy on a silver tray, bore an English stamp. She was thrilled to receive it. In the envelope were two sheets of lightly perfumed writing paper. After reading both pages slowly, she turned back to the first page and started again.

'Did Alice tell you she was planning to go back to nursing while we were away?' she asked.

James shook his head as he scooped the skin from the top of his coffee.

'She says here, she is staying with her mother in Ilkley and intends to go back to full-time work at the hospital, and to live-in at the nurses' quarters.' Lucy raised her eyebrows. 'It appears Rachel is going to live with Pansy and Miss Pugh on a permanent basis.' Lucy looked at James. 'How strange!'

'Did she give a reason?'

'No. Apart from the fact she says she enjoys working.' Lucy finished the letter and handed it to James.

After reading it he frowned. 'She says she has asked Mr Fothergill and

Grace to keep an eye on the cottages and feed the animals while we are away. That means Grace is going to be kept busy because Mr Fothergill won't be going far on that leg of his.' Folding the letter he handed it back to his mother. Gazing up at the fan rotating slowly above his head, he watched it for while as it wobbled in its housing. 'What would you say if I went back to England? Would you be all right on your own?'

'Do you think it necessary?'

'Yes,' said James. 'I do.'

The following morning they took a taxi to the Bombay shipping offices where James secured a berth on a cargo vessel sailing for London the following week. At the post office, Lucy sent a telegram to Wainwright's friends in Nashik accepting their offer of hospitality.

Three days later, a chauffeur-driven car collected her from the hotel for the drive to Nashik. The journey was long, hot and at times, intolerably bumpy. It took most of the day. But, as Wainwright had promised, the mountain air was a welcome change from the city. It was also sweetly perfumed with the masses of flowers which bloomed in profusion on every hillside. Lucy thought the area delightful and agreed to stay with the elderly couple for two or three weeks. She hoped when she returned to Bombay, there would be news about the properties which she had offered for sale.

Beneath a yellowed canopy of mosquito netting, James lay naked on the hotel bed, counting the hours until his sailing day. He thought mostly about Grace and about seeing her again. He wondered about Mr Fothergill and the farm and hoped the weather had improved. He thought about Alice and wondered why she had suddenly decided to leave the cottage and return to work. He wondered if it had anything to do with his growing attraction for Grace Fothergill? No doubt he would find out when he got home.

Six weeks later, James was standing in the front room of his cottage staring at the empty shelves in his glass cabinet. All Edward's fine ornaments had gone. The marks in the dust were the only clue as to what had been there. 'Tell me what happened,' he said quietly.

Grace sniffed and wiped her face. 'When I came down to feed the chickens one morning, I noticed the door to Alice's cottage was wide open. I thought maybe she'd come back to get some things, but when I went in I found the place in a mess. Pots and pans scattered on the floor, the cupboard door hanging off, every one of the dresser drawers smashed and the curtains ripped from the rails. I drove straight to the police station and got the constable. We went through the two other cottages together and they were in the same state. I couldn't tell him what was missing but I knew you had lots of lovely things and they were all gone. I'm sorry,' she said. 'Dad and I stayed here a couple of nights but after that we had to go back to the farm. Dad said whoever did it got what he wanted and probably wouldn't come back.' She shook her head. 'I'm sorry, James.'

'It's not your fault,' he said. 'I wish Alice had been here, then this might never have happened.'

James looked at the list of items missing from the three cottages. It was not comprehensive, and there were probably many more things missing than he could remember. He should have shown more interest in Edward's things, but trinkets and ornaments never really interested him.

Constable Merrifield was sympathetic but could offer little hope the items would be recovered. 'Quite a haul!' he said. 'What surprised me,' he added, 'there was no sign of a forced entry. Looks like the burglar had a key. You don't think it could be anyone you know do you?'

James shook his head.

'Hopefully some of the items will turn up. Whoever took them knew they were worth a few quid otherwise they'd have been smashed.'

'Is there anything I can do?' James asked.

'I suggest you scout round the markets. And take a look in the antique shops. You never know your luck.'

Chapter 22

Decisions

'Pull up a chair, lad,' Mr Fothergill said. 'Try some soup. It's not bad.' James smiled at Grace. It smelled good.

'You said once you were looking at getting a few acres,' the farmer said. 'Putting a few cows on it. Were you serious?'

'Yes, I was.'

'But your mother said you was going to go to college, become a doctor or teacher, or some such sort.'

James sighed. 'I thought so too a few years ago. I think Mum still has hopes. She says I've been wasting my time since I got left the money. Maybe she's right.'

'Well I don't want to know your business, but if you're interested in doing a bit of farming, I've been thinking of putting part of the farm up for sale.'

Grace pushed the stool towards her father and lifted his foot on to it.

'I ain't getting any younger and this damn leg don't work so good since I took that tumble in the snow. Me and the missus hoped the boys would take over when we was too old, but the war put paid to that. So now it's just me and Grace.'

Looking straight at his daughter, the farmer spoke as though his daughter was not in the room. 'She's a good lass but she's been wearing herself out lately minding me and the dairy. I can sit all right and do the milking but she's got to fetch the beasts in and fill the racks. Then there's the horses, the cart, delivering the milk, and the churns to clean. When I asked her about ploughing the paddocks for this year's crop she was ready to take off. Get a job in the city.'

'I was tired, Dad. That was all. You know I wouldn't leave you.'

'Aye, I know you wouldn't, lass.' He turned to James. 'But I got to be honest with myself. It can't go on like this forever. Different if she was a farmer's wife. But she ain't and it's no life for a girl on her own.' He saw the look exchanged between Grace and James. 'Now,' he said. 'Don't get me wrong, I'm not suggesting you two get married. But I do have a proposition.'

'Let's hear it,' James said.

'The farm's getting run down because we're trying to do everything by hand. Now you're pretty good with mechanical stuff. You've even got Grace driving the car like she's some racing driver.'

'Dad!'

'You buy some land off me, lad, and with the money, I'll rebuild the dairy, install some mechanical machines for milking and I'll buy a truck for delivering the cream. Aye, and a tractor if funds will run to it. What do you think?'

'I like the sound of it but I'll have to give it a bit of thought.'

The farmer beckoned his daughter. 'Come here, lass.'

Grace walked over to her father and rested her hand on his shoulder. Sliding his arm around her waist he looked into her face. 'Me and Grace can make the place run, but we're fighting an uphill battle and losing. But,' he said, 'with a bit of careful planning, we can make this farm into a good paying concern. I've done me sums. We can run more livestock. Buy a new bull. Increase the volume of milk. And our Grace is pretty good at making cheeses, if she's given the time. Think about it serious, lad. But,' he said, as he leaned across the table to James, 'if you decide, you've got to remember farming's not for a week or two, or even a season or two, it's for life. But if you give it a go and we work it right, we can both make a decent living. It's up to you.'

'Colonel Winters?'

'Welcome, Mrs Oldfield. I am very pleased to meet you.' The colonel's accent was English southern counties, the sincerity of his greeting, West Riding. He was smartly dressed in a dark suit which would have been more appropriate in Bradford than Bombay. He was at least seventy-five years of age, wore gold-rimmed spectacles and carried a walking cane. Taking Lucy's arm, the retired colonel escorted her up the stone steps into a rather austere sitting-room. Though the entrance to the building had been light and airy, this room was heavy with mahogany and the worn leather bindings of innumerable books. Having invited her to sit down, he settled himself on the settee opposite. A marble-topped coffee table separated them. After barely raising his hand more than a few inches, a waiter appeared and bowed.

'A lemonade for the lady and the usual for myself.'

As they waited for the drinks to arrive, Lucy looked around. The fronds of a tall palm tree growing from an earthenware pot curled over at the ceiling. Beside the ornamental fireplace were two stools made from the feet of an elephant, the steel-grey skin was coarse and wrinkled, the enormous toenails highly polished. Above the mantelpiece a pair of huge tusks hung like crossed swords. Lucy wondered if they were from the same animal.

'I did not know ladies were allowed into gentlemen's clubs.'

The colonel smiled. 'We maintain our inner sanctum but we like to provide an area for members' guests, most particularly the ladies.' He leaned forward slightly and lowered his voice. 'If truth be told, most of the members would give their right arm to be accompanied by a lovely lady like yourself, though if you asked them outright they would probably argue they are quite content without the company of the fairer sex.'

Lucy sipped her lemonade. It was freshly squeezed and cool.

'But tell me. How is Captain Wainwright? Haven't seen the blackguard in fifteen or twenty years. And that wife of his, Lydia. I heard she was not well.'

'I'm afraid Lydia passed away after a long illness. But Captain Wainwright is very well and sends his regards.'

'Must look him up when I am in England. Must go back to the old Dart sometime. It has no doubt changed since 1910.'

Lucy smiled politely.

Colonel Winters clicked his fingers again. This time the servant appeared with a box of cigars. Before taking one, Colonel Winters turned to Lucy. 'Do you mind if I smoke?'

'Please go ahead.'

The swarthy hand held the flame while the colonel sucked on the cigar. The blue smoke had the distinctive smell of first-class railway compartments, P&O smoking-rooms and gentlemen's clubs.

'Now,' he said, shuffling in his seat. 'You said when you phoned you had a problem.'

Feeling a little embarrassed, Lucy returned her glass to the table, sat upright and broached the subject. 'I don't know if you can help me, Colonel, but you are the only person I can turn to.'

The gentleman relaxed into the leather chair and listened as Lucy explained her problem. It related to the sale of a large Victorian house left to her by Edward Carrington.

'Ah, dear Edward. We were all sorry to learn of his death.'

Lucy continued. 'The rates and taxes have been paid each year, but the place has been left for a long time without a regular tenant. Unfortunately, the so-called resident staff either died or absconded and the property has been completely overrun by squatters.'

The colonel shook his head sympathetically.

Lucy explained that when the agent had showed her the building she had estimated over 200 people were living in it. 'They have taken over every room, upstairs and downstairs, the attic, the bathroom, the pantries, even the closets. The toilets aren't working; there's no running water; the place is filthy and infested with rats and cockroaches. I'm afraid the stench almost made me sick. It was unbelievable.' She took a deep breath. 'And if that is not bad enough, the gardens, which I imagine were once sculptured and ornamental, have been replaced by a shamble of shelters made from bits of canvas and cardboard.'

As the colonel puffed on his cigar, Lucy continued. She told him she had instructed the agent not to advertise the property until the squatters had been evicted and the place cleaned. The company's representative had promised he would attend to the matter personally, at the same time insisting that the additional costs should be paid in advance together with a hefty retainer for his services prior to the house going onto the market.

After several letters, frustrating phone calls and two rather perilous excursions to the property, Lucy said she had come to the conclusion that absolutely no effort was being made to evict the residents. Though she felt sorry for the people who were to be made homeless, she nevertheless had to conduct her business.

'While the house remains the way it is,' she said, 'no one in his right mind would even consider buying it.'

Colonel Winters laid his cigar in the alabaster ashtray.

'I will require the address of the property and the name of the agent. This business may take a little time and involve some expense.' He looked at Lucy quizzically.

'Cost is no object,' she assured him. 'And even if it were, any expenses would be offset by the sale once it goes through.'

'As I thought. Leave the matter with me.'

'May I ask how you hope to remove all the people and when you do, how you will keep them out?'

'That I cannot answer, as I have not yet worked out a strategy. Speaking from experience, I can say dealing with some of the local government bodies is a long and painstaking procedure, and those avenues would get us nowhere in a hurry. In this instance what we need is a more dynamic approach. The first move will be the erection of a high fence around the grounds and the installation of a squad of security guards. If necessary I will call on my friends in the police department.' He paused. 'In fact, I will speak with the recently retired commissioner who is, right this moment, within these walls. Once the vagrants are evicted and the house is empty, I suggest you refurbish it before presenting it on the market.'

Lucy found it hard to thank him enough.

'It is my pleasure, madam. Not only does it give me the opportunity to help you and return a favour to an old friend, but it gives me something to get my teeth into. One gets bored here with the same routine day in and day out. I have played so many games of chess in the last few years it is a wonder I do not walk diagonally across our checkerboard floor.'

'Thank you again, Colonel Winters,' Lucy said, as she shook hands with him.

'My dear lady,' he said holding her hand in his, 'I will enjoy this exercise immensely. And when the house sells, you may treat me to a box of those rather fine imported cigars.'

It was a long time since James had wandered on to the moors on his own.

Sitting on a rock, he gazed across Wharfedale to the grey-green hills in the distance. He had always loved the countryside especially the open moors. It had a peacefulness he found nowhere else. Below, in the valley, the river snaked lazily through verdant fields. Downstream the clusters of smoke-blackened houses blemished the natural landscape. The thought of working in a dirty city was repugnant.

But James knew his mother had always wanted him to improve himself, go to university. So had Edward. He had even left money in trust for that purpose. But Edward was dead, and James now found himself torn between his desire not to disappoint his mentor and his wish to work on the land. He sighed, knowing full well that study and professional qualifications were not what he wanted.

But time was running out. He had to make a choice. His car was getting older and would not run forever. He was living on the interest from his savings, but they were rapidly diminishing as he was eating into his capital. One day he would likely inherit most of his mother's money. But she was fit and only fifty years of age. Even though James knew she was a wealthy woman, he would never ask her for money. Besides, the trip, on which she had taken him, halfway across the world to India, had not been cheap.

But what she had said was true; for several years he had had neither job nor income. He had done repairs to the cottages and pottered about with the horses, grown a few crops on the meadow and helped raise a few calves and hens. He had read many books, learned a lot, but earned nothing. He had been thoroughly self-indulgent. And all that time Grace had worked like a navvy, no doubt observing him. What on earth did she think of him?

Here he was, twenty-five years of age with no trade, no job and little income, at a time when the queues of men seeking work were growing throughout the length and breadth of England.

If Mr Fothergill were to advertise for help, he would have no difficulty finding men eager to work on the farm. Men were becoming desperate. Some would work just for the milk to feed their bairns. Milk was essential and always would be. Being part of a dairy farm was a damn good proposition.

It was a good offer and James knew it, but since he had first mentioned the idea of farming, the price of land had risen and his capital had been depleted. Now, when he really wanted to buy some land, he did not have enough money. If there was no other way, he could ask his mother for a loan, but he did not know when she would be back. It might be weeks or months before she returned to England and Mr Fothergill was waiting for an answer. Summer was round the corner and the fields were still lying fallow.

As he sat pondering his decision a sparrowhawk dropped vertically into the heather. After a few moments it flew up, its prey gripped tightly in its talons.

James knew instantly, he must grab the opportunity while it was available. But he also knew, if he was to accept Mr Fothergill's offer, he would have to find some other way of getting the money.

Chapter 23

Cyril Street

The white-clad waiter was a tall willowy man. His turban made him appear even taller. Lucy took a sandwich from the tray and thanked him.

'You don't mind this heat?' The voice came from a man drinking tea at the next table. He flipped the crumbs from his lap and turned to face her.

'No, I don't. It's the moisture in the air, I hate. Makes everything feel permanently damp.'

'You might like Australia then.'

'Might I?'

'Maybe. Hot there, but not as humid they tell me.'

'You are travelling on, are you, Mr. . . ?'

'Street. Cyril Harley Street.' He laughed. 'Sounds more like an address than a name, don't you think?'

'Lucy Oldfield,' she replied offering her hand. 'Missus,' she said, 'but actually it's miss.'

'You are very forthright! I like that.'

'Why not?' she said, as she invited him to join her. 'I have become used to that title over the years. I think, because I was single and had a child, people called me missus out of politeness. For a long time I was happy to accept it. Preferred it, I suppose, to being thought of as a loose woman.'

'And were you?' he said with twinkle in his eye.

Lucy grinned. 'That I am not telling, Mr Street.'

'Call me Cyril,' he said. 'Care to walk out on the terrace? I think there might be a little breeze outside.'

The hotel's restaurant was open on all sides. Doors. Shutters. Windows. But neither the balmy breeze blowing in from the ocean nor the ceiling fans provided any relief from the sultry atmosphere. The air on the terrace was little different.

'Are you staying in Bombay long?' Cyril asked.

'Not much longer. I'm waiting to conclude some matters. It's taken a little longer than I expected. But it's been interesting to see how business is conducted in the colonies.' Lucy dabbed sweat from her brow. 'It's over six months since I left England and about time I was heading home.'

'As you have been in no hurry, I assume you have enjoyed your stay, and you have no one back there desperately awaiting your return.'

'You could be correct.'

'In that case, would you care to dine with me this evening?'

'You do not waste any time, do you?'

'At my age, madam, my adage is waste not, want not!'

'All right, Mr Street, you have won me over for a meal. But a meal only.'

'Well at least it's a start,' he said. 'Shall we say seven?'

'Seven on the dot. I will look forward to it.'

'For you,' James said as he handed Grace the bunch of pink carnations.

'You shouldn't have,' she said, as she sniffed the flowers and smiled. 'I thought we were here to look at the stalls?'

'We are.'

The city market was crowded with shoppers. Under the glass-domed roof, the still air echoed with the raucous voices of traders competing to sell their wares. The individual shops looked the same as James remembered from his childhood: books, toys, drapery, and shoe shops set amidst the aroma of freshly baked bread and the scent of the cut flowers. Leeds market stocked almost everything: pots and pans, polishes, brooms and buckets, dusters and dishcloths.

James and Grace ambled between the maze of assorted outlets, to the lane consisting entirely of butchers' shops. Outside each establishment, chalkboards advertised tripe, dripping and kidneys. Inside, butchers smelling of blood and mutton hacked bone and cartilage with sharpened cleavers. A hungry dog sniffed at the doorways, but instead of scraps received shouts of abuse.

The fish market had a different smell but James didn't notice as they walked through. He was looking for the stalls selling second-hand goods and whenever he spotted one he scanned the wares hoping to recognize something familiar, an item which had once belonged to his mother or Edward. Not knowing exactly what had been stolen, Grace wandered on.

'Nothing,' he said, as they left the indoor market and wandered outside to the stalls which mostly sold fruit and vegetables.

'Lovely apples! Granny's! Cox's! Pick your own.'

' 'Ere 'ave a taste,' a leather-faced lady said, thrusting a segment of orange into Grace's hand. 'Don't come no sweeter than that!'

Grace sucked on the fruit, the juice running between her fingers.

The sun had disappeared and a chill wind had whipped up while they were indoors. Cloth canopies flapped. A tin tray clattered as it blew over and skidded along the ground. James retrieved it and returned it to the stallholder. It had come from a second-hand stall neither had noticed. Amongst the items on display was a teapot. It was a common white pot, stained inside and with a web of clay-coloured cracks running right through it. James had seen a similar pot in Alice's kitchen. He remembered the time she had scalded her wrist when the steam had escaped through a chip in the lid. This pot had a chip in the same place.

'How much for the teapot?' James asked.

'Tanner to you, guv.'

James replaced it and looked around.

' 'Ave a look,' the man said. 'Come on missus, got all sorts o' stuff.'

Most of the items were damaged or stained – odd cups and saucers, bottles, books, tins, biscuit boxes, single serviette rings. Nothing of value. James scrutinized every item carefully till he was satisfied that apart from the teapot there was nothing else he recognized.

'Any idea where this came from?' he said holding the pot at arm's length.

The man shook his head. 'No idea.'

'Any other things came with it?'

The man shook his head cautiously and turned his back.

'Would a pound jog your memory?'

The man shuffled around. 'Might do.'

'I'm not interested how you got it or who you got it from, I just want to know if there was anything else came with it.'

'Might have been.'

James reached in his pocket and took out a bank note.

The man looked around furtively.

'Well,' said James rubbing the paper between his fingers.

'There was quite a bit of stuff.'

'If it's what I am looking for I'm prepared to buy it off you at a reasonable price. Where is it?'

'Sold it,' the stallholder sniffed. 'Not my sort of stuff. Good stuff, if you know what I mean.'

'Tell me who bought it and the money's yours.'

'No idea, guv! Honest! Sold it to a bloke who came looking. Seen him before. Bit of a toff. Fancy dresser. Only wants quality. Don't think he's a collector. Reckon he's got a shop 'cause he bought the lot.'

'How much?'

'That's my business, guv! I bought it fair and square.'

'Who from?'

The man shrugged. 'Fella comes round at times. Brings me stuff by the sackful.'

'Is it stolen?'

'I don't ask questions. Just gives him a price.'

'And this other man who came and bought the stuff, the toff: would you know him again?'

'I'd know him if I saw him. Never forget a face.'

James took out a paper and pencil. 'Can you write?'

' 'Course I can write, I'm not stupid!'

'Good. This is my address and here's your money. And there's another quid for you if you can get the name of the man who bought the rest of the stuff from you.'

'And what about the fella I got it off in the first place.'

'You get his name and address and I'll give you the same again.'

The man pushed the piece of paper into an inside pocket. 'You'll be hearing from me, governor.'

James nodded and took Grace's arm. They had only gone a few yards when the man shouted after them.

'Hey, guv!' The man was beckoning. 'I got a pile of odds and ends the toff didn't want. Said it was rubbish. That's where the pot came from. Want to have a look?'

James nodded.

Dragging a Hessian sack from under his counter the man unravelled the twine tied around the top. Reaching his hand in to the bag, James lifted out various items, one by one, and laid them carefully on the ground.

'You won't find anything of value in there!'

The man was right. The clock's face was broken. The glass vase was badly cracked. The pages of the book had become separated from its binding. There was a pile of old sheet music. A posy of dried flowers. An umbrella with bent spokes. A tortoiseshell hand mirror with a crack across the glass. A picture frame without glass. James looked at the sepia photograph. It was faded and slightly scratched. He recognized the girl in nurse's uniform. 'Alice,' he murmured.

'Is that some of it?' Grace whispered.

James nodded.

'You can have the sack for a quid.'

'Your customer was right,' James said. 'This stuff is worth nothing.'

'All right! Ten bob to you, guv.'

'I'll give you five bob for the lot including the teapot.'

'Done!' said the man.

'And don't forget, those two names. Addresses too if you can get them.'

'Please come in Mr Oldfield and take a seat.'

James thanked the solicitor and sat down opposite the two elderly gentlemen.

'How is your mother?' Mr Armitage asked.

'I gather she is well and enjoying her time in India despite everything not going quite as she would have wished.'

'Ah! Yes,' he said. 'We received a letter from our contact in Bombay. He said there were some problems. Legal matters have a habit of becoming tedious. I hope the delay will not cause your mother too much inconvenience.'

'On the contrary, I think she welcomed the opportunity to extend her stay, although I don't know how she will cope with the heat of the tropical summer.'

'How right you are,' the elder of the two solicitors said.

'Now, Mr Oldfield, regarding the matter you put to us last week.' Mr Proctor took a file from his desk drawer and leafed though the papers. Selecting one, he held it at arm's length, read it and passed it to his partner. From the coat of arms embossed on the top of the cream paper, James knew it was from Lord Farnley.

'This is a very commendable character reference you have provided.' He pulled out another sheet. 'And also this one from Captain Wainwright.' He cleared his throat. 'As trustees of any estate we are obliged to carry out the terms of the will according to the wishes of our clients. We must deal with any request to deviate as we feel our client would have dealt with them if he were still alive.'

James nodded.

'In this submission, you are asking that the money which Mr Carrington set aside for your tertiary education, is paid to you as a lump sum. That you intend to use the money to purchase some land.' He turned the page and examined the title deeds of John Fothergill's farm. After rereading James's proposal he continued.

'Mr Oldfield. My partner and I have come to the following conclusions: had the money been required for the purchase of a vehicle or a holiday or suchlike, we would have declined your request. However, the purchase of land is regarded as a good investment, possibly sounder than leaving the money in the bank which is where it is at the moment. However,' he added, 'once you have invested the money we cannot stop you from selling the asset in a year's time.'

'That is not my intention, sir.'

'We thought not. This brings me back to another point. Mr Carrington's wish was that the money was to be spent on furthering your education. Yet you say you have no desire to pursue a professional career.'

'That is correct.'

'We have noted Captain Wainwright's letter which states that Mr Edward Carrington did not follow the military career his father had intended for him because the army was not his chosen path. Because of this fact, we feel, if our client had been alive today, he would have been sympathetic to your request. He would not have forced you to attend university purely to please him. We also think he would have supported you in whatever you chose to do.

'Edward Carrington, besides being an astute man, was a man with a good heart. We believe he would have wanted you to follow your heart.' With that said the solicitor replaced the papers in the file and closed it. 'We will arrange for the money to be transferred from the trust and placed into your personal account.'

'And may we wish you every success in this new venture,' his partner added.

*

My dear James

I hope you and Grace are well. I received your letter and was interested to hear you are spending a lot of time at Fothergill's farm. As you do not mention Alice and the baby, I hope all is well with them too. Have you visited Pansy in Ilkley lately?

As for me, I am very well and still enjoying my time in Bombay. So much so I will not be coming home as planned – at least not for some time.

I have met a very nice gentleman here. His name is Cyril Street. He comes from Kent, though originally he was from the north. He is travelling around the world stopping at the ports which interest him along the way. He has been in Bombay for several months.

Hearing him talk about the places he'll be visiting has made me wish I could see a little more of the world. Not wanting to travel alone, I have arranged for a passage on the same vessel as Mr Street. We are booked to sail on the SS Gothenburg which is leaving Bombay the first week in October. The ship will be calling in at Colombo, Rangoon and Singapore. From there we will catch another vessel to Sydney, Australia. My friend, Mr Street wants to purchase some land on the southern continent. He says land is the best investment these days.

Recently I read in the newspaper that poverty and hardship are increasing in Britain. I'm indeed fortunate in my financial position. Write and tell if there is anything you need.

By the time you receive this letter we will be at sea. You can write to me care of the General Post Office in Sydney and I will collect the mail when we get

there. At this stage, I don't know when that will be.
Take care of yourself

Your loving Mother

James smiled, folded the letter and slid it back into the envelope. He was relieved to hear all was well and surprised to hear his mother had found a travelling companion and was not coming home immediately. He hoped she was making a wise decision and in a way envied her. He remembered how much he had enjoyed his visit to India, an experience he would never forget. But James preferred to be at home and welcomed the challenge of being a farmer. Above all he wanted to settle down and had been waiting for his mother to return before asking Grace to marry him.

As he put the letter away, he decided he could wait no longer. He would be seeing Grace that evening and would ask her then.

Chapter 24

Marriage

James and Grace were married at the Leeds Register Office.

Grace wore a cotton frock patterned with tiny rosebuds, a pink hat with a net veil, white gloves and white high heeled shoes. Later she regretted she had only bought the shoes the week before as she had no time to wear them in and they made her feet sore. There were no bridesmaids or best man – just the two witnesses, Mr Fothergill and Pansy Pugh.

Pansy caught the 8.30 train from Ilkley and met them in City Square. She brought Rachel with her but apologized that Alice couldn't come as she had to work. It didn't bother either bride or groom that they had few relatives or friends attending the ceremony, though James was disappointed his mother wasn't there. The only other person he would have wished to be present was the man who had been like a father to him, Edward Carrington.

After the civil service, the wedding group went back to the farmhouse for a meal. Grace had prepared it all beforehand; roast lamb, potato and pickles, and apple pie. It didn't take her long to whip up a basin of fresh cream, but by the time they sat down to eat it was almost three o'clock.

It had been several months since James had seen Pansy and he thought she looked well, still thin and pale-cheeked, but content. Rachel was growing quickly, but unlike Alice who had been boisterous and full of adventure, Alice's daughter was shy. Being brought up in the house of Miss Pugh, she had little contact with other children and, as a consequence, her behaviour was that of a child of the Victorian era. Even the dresses Pansy chose for her were rather old-fashioned and too long which added to her delicate appearance.

As James tried to encourage Rachel to talk she clung tightly to her grandmother's arm.

'She'll grow out of it quick enough once she gets to school,' Pansy said. James asked about Alice.

'She's well and still working hard,' Pansy said, dabbing a speck of dirt from Rachel's cheek. 'She's a sister now. Got a ward of her own.' She sounded proud, then suddenly her tone changed. 'I wish she had met a nice young doctor instead of getting tied up with that Bertie Bottomley.'

'Does he ever get in touch?'

'No, he's long gone. And good riddance, I say. Alice's better off without him.' Pansy sighed. 'I feel sorry for her at times. She works long hours and only sees Rachel once a week when she visits. Life must be lonely for her.'

'Why doesn't she come back to the cottage?'

'Keeps saying she might one day. Don't think she liked being here on her own when you and Lucy were away. Maybe she'll come back once you and Grace settle down. But,' she said, in a more positive tone, 'I know she loves her job.'

'You must be proud of her,' Grace said.

'I am. But that's enough talk about me; tell me what you're doing at the farm.'

James looked over to the man who was now his father-in-law. 'I bought half the farm,' he said proudly.

'And I'm aiming to make a farmer out of him,' John Fothergill said with a grin.

'Do you think you'll succeed?' Pansy asked.

'He's doing all right so far. And we ended up with a good harvest this year, even though some of the seed went in late.'

'And the dairy's improved,' Grace added, tucking her arm inside James's. 'Dad said we're already getting more milk, and with the extra feed we'll have more calves for the market at Christmas.'

John Fothergill put his finger to his mouth. 'Shhh! Don't want him to get a swelled head, but I think that calls for a toast.' He got up from the table and hobbled over to the pantry. 'It's only sherry but it'll do the job.'

There was almost half a tumbler each. Ample to drink the health of the newly married couple.

As the afternoon wore on, Rachel fell asleep on the sofa and by five o'clock Pansy was anxious to get back to Ilkley and Miss Pugh.

'And we'll be back early in the morning for the milking,' James called to his new father-in-law, as he and Grace prepared to take Pansy home. 'I'm taking this young lady to a hotel for the night,' James announced. 'She says she's never stayed in a hotel before.'

Grace blushed.

There were tears in the farmer's eyes, as he hugged his daughter. 'Now you look after her!' he said to James. 'And don't worry about the morning. I'm not altogether useless! If the cows have to wait a while, it won't kill them.'

Dusk was falling as they waved goodbye. With her head resting on Pansy's lap, Rachel slept all the way to Ilkley. Grace sat close to James, her hand resting on his leg.

With only a fine sliver of new moon on the rise, it was almost black when they reached Miss Pugh's house. Grace declined Pansy's invitation to a cup of tea, and the newly-weds said goodnight.

As James closed the car door, he leaned across and kissed his wife. 'I'm sure it's past your bed time, Mrs Oldfield.'

Grace grinned 'Do you really think so, Mr Oldfield?'

'I know so!' he said.

It was almost two weeks after the wedding before James, Grace, Mr Fothergill and the cows, were settled in to a regular routine. James took over all the heavy work on the farm and most of the driving, allowing Grace more time in the house for baking.

Within weeks of the change, John Fothergill was loosening the notches on his belt. He was partial to his daughter's curd tarts, but a plate of hot scones and a pat of fresh butter was his favourite. At first his appetite for sweet stuff was treated as a joke but before long the extra weight he gained began placing additional strain on his leg.

Since the accident he had walked with a limp. His leg had healed but the doctor said the hip joint was damaged. It was obvious it gave him a lot of pain. Unable to climb the stairs, he slept downstairs at the farmhouse in the room his wife had used. He refused to accept a walking stick; instead, when he hobbled to the shed at milking time, he leaned heavily on a staff. As he was unable to do much around the farm he spent most of each day watching Grace working in the kitchen.

Naturally Grace was concerned about her father. She and James considered moving into the farmhouse with him, but the farmer insisted he was all right on his own and, as James liked his own cottage and the privacy it offered them, Grace agreed she would live at Honeysuckle Cottages. It was very close and only took a few minutes to walk from the cottage to the farm and only two minutes by car.

For more than a week after she moved in, Grace felt confined. The kitchen was tiny, the rooms small, the ceiling low. Quite different to the spacious interior of the farmhouse. Every morning Grace was up before James, anxious to get back to the farm to check on her father.

At first James worried that she was doing too much, helping with the milking, separating the cream, making and tending the cheeses, keeping the farmhouse and cottage tidy and cooking for her father. But Grace said her work was much easier than before he had started working with them.

As James was more active than he had been since his time in the army, by evening he would fall into bed exhausted. But he enjoyed the outdoor work and being with Grace for much of the day. He liked delivering cream and driving in the surrounding district. Being outdoors in all weather didn't bother him.

A week after the wedding, the postman delivered a letter for James. The crumpled envelope was daubed with dirty smudges around the stamp and across the back where it had been sealed. James's name and address were scrawled in pencil in a combination of capital and small letters. It was from the man on the market stall. He signed himself, 'Tom'. There was no surname. In the letter he said he would give James some news if he visited him at Leeds market. James waited until Saturday morning to go.

'I got that info for you, guv,' Tom said. 'You said it was worth a quid.'

'You give me the information and I'll tell you if it is.'

'I found out where you'll find the toff who bought the stuff you're looking for. He has a shop, like I thought. It's on Pembroke Way, behind the hotel in Headingley. He didn't want to give me his name.'

'You're not making this up, I hope.'

'Honest, guv!' the man said, holding out his grubby hand. 'Would I do a thing like that?'

James ignored the question as he handed over the pound note. 'No news on the other fellow?'

Tom shook his head. 'Not yet, but he'll be around soon. Not usually this long between visits. Trust me, guv! I'll let you know. Same arrangement as before?' he asked.

'Same arrangement as before,' James added.

There were two antique shops near the Pembroke Hotel, one on either side of the narrow lane. The first was dark and dismal inside. It was crammed with all manner of bric-a-brac but few items appeared to be of any value. While James browsed, the man behind the counter never lifted his head from the newspaper he was reading. With the list of missing items in his mind, James knew exactly what he was searching for. The air in the shop was musty and reminded James of mice. After searching unsuccessfully for over ten minutes, he was pleased to step outside and breathe some fresh air.

When he spied the row of Ghurkha soldiers lined up in the window, James knew the second shop was the one he wanted. The bell above the door tinkled as he walked in. The proprietor was smartly dressed in a blue striped suit with a patterned waistcoat. He greeted James and offered his assistance. When James said he was content to browse, the man excused himself and hovered behind the counter watching James's every movement.

Like the previous business, this one was equally packed with merchandise, but in this shop most of the antiques were of items of value. Seeing the toy soldiers made James sure he would locate more of Edward's possessions. As he scoured the shelves, recognizing various ornaments, James ticked them off his mental list. He was careful not to touch anything in the shop and tried not to show any evidence of interest in his face. But his expression changed to a frown when he realized his inventory had more than a few omissions. He had completely forgotten about the ivory crocodile and the old bugle which had always hung in the hall. And there was an ebony elephant with the loose tusk, the scrimshaw, the cribbage board and the old doll with the black wig which he had made from a piece of goat skin for Alice when she was a little girl. How did he forget to list those?

On intuition, James paid another visit to the market the following week. He felt guilty leaving Grace and John at the farm but started work early and managed to get through his morning's chores before he left.

His visit paid off. The man who had originally brought the sacks to the market had been back with a suitcase full of other goods.

James wasn't surprised that the man's description fitted that of Stanley Crowther, though Tom said his name was Wilkinson. He did not have the man's address and said Wilkinson had got angry when he started asking questions.

After examining the contents of the suitcase, James paid the second-hand dealer thirty shillings, a sum far in excess of what he thought the items were worth. He was also obliged to pay out the pound note which they had agreed on.

Armed with the suitcase, a surname and the address of the dealer in Pembroke Way, James paid a visit to the police station.

Three days later, James and Constable Merrifield drove to the antique shop where the toy soldiers were still lined up in the window.

The dealer remembered James but was not pleased when he learned the purpose of the return visit. After presenting the proprietor with a list, the constable informed him that selling stolen property was an offence and that the goods were to be confiscated. The shopkeeper was irate and insisted he had bought them from the market stall in good faith, unaware they'd been stolen.

The only consolation the officer could offer him was that when the matter got to court, the onus would probably fall on the stall holder. He said the police had questioned him the previous day and in his opinion, the man was lying when he said he didn't know the goods were stolen.

After placing all the recovered items into four large boxes, James loaded them on to the back seat of the car while the policeman took down the antique dealer's personal details. Glancing in the car's mirror as they drove away, James could see the man standing in the road shaking his fist and cursing.

With only six items unaccounted for, James felt pleased. He presumed the missing items had been sold and that the probability of tracing them was unlikely. The fact the stolen goods would be held at the station until the case was brought before the magistrate, didn't worry James. He was, however, disappointed the man who called himself Wilkinson had not been apprehended. The constable had grave doubts the man would be caught.

'If he's the same Wilkinson we had around these parts a while ago, he's a slippery customer and if he gets the slightest whiff we're on to him, he'll be off like a flash!'

James felt pleased he had been able to resolve the matter without worrying his mother while she was away. He had not written to tell her about the burglary as she could do little from overseas. To his knowledge, nothing of value had been taken from her cottage and, as almost all the goods had been returned, he doubted he would bother mentioning the burglary at all.

An invitation was extended to all the first-class passengers to attend the shipboard party to celebrate Lucy Oldfield's marriage to Cyril Street. It was a spectacular affair. From early evening champagne corks popped and the small orchestra in the grand ballroom played non-stop, the popular tunes interspersed with plenty of leisurely old waltzes. It was an elegant party, the garlands of flowers, coloured streamers and balloons, dull in comparison with the flash of diamonds and the shimmer of sequins which glittered from the ladies' ball gowns.

It was not until the early hours of the morning that Lucy and Cyril escaped to the cool air of the promenade deck. Around her shoulders Lucy wore a short mink cape, a wedding gift from Cyril.

As they stood by the rail, gazing across the waters of Bass Strait, in the distance they could see the cliffs of the Australian coastline shining in the moonlight.

'Like the white cliffs of Dover,' Cyril said.

'Yes.'

He put his arm around her. 'Happy?'

Lucy nodded.

'Homesick?'

'No,' she said. 'Home is where the heart is, isn't that what you say?'

Chapter 25

Home again

Grace grew increasingly anxious when she heard Alice was planning to move back into Pansy's old cottage, whereas James was delighted at the prospect and mentioned the fact almost every day. He made time to weed Alice's garden, even though their own garden, and Lucy's was equally overgrown. He also washed the downstairs windows of the end cottage and replaced the hinges on the gate which Crowther had broken. Though she never said anything, Grace was concerned. Would James be wanting to spend time with Alice when she came back? And would Crowther reappear and start bothering them?

As each day passed Grace found it harder to hide her feelings and the idea of moving to the farmhouse became more and more appealing. If they stayed in the cottage she knew she would feel vulnerable, jealous. Alice was a clever girl, a nursing sister, well educated, and always well dressed. Alice was also intelligent and nicely spoken, while she was just a farmer's daughter, who had left school at twelve and who could boast no fancy clothes or ways. Alice was not only pretty and slim, but, even in her white satin nurse's shoes, taller than her. The baggy trousers Grace wore every day, the broad leather belt and mud laden Wellington boots, made her look even shorter and fatter than she really was. The fact she was pregnant didn't help matters.

'Who cares what someone wears! I don't!' said James, pulling his wife to him and hugging her. 'You always look smashing to me. And besides,' he said, 'in a few months' time you'll be glad to have Alice around.'

Grace smiled and kissed him. As usual, he was right and she was being foolish, but she found it difficult to talk to him about her feelings. As he and Alice had grown up together, they were as close as any brother and sister, and it appeared to Grace that James's instinct would be to defend Alice whatever happened.

Two things puzzled Grace, though. Why had Alice left Rachel to be brought up by Pansy in Ilkley? And why was she now planning to move back into the cottage on her own, yet not bringing Rachel with her?

'Seems odd to me,' Grace said casually, 'not having the little lass with her. I can promise, when I have the baby, I won't let her out of my sight.'

'And what will you do when you're milking?' James joked.

'She can sit on a stool and watch. Never too soon to learn!'

'It's going to be a girl, is it?'

'Of course,' said Grace, holding her hands hard against her belly.

'Is there anything else of yours in here?' James asked, as Alice rummaged through the four large boxes which he had just collected from the police station.

'The rest of these things came from your mother's place,' Alice said. 'Including this.' As she spoke she pulled the old doll out of the box. The lace trim on the frock had yellowed and the black goat skin pate looked stark against the pale bisque cheeks. Laying it gently on the table, Alice watched as the eyelashes closed across the luminous blue eyes.

'I loved this doll when I was young,' she said. 'When I was afraid of the dark, I would take her to bed with me and talk to her under the covers. I didn't feel scared when she was with me. I suppose I thought she was real.' She turned and smiled at Grace. 'Silly isn't it, how you think when you are a child.'

Grace nodded and smiled sadly, but her eyes were not on the dilapidated doll, she was looking at the hands holding it, ugly hands, the skin coiled and scarred from being burnt.

'Why don't you keep it?' James said, closing the box's lid. 'Mum gave it to you. She's no reason to want it now.'

Alice held the doll to her chest and thanked James saying it would be nice to have its company in the empty house. Grace offered to help her unpack her suitcases, but Alice said she could manage alone.

The rain, which had started soon after she arrived, was getting heavier. Alice ran back to her cottage trying to avoid the puddles and small streams forming on the lane, but the water splashed over her shoes and saturated her stockings.

The cottage had suffered from being left vacant. It felt cold and damp and the smell of mould hung in the air. After rubbing the rain from her hair and drying the doll's head, Alice kicked off her shoes and ran upstairs to find her slippers. As she walked across the bedroom her toes squelched on the bedside rug. It was sopping wet. Looking up she could see water, dripping from around the covered hole which led up into the roof.

She wondered why the ceiling was wet. There was no window in the attic. Nowhere the rain could blow in. As she stood there, water droplets continued dripping on to the already saturated rug.

Returning from the kitchen with a stack of pans and bowls, Alice dotted them across the floor like stepping stones. In the morning she would tell James. Ask him to climb into the roof cavity to investigate the leak. Perhaps when the tree branches were moving in the wind, they had dislodged one of the slate shingles. Whatever the reason she knew James would fix it.

As she unpacked her clothes and hung them neatly in the wardrobe, she could not escape the constant plop-plopping of the water as it dripped into the pans.

It was hard for Alice to get to sleep that night. Rain lashed against the window and water continued to seep in. Across the roof, the tree branches scraped eerily on the shingles and, in the white flashes of the storm, the blot of mottled mould on the ceiling appeared to move and roll like a gathering thundercloud.

As she pulled the doll into bed beside her, she saw its eyelids close. It was well over two hours before Alice's eyes closed.

James woke Alice at midnight and Andrew Oldfield was born at two o'clock the following morning. His arrival was three weeks earlier than expected and Grace was relieved Alice had been close by.

As day broke, she felt guilty knowing Alice was on duty at the hospital that day. But Alice would hear nothing of her concern. She had been pleased to assist the new baby into the world.

*

The River Wharfe meandered lazily. Sunlight bursting through the trees flickered on the fresh green leaves and glinted on the water. The woodland path was soft underfoot. To the left, the lush ground was a carpet of blue. Masses of bell-shaped flowers bowed their heads towards the earth shedding tears of morning dew. To the right was the river. A pair of squirrels raced along the path, stopped for a moment, tails erect, then scampered across of mesh of twisted roots and up the crumpled bark of an ageing tree. In the silence of the woods the sounds of birds echoed in the still morning air.

Alice loved her weekly visits to Ilkley, especially in spring. Rising before dawn, she always caught the early train so she could share breakfast with her mother and Rachel. And as soon as the meal was cleared away, they would pack a picnic and set off for the day.

Alice hated staying indoors on her day off, and as Miss Pugh's big house in Ilkley was rather dark and depressing and had a distinct musty smell it reminded her of the hospital. Unless the weather was really bad she always preferred for them to go out. Though Alice sympathized with the spinster's mental condition, and admired her mother for looking after her, she was relieved that her great-aunt never asked if she could join them.

On the days they spent together, Alice, Rachel and Pansy walked for miles around the local countryside. Though Pansy still looked thin and frail, she was used to walking. Rachel would walk until she was tired, then the two women would take turns to carry her on their backs.

If the ground was not too slippery, they would take the steep path up the side of Heber's Ghyll, the stream which arose on the moors and gurgled down through the shaded undergrowth to the river in the valley. At the top of the ghyll where the trees stopped and the moors began, they would stop to drink the crystal water pouring from a freshwater spring, or ponder the strange centuries-old shapes carved on the weathered stones.

On a fine day they would hike through the heather to the Cow and Calf rocks, always stopping at the bottom of the cliff face, never venturing to climb. Some days they would stroll down to the Wharfe and wander along the open fields which the river ran through. Sometimes when they reached a pebbled beach, Rachel would paddle in the shallow water while the two women would sit and chat while the curling current drifted lazily by.

'I've decided I'm going to leave the hospital,' Alice said to her mother, as Rachel danced in the bed of bluebells. 'I'll get a day job, like the one I had in the nursing home. I want Rachel living at home with me before she's too old.'

Pansy squeezed her daughter's hand. 'I'm pleased to hear you say that, dear. I love the little lass, but I know she misses you. It's only right she should be with you.'

'I don't know why I didn't think of it before. Now I'm settled back at the cottage it seems the obvious thing to do.' Alice sighed, as she voiced her thoughts out loud. 'Over the years I've been too involved with work. Now it doesn't seem important any more.'

'But you've been a good nurse and your training won't go astray.'

'I know,' said Alice. 'But I wish I hadn't been so blind.'

Rachel presented her grandmother with a bunch of bluebells before running back into the glade to gather more.

'Little Andrew is already walking and Grace is expecting another baby around Christmas time. Rachel will have someone to play with.'

'I'm pleased, Alice. But I'll miss her.'

'Then you must come to the cottage and stay with us.'

'It's hard for me to leave my aunt for long. The old dear is apt to go wandering if I'm not around.'

Alice looked disappointed.

'But we'll see. You never know what's round the corner.'

As the sun's rays poured between the treetops, Alice and Pansy ambled along the path hand in hand. Knee-deep in blue, the child wandered through the woodland, stopping at times to pick another flower. A pair of chaffinches busy at their nest attracted her attention. A dragonfly hovered in the air. She heard a cuckoo and watched a nosy butterfly settle on the flowers in her hand. Above her head she saw a swarm of tiny flies, and looked around for squirrels when she heard the bushes rustling.

Engrossed in conversation, the women wandered on, their minds removed from the sights and sounds of the river-bank. They didn't hear the startled shriek of a bird or the crack of dead twigs broken underfoot. They didn't see the man who was following them, loitering in the undergrowth.

Chapter 26

The Car

Lucy's letter bore an American stamp. As they sat by the fire in the evening, Grace asked James to read it to her.

My dear James and Grace

As I write, the ship is steaming slowly through the Panama Canal. How different the scenery here is from the canal at Suez. Being near the equator, the weather is hot and sticky and Cyril and I are looking forward to being back on the open sea again. We change ships at New York but will not stay there as we do not want to be crossing the North Atlantic once the winter storms have blown in. From New York the ship steams via the Azores and we will disembark in Southampton.

I was overjoyed to hear that I have a grandson and congratulate you and Grace on the birth of Andrew Edward Oldfield. I only wish I could have been home in time for his arrival. But I am glad Grace and baby are well, and to hear Alice is living back home. It will be wonderful for us all to be together again at Honeysuckle Cottages. Perhaps one day Pansy will come back too.

I hope it will not come as too much of a shock but Cyril and I were married some weeks ago. You will remember I mentioned our friendship when I wrote from India. We were attracted to each other when we first met and, as Cyril does not believe in wasting time, we decided to get married straight away. Being practical, as we both are, we decided it was foolish to pay for two cabins on the ship and two rooms in the hotels, therefore when the ship docked in Fremantle in Western Australia we arranged for a special marriage licence. As our relation-

ship had been a topic of gossip amongst the first-class passengers, it seemed fitting
to have a party on board to celebrate. I was hardly the young blushing bride, but
it was a memorable day.

I feel sure you will both like Cyril. He is a kind and gentle man with a lively
sense of humour. He has the patience and tolerance of Edward, and a consid-
erable amount more energy. Hopefully we will be home within two months.

Give my regards to John Fothergill.

Your loving Mother

'She sounds happy,' said James.

Grace agreed. 'And they will be home before Christmas.'

James smiled. 'Yes,' he said, as he gazed out of the window. As the
wind swept waves across the grass, he tried to picture his mother on the
deck of a ship sailing somewhere on the North Atlantic. He remembered
his voyage to India and wondered if he would ever travel abroad again.
'I'm tired,' he said.

'Go to bed. I will follow in a few minutes.'

James kissed her. He felt more weary than usual. The last few weeks
had not gone well and there was little for him to feel positive about. The
heavy rain had come at the wrong time damaging the crops which were
ripening and almost ready for harvest. A month ago the top field had
swayed golden in the breeze, waving like the surface of the sea bathed in
a glorious sunset. Now the field was spoiled, flattened, the whole crop
turning black and mouldy on the ground. A full year's work had gone to
waste.

Apart from the wheat, the drenching rain had turned the bottom
meadows into swamps. The cows, sinking to their bellies in the mire, were
coming in for milking with filthy udders. The farm's tracks were gouged
with muddy ruts and potholes and James's legs ached constantly from the
weight of clay caked around his boots. He was tired of being soaked to
the skin, tired of the wind's bitter chill striking through him like a steel
blade and tired of everything going wrong. At times he wanted to give up,
to ignore the cows and the farm, to stay indoors with Grace.

Lying in bed, he asked himself if he was cut out to be a farmer.

The thirty gallons of milk wasted during the week was due to his own
stupidity. No one else was to blame. He had been hurrying. Stubborn. Not

listened to Grace when she had advised him to be careful. He had known the roads were bad but had been driving too fast. He remembered the truck rocking from side to side. Remembered his sudden sense of panic expecting it to topple. He had felt the wheels lock, struggled with the wheel, but could do nothing. Within seconds the front end had embedded itself into a deep ditch.

Along the road, he had left a trail of spilled milk and littered the verge with dented churns. Fortunately there was no damage to the truck or himself, but it took three hours and the help of another farmer to pull the vehicle out of the ditch, and besides that, the missing milk delivery upset several of his regular customers.

John Fothergill had never made a fuss. He had been concerned but seemed philosophical and glad that James had not been injured. 'These things happen,' he said. 'Not a lot you can do about it.' He calculated that the number of cattle they were feeding for the Christmas trade would compensate for the loss of crop. They could buy extra stock feed if needed. Despite their losses, he seemed quite positive. James, however, wasn't convinced. Market prices fluctuated and though at present the cattle looked good, if the rain continued much longer their condition would start to decline.

As he lay on the bed almost too weary for sleep, he thought about Grace. She was pregnant again and, whether she wanted to or not, soon she must stop working. That was going to mean even more work for him.

What the farm needed was an extra hand. But could they afford it and still support the two households? He must speak seriously to John about taking on some help. Perhaps a young lad to work full-time or a man to work part-time in the dairy and drive the truck.

He didn't know how Grace and her father had managed to run the farm on their own and wondered why he couldn't manage. What was he doing wrong? As he rolled over, he heard Grace's footsteps on the stairs. They must find time to talk about these things. Yawning, he heard her close the bedroom door but by the time she climbed into bed beside him, he was asleep.

'James! Help!'

James dropped the pails when he heard Grace's cry and ran back towards the farmhouse splashing through pools of mud.

'It's Dad,' she cried, when he was near the house.

John Fothergill was sprawled on the ground outside the back door. He was soaking wet, his face half submerged in muddy water but he was still breathing.

'I thought he was with you!' she yelled. 'I've just found him. I don't know how long he's been here.' Taking her father's arm, she tried to pull him up.

'Let me!' James said

'Is he all right?'

'He's alive, but we've got to get him inside and warm or he'll not be for much longer.'

James grasped his father-in-law under the arms and dragged him into the house. A trail of mud followed them down the hall and into the bedroom. The old man groaned as James hoisted him on to the bed.

'I'll go fetch Alice. She'll know what to do.'

Grace nodded. What would she do now? Her father couldn't stay in the farmhouse alone, at least, not while he was sick. She could never sleep in the cottage for fear he might fall again. She would have to stay with him.

When more than an hour had elapsed since James left, Grace started to worry. She was afraid he might have met with an accident, worried that the truck might have gone off the road again, or got bogged in a ditch. She had wanted to go out searching for him but dare not leave her father. She didn't know that Alice wasn't home and James had gone to the village looking for the doctor, that he had waited in the surgery for almost an hour but the doctor didn't return from his calls.

But by the time James got back, John Fothergill was beginning to feel better. Grace had removed his wet clothes and managed to get some warmth back into his cold body. While he remained still, the farmer had little pain, but with the slightest attempt to move, the pain was excruciating.

Grace was worried about him, but she was worried about James too. He looked exhausted. He was trying to do everything and it just wasn't possible. If he didn't slow down soon he would make himself sick.

With Mr Fothergill confined to bed, James and Grace slept at farmhouse for the following week. There was little the doctor could do for him save recommending bed rest and prescribing something to ease the pain in his hip. The farmer didn't argue as it was impossible for him to move.

As Grace's pregnancy advanced, James could read the strain in her face. He knew her energies were being stretched to the limit. One afternoon he found her crying over a sheet she had torn in the mangle.

'Leave it, love. It doesn't matter,' he begged.

'It does matter!' she sobbed. 'I shouldn't have let it get stuck.'

He knew she was not coping. They were all under strain.

James didn't want to drive Alice to Ilkley. He wanted to stay at home with Grace and catch up on a few jobs around the cottage. He knew once they got to Ilkley, Alice would be obliged to stop and talk with Pansy and Miss Pugh, which meant they probably wouldn't get back until late in the afternoon.

But he had promised Alice he would take her to collect Rachel and he couldn't let them down. At least it wouldn't happen again. This time Alice was collecting Rachel and bringing her home to stay permanently.

'Why don't you come with us?' James asked Grace 'There's plenty of room in the car. The ride'll do you good.'

'I can't leave Dad,' Grace said.

Despite not wanting to leave either his wife or the farm, James enjoyed the half-hour drive. He had little opportunity for such luxuries these days.

With the car roof down, the air was exhilarating. Alice, her head wrapped in a silk headscarf, seemed more relaxed than she had been for a long time. She was looking forward to having Rachel share the cottage with her.

Speeding past open fields and clusters of houses in the villages, James asked Alice about her new job in Horsforth and how she was enjoying being back at the cottage. She asked him about Mr Fothergill, the farm, Grace, and when the next baby was due.

As the conversation drifted to more trivial matters, James relaxed. Sitting beside Alice reminded him of the times they had spent riding when they were teenagers. Those had been good times, happy times without any stress. He had almost forgotten the fun they had had in each other's company and how much she had meant to him. He looked across at her eyes watering in the wind, her hair streaming from beneath the scarf. How attractive she was. Mature. Intelligent. Well dressed. The tweed suit she was wearing was well tailored. The silk stockings, smooth and shiny. Her shoes, the latest fashion. Was this really the waif he had found huddled in the heather? How they had both changed.

It was an emotional parting for Pansy and her granddaughter. Pansy had treated Rachel as if she were her own daughter and Rachel regarded her as her mother. Now the little girl was moving back to live with her real mother, a woman she knew little about, back to Horsforth, a place she was not familiar with.

The goodbyes were protracted.

Miss Pugh was in surprisingly good spirits and appeared to be in full control of her senses. 'You mustn't worry about Pansy,' Miss Pugh said to Alice. 'I'll look after her.' Her tone was confident and convincing. The spinster was certain it was Pansy who was in need of care. 'We manage well together, don't we dear?'

Pansy smiled. 'Of course we do, Aunty.'

The old woman drew Alice aside and whispered in her ear, 'Don't you worry about her, my dear. She'll be all right. She'll have this place when I'm dead and gone.'

Alice thanked Miss Pugh politely and told her that she and Rachel would be visiting every week.

'But it's such a long way to come,' Pansy argued.

'While the weather's fine and the trains are running, we'll come. You know I love to get out on the moors or walk along the river. I've spent too many years cooped up indoors. Besides, I know Rachel will want to see you.'

Rachel cried as she hugged her grandmother.

'I will see you next week,' Pansy said. 'The time will fly.'

Rachel had only one small suitcase and a paper carrier bag with a few books and toys. James laid them on the front seat. As he drove back to Horsforth, Alice and Rachel talked quietly. James couldn't hear what they were saying and didn't try to join in the conversation.

The following week, Alice and Rachel didn't go to Ilkley as planned, instead Pansy came to visit them, at the cottage, on the Saturday.

Alice had arranged a party for Rachel. It wasn't her birthday, but as she had never given her daughter a party before, coming home seemed like a good enough reason to celebrate.

Prompted by the party and the fact Mr Fothergill could no longer manage on his own after the fall, Grace decided he should move into the cottage with them. James collected a single bed from the farm and assembled it in the front room of the cottage. During the day the farmer sat in Edward's leather armchair, his legs resting on a stool.

At first Mr Fothergill wasn't sure about living away from the farm. He had grown up in the rambling old house which his grandfather had built and this was the first time he had been away. But he knew his incapacity was causing problems and hated being a burden.

'If I was a cow you would shoot me,' he said to James one day. 'Damn nuisance. Rheumatics that's all it is.'

But he never joked to Alice about his leg. 'I wish sometimes the doctor would take it off. I'd manage better without it.'

It was a fun party. Alice made paper hats and toffee apples. They played charades and James amazed them with the card tricks he had learned in the army. Later in the afternoon they trooped into Lucy's cottage for a sing-song. If some of the keys were out of tune, no one cared. It was a long time since Alice had played.

Grace left early as her father had stayed at home and she wanted to make sure he was all right. When she walked through the door she could hear him snoring loudly. It was obvious he was oblivious to the sound of voices raised around the piano next door.

From the front window she could see the Tourer parked on the lane. The roof was still down, but the bonnet was up and the engine was being cranked over. She wondered why James had left the others and where he was going. Perhaps he was planning to take the children for a ride, perhaps he was going to the farm? She thought it strange that he hadn't said anything.

As she watched, the man leaning down beside the radiator grille stood up. Despite the goggles half covering his face, Grace knew it wasn't James.

Running out the door, Grace shouted, 'Hey! You! What do you think you are doing?'

The man leaned down and cranked the handle again. The engine fired. Quickly closing the bonnet, he jumped into the car.

Grace reached the lane as the Tourer started rolling. Jumping on to the running board, she grabbed hold of the passenger door. 'Get out! This isn't yours! Stop thief!' she screamed.

The driver accelerated. The car gathered speed.

James heard Grace's screams, but by the time he reached the lane the car was halfway down the hill. He started running. The car was going faster. Twenty miles an hour – twenty-five miles an hour – too fast to take the bend!

The brakes were little use on the loose gravel. The narrow tyres skidded towards the verge. When it hit, the chassis bounced and Grace was tossed backwards on to the wet grass which sloped steeply away from the road. Landing on her back she slid to the bottom of the slope like a sledge down a hill of fresh snow.

James watched helplessly. When it reached the corner, the car turned in a complete circle, ran on two wheels, then tottered slowly on to its side before coming to a halt. Though the engine spluttered and died, the front wheel continued spinning in the air while steam and water spouted from the radiator.

A man was lying on the road at the far side of the car, blood smeared across his face. But James didn't care about him. It was Grace he was worried about. She was lying at the bottom of the slope. Sliding down the grass to her, he lifted her hand. She didn't move.

'Grace!' he cried.

Chapter 27

The Strid

Grace groaned as she lifted her head. 'I've been kicked by a cow before today, but never felt quite like this!'

James kneeled down and helped her sit up. 'Promise me you won't ever do anything like that again. You could have been killed!'

'Are you all right, Grace?' said Alice, as she slid down beside the pair.

James jumped up. 'Stay with her! I want to find the bastard who did this!'

Scrambling back up the hill was not easy. Though James dug his fingers into the soil, his feet would not grip on the wet slope. After a few unsuccessful attempts, he resorted to the longer route round the bottom of the hill. It brought him out further down the lane. Striding back to his car, he wondered what damage had been done? The windscreen was still intact and the headlights were in one piece. He could see the running board was twisted. The Tourer was resting on it.

As he walked round to the far side of the vehicle he expected to find the man lying on the gravel, but he had disappeared. The only trace of the offender was a few spots of blood.

James was angry. He didn't care about the man's injuries, he wanted to see him punished for what he had done to Grace.

'Coward!' he yelled, scanning the bushes. 'You'll get what's coming to you, one of these days!'

James led the constable upstairs and knocked on the bedroom door.

Having complained of feeling unwell after the accident, Grace was in

200

bed. Alice had insisted she rest, having grave fears she might lose the baby which was due in a few months' time.

Grace fastened her bed jacket. 'Come in!'

'Can you describe this man?' the policeman said.

'I'm sorry,' Grace said. 'I couldn't see his face. His cap was pulled low on his forehead and he was wearing a pair of goggles. All I remember was a drooping moustache, brown and straggly, and the look in his eyes as the car speeded up.' A shudder ran through her. 'I think he was laughing.'

James looked at the constable, but refrained from speaking.

The policeman closed his notebook. 'Thank you, Mrs Oldfield. If you think of anything else, please let me know.'

'I will.'

The constable collected his bike from the front garden and wheeled it out to the lane. 'You said you thought the man was injured.'

'There was blood on his face but he disappeared so quickly, I don't think there was much else wrong with him.'

'I hope it's not that fellow, Wilkinson or Crowther or whatever he calls himself. I was hoping we'd seen the last of him.'

'Do you think it could be the same man who robbed us?'

'Damned sure it is,' the constable said as he wheeled his bike on to the lane. 'Shame the magistrate had to dismiss the case through lack of evidence. This fellow is cunning. Like a fox, he is. Goes to ground for a while then when he feels safe, out he pops. But it's the first time I've heard of him trying to pinch a car.'

'Have you had any other reports in the area?'

'Not here. But I heard of a case last week in Otley. A poor woman who lived on her own was robbed and beaten up. Left her in such a state she could hardly talk. All she could tell the local Bobbies was that the man had a moustache. Hardly enough to go on! But I wouldn't be surprised if it was the same fellow.' He looked James in the eye and spoke quietly. 'That young wife of yours is lucky to be alive. I suggest you keep a good watch around the place.'

Tapping his helmet firmly on to his head, the policeman swung his leg over the bike's saddle. 'I'd give my right arm to get my hands on that man! Deserves to be put away for life in my book.'

'We'll watch out,' James said. 'Thanks.'

*

Though Lucy and Cyril's arrival was expected, the car's engine had hummed so quietly up the hill no one heard it coming. The car was brand new and expensive, the latest from the Armstrong Siddely factory. Even in the greyness of the day the chromework gleamed.

'They're here,' Grace shouted, when she looked out of the window.

James was first outside to hug his mother and shake hands with her new husband.

'It's so good to be home again,' Lucy said.

How well she looked, James thought. And happy.

'Nothing has changed,' she said, as she stood at the gate and ran her eyes over the three adjoining cottages.

But in James's mind a lot had changed in the two years since his mother had left to settle affairs in India. He and Grace had married. Andrew had been born and another baby was due at Christmas. Mr Fothergill now lived with them permanently, as he could only manage to walk a few yards and only with reluctance allowed himself to be pushed around in the Bath chair James had bought for him. Alice, of course had returned to Honeysuckle Cottages and settled into her new part-time job at the nursing home. And Rachel was living there too, although neither he nor Grace saw much of her. When Alice was working, Rachel was minded by a lady in the village, and every Saturday the pair travelled to Ilkley to spend the day with Pansy and Miss Pugh. James had seen little of Pansy recently as her aunt's mental state had deteriorated considerably and she didn't like to leave her alone for very long.

As they settled around the fire, Grace served tea and Lucy asked about the farm.

'Things are improving,' James said, as he glanced at his wife. 'We went through a bad spell for a while, didn't we?'

Grace nodded as Andrew crawled on to her knee. His eyelids were drooping.

'We've got a labourer and a lad working for us now,' James said. 'Local men. Both good workers. Makes such a difference,' he said. 'Money's a bit tight at times, but we manage.'

'When the baby's born I'll be able to do more,' Grace added. 'I hate being useless.'

John Fothergill shuffled in his chair but said nothing.

'Well I must say you look happy, James. Married life must suit you.'

'And you look happy too, Mum.' James turned to Cyril. 'You must be good for her!'

They all responded to his broad smile. 'Good for each other,' Cyril said.

While James and Cyril talked about the farm, Mr Fothergill was content to sit and listen.

James was filled with enthusiasm for the farm. He was eager to show his mother the changes he had made to the dairy, and the modern milking equipment they had installed. He wanted to take Cyril out to the far meadow to show him the red Angus bull they had bought to cover the black heifers. 'Less trouble with the calving,' he said. And to show them both over the parcel of land he had just managed to lease to run the small beef herd on.

'We'll have a bumper season next year,' James said.

John Fothergill leaned forward in his chair towards Lucy. 'He's got his head screwed on right, that lad of yours. Done far more than I ever did with the place. I could never see further than the end of my nose, but young James here, well, there's no stopping him.'

'Only problem is finance,' said James seriously. 'Can't do anything without capital. That's something I want to talk to you about, Mum, but it can wait until later.' He paused. 'Now tell us about your travels and about yourself, Cyril. My mother has been keeping me in the dark. I want to hear about this man who swept her off her feet.'

'Me!' he said. 'Don't blame me. If anyone was doing the sweeping it was this mother of yours.'

Lucy smacked his hand playfully. 'You wait till I get you next door!'

He laughed. 'See what I mean!'

The evening sky was changing colour. Across the meadow the hilltops glowed with the dying rays of the sun.

'I want to sell the cottage,' James said to his mother. 'Grace and I have been talking about it for some time. It would be more sensible for us to live at the farm rather than walking there every day. Besides, Grace misses her big kitchen. And there will be plenty of room for Andrew and the new baby when it arrives. Apart from that, John will be happier in his own place.'

Lucy thought for a moment before answering. 'But you could lease the cottage and get a decent rent for it.'

'We considered that idea, but right now it's the capital we need. If we sell, we can put the money back into the farm. It'll pay big dividends in the long run.'

'I know John Fothergill's a good man,' Lucy said, 'but is it wise to put all your money into a farm that's not yours?'

'It is though!' he said. 'John signed over the title to me and Grace. It's all legal. He said he didn't want problems with it when he was dead. He's a good man, Mother, he really is.'

Lucy agreed, John Fothergill was good.

'Do you and Cyril want to buy my cottage? You could knock down the adjoining wall and make the two places into one. The cottage is in need of modernizing.'

'It's possible,' said Lucy slowly. 'Though Cyril and I haven't decided what we shall do in the future. Somehow, I don't think we will stay in Yorkshire.'

James was not surprised.

'There are places we like overseas. And we both enjoy the sunshine. But Cyril likes his home in Kent and I have to admit it's a lovely place. The house is set in a big garden with huge rhododendron bushes around the lawns. I've never seen them in full bloom but he tells me they look beautiful. And Kent is such a nice county.'

As they walked across the back meadow, Lucy's mind drifted. It was a long time since she had felt the field beneath her feet. She smiled. 'I remember struggling across this ground with the hand plough. Me, Pansy and Alice worked this meadow every year while you were away at the war. And I remember the horses too. How patient they were.'

James's smile was wistful as he remembered Goldie, his horse that lived out its years in the paddock and was only put down when it went lame. He thought too of Edward's mare. The horse that was stolen and never recovered.

'You and Edward used to enjoy your rides together,' Lucy said. 'He was such a good man. Without him none of us would be where we are today.'

'We should go inside,' James said. 'You are getting cold.'

'No, just a shiver,' she murmured. 'And a few memories.'

Cyril bought the tree for Christmas. It was the tallest one they had ever had in the house, its tip touched the ceiling. He also bought the coloured lights which were a change from the tinsel and paper decorations of previous years. This year all the presents were wrapped in fancy paper and the pile was higher than it had ever been.

Rachel was so excited, constantly rushing outside looking for her grandmother when it was time for her to arrive. When the car pulled up she ran down the path, arms outstretched to welcome her. In the crisp air their combined breath puffed like steam from an engine. Rachel jumped up and down, tugging at the shopping bag on Pansy's arm, dragging her grandmother into the house.

'Isn't it wonderful all being together like this?' Lucy said. 'It has been so long.'

Christmas dinner was a feast. Turkey and pork and all the trimmings. The turkey had been raised and fattened on the farm, but James had bought the pig at the market.

'We should build some sties,' James said to his father-in-law. 'Get two or three gilts and a boar. We've got plenty of grain and I'd have no trouble selling the piglets.'

Mr Fothergill agreed. The idea was worth thinking about.

Rachel wasn't interested in pigs, apart from the gingerbread ones Lucy had made with currants for eyes and a candied peel tail. For Rachel it seemed to take forever before the adults were finished at the table and Mr Fothergill's chair pushed back into the front room.

By the time they all sat down, Lucy's front room was crowded. Cyril and Lucy shared the sofa, John Fothergill's Bath chair was squeezed in beside the fireplace, Alice perched on the piano stool with Rachel beside her, while Grace sat opposite her father, bouncing Andrew on her knee. James was content to rest on the chair arm, while Pansy sat by the window.

Once everyone was settled, the presents were opened. Amidst the litter of string and wrapping paper, Rachel and Andrew took pride of place on the rug.

'This is the best Christmas I can remember,' whispered Lucy, as she leaned against her husband and placed a kiss on his cheek.

That evening Alice and James took turns at the piano. They played almost every carol in the book and a few of Cyril's favourite hymns. Even John Fothergill joined in until he was suddenly overcome by tiredness. When he started snoring, Grace offered to go home with him. She too was very tired and ready to leave. With the baby almost due she had been feeling weary lately.

Amelia Rose was born at three in the afternoon exactly a week later, on New Year's Day.

That winter was fairly mild. Apart from the water troughs freezing over, and an occasional flurry of snow which didn't settle, James had no problems getting to the farm. The dairyman who worked for them lived nearby and besides being reliable, was an early riser. Every morning he had the cows in the shed before James arrived.

After the birth of the baby, Grace was happy for them to remain at the cottage until she was a few months old. They decided that they would put off moving back to the farmhouse until spring arrived.

Mr Fothergill had also lost the hankering to go. The rambling house took a long time to heat and was bitterly cold without a fire, but the front room of James's cottage, where he had his bed, was always warm. This was the first winter in a long time, he had not suffered from the cold. Even when Cyril took him for a drive, the car's heater warmed his legs. He liked being taken out, sitting at the front, watching the season as it slowly changed, the criss-cross framework of winter trees preparing to burst into a canopy of soft green. John Fothergill always looked forward to spring.

The Sunday after the May Day celebrations, Alice paid her weekly visit to her mother. As Lucy and Cyril had gone to the seaside for a few days and taken Rachel with them, she went alone.

When Alice arrived at the Ilkley house, she was pleased to hear Miss Pugh was well. That meant that she and Pansy could go out for a few hours without worrying about the elderly lady. It was a nice day so they decided to catch a bus to Burley-in-Wharfedale. From there they would amble back to Ilkley along the riverbank. It was a long walk, but one they always enjoyed.

Through the valley, the river meandered silently. At its widest point, the crystal water magnified each speckled pebble, log and darting fish as clearly as features in a goldfish bowl. For much of the way, the footpath was soft and flat. But as the river narrowed through the wooded glades, the banks grew steep, the path slippery, occasionally obstructed by a fallen tree or trickling stream. The women didn't mind. They scrambled over and wandered on. They loved the scenery, enjoyed each other's company and chatted avidly. Without Rachel with them they were able to stride out at their own pace.

When they reached a clearing they stopped. Ahead, a broad expanse of rock barricaded the river's course. Stretching from one bank to the other, it halted the water's flow. With only a narrow gap in the shelf to pass through, the water gurgled loudly as it gushed through, disgorging itself into a swirling pool whose frothy surface churned white with foam. Constantly full, the pool overflowed, spilling its content down across the rocks, feeding the broad riverbed, allowing the Wharfe to refill and resume its leisurely journey downstream.

On the left bank, Alice and Pansy found their special seats; two weathered rocks, green with moss and shaded by the overhanging trees. Overhead, the sun was warm. It was a place the women often chose to stop, to sit and talk, and watch the swallows swooping in endless circles across the sparkling water.

Behind them leaves rustled. The bushes parted. A man laughed.

'Stanley!' breathed Pansy, as memories flashed back. The face, expression, the evil grin, masked by the whiskers covering his upper lip.

'So ladies, we meet again! It's been too long!'

'Ignore him!' Alice cried.

'Two birds with one stone!' he laughed sliding his hand on Pansy's knee.

She tried to pull her leg away as Alice stood and swung her handbag at his head. His left arm shot out and sent her toppling back across the rocks.

'Leave us alone,' Pansy screamed.

'There's no one going to help you here,' he leered, as he forced her back against the bank and pushed his hand beneath her skirt.

'Leave her alone!' screamed Alice as she tried to pull him from her mother.

He swung at her and hit her full in the face then muffled Pansy's screaming with his hand.

As if from nowhere, a small dog appeared and snapped at Crowther's feet.

He kicked at it but missed.

In the distance Alice heard someone whistling for the dog.

'Help!' she shouted, as she glimpsed three figures wandering down the path. She yelled again. This time they heard her and started running.

When Crowther saw them they were not more than thirty yards away: three fit young men each brandishing a walking stick. Crowther glanced to the bushes and along the track. He'd never escape them through the undergrowth or outrun them on the track. The path was slippery, the young men fitter than he. Had there been only one he would have stood his ground.

He cursed and ran across the bed of rock towards the point the river gurgled through the gap, a width of five or six feet. He'd jumped it once before when he was younger. He only needed speed to clear the distance.

'Come back!' the man cried, as his dog bounded after Crowther snapping at his trousers.

'Don't jump!' another yelled.

As the dog jerked on his trouser leg, Crowther hesitated but he was too close to change his mind. He leapt, landing his toes on the other side. But the rock was smooth and damp with moss, and for a second he stood, as if hanging on by an invisible rope. Suddenly his arms began to flay the air, turning faster and faster as he fought to regain his balance. Letting out a choking cry, he desperately tried to grip the air, but there was nothing to stop him falling backwards.

The women watched helplessly as his feet slipped from the rock and he dropped into the rushing water.

Standing close to the edge, the terrier wagged its tail. The man he'd chased had disappeared. After sniffing the air, it turned and trotted back to its master.

'Damn fool,' one of the young men cried.

Stepping cautiously, Alice moved towards the gap and gazed into the water. There was no trace of Stanley Crowther. Not even his cap.

'Be careful, lady,' the man said.

'Is it dangerous?'

'The Strid?' he said. 'Don't look dangerous. But no one who's ever fallen in has surfaced at the other end.'

Alice looked at the crystal water flowing downstream from the pool. 'But it's shallow there. Couldn't he swim out?'

'You don't swim out of the Strid, missus. The rocks we're standing on are riddled with caverns. The river swirls into them and carries everything with it. It never gives back what it drags down.'

As Alice stepped back, her legs were shaking.

'One thing's for sure,' the young man said. 'That man will never trouble you again. I can guarantee you that!'

Chapter 28

The Storm

It was late when Alice got back to the cottage. She was relieved Lucy and Cyril had gone away and taken Rachel with them. She wanted to go inside and close her door on the outside world. Though Crowther was dead, she felt no desire to celebrate.

When Lucy returned two days later Alice said nothing about the incident, and the story she related about her bruises – saying she had fallen on the rocks beside the river – was not entirely untrue. The following day, she did not go to work; instead she travelled by train to Ilkley to meet her mother. At the local police station the two women made formal statements.

'It's unlikely we'll ever find a body,' the constable said, confirming the comments of the young men who had helped them.

'Did you see him fall? Did you see him go under? Did the water pull him down?'

Alice answered as best she could. She could still visualize his face; his eyes wide, his mouth gaping, gulping for air as the force of water dragged him under.

As she rode home her mind was blank. She was conscious of nothing but the clatter of the train on the railway lines, the carriage swaying, the flash of fields and factories as they flew by. The only thought nagging at her brain was the fear the police would visit her in Horsforth. She wanted to forget Crowther, get far away from his memory, forget the face now etched in her mind. The face which would return in the darkness to haunt her!

*

For Lucy and Cyril, their time in Horsforth was like an extension of the long holiday they had enjoyed together. They went out several evenings a week, sometimes to a picture house to watch a film, or into Leeds to one of the city's theatres; to a musical recital at the town hall, or, on a fine afternoon, to stroll across the park at Roundhay, or take a rowing boat out on the lake.

Lucy enjoyed the evenings when the children would play together on the floor. She would listen when Rachel tapped notes out on the piano and was sorry Alice had never had time to give her lessons. During the day she missed James. He was always busy on the farm, away from home all day from early morning till late afternoon.

Grace was a good mother. And the new baby, Amelia Rose was growing quickly. Lucy knew Grace was becoming more anxious to move back to the farmhouse.

Grace rolled over in bed. The sound of the storm was making sleep impossible. It had rumbled around the district for over an hour but now it was directly overhead. The crash of the thunder came at the same time as the flash of light. The ornaments on the dressing-table rattled.

James got up. It was pointless lying in bed. He couldn't sleep. He decided to make a cup of tea and bring it back to bed. He knew Grace wasn't sleeping either.

Before he reached the door a flash of white light startled him. A crack, like the sound of a leather whip, accompanied it, then a hissing noise and a rumble like the sound of a rock face crumbling.

Grace sat bolt upright. 'What on earth was that?'

In the flashes of light through the window James could see nothing for the rain beating against the pane. Outside, the wind was howling. For a moment the lightning stopped, but in the darkness he could still see light outside, flickering. It was coming from the other end of the cottages.

'Something's wrong!' he shouted, pulling his trousers over his pyjamas.

Grace slid from the bed and grabbed her clothes.

As soon as he stepped into the front garden, James knew the chestnut tree by Alice's cottage had been struck. Branches draped across the roof were alight.

Rachel's face was at the upstairs window. Her mouth was open –
screaming – but the wind and storm were swallowing her cries.

'Get the fire brigade,' James shouted, as Lucy and Cyril appeared at
their door.

'I'll go,' said Grace

Cyril followed James to the back of the cottages.

The sight that greeted them was shocking.

The old tree had been rent in half and split open. Flames were burning from the centre like the incandescent flame of a huge pressure lamp.
The enormous bough, which usually draped its shade over the house, had
sheered from the trunk, slicing through the shingled roof, completely
demolishing the back bedroom. The burning branches, rubble from the
bedroom wall, the rafters and the slate were piled on the heavy beams
which formed the kitchen ceiling.

'My God!' Cyril cried.

'The ladder!' James yelled. 'We've got to get them out!'

Clad only in pyjamas and slippers, Cyril ran to get it.

At the front of the cottage, Rachel had opened her bedroom window.
Smoke was billowing around her. She was frightened. Coughing.

'We'll get you down!' James shouted.

'Mummy!' she yelled. 'Mummy!'

As James grabbed her, he could see the adjoining wall between the two
bedrooms was still standing. The doorway to the staircase was filled with
smoke and branches.

'Where's your mummy?' he yelled, as he passed her down to Cyril.

'In bed,' Rachel sobbed.

James shook his head. She couldn't be in bed. There was no bed. No
bedroom. No roof. The back bedroom of the cottage had gone. All that
remained was the pile of burning rubble.

'Don't go in there!' Cyril shouted, as James climbed back up the ladder
and through the bedroom window. A moment later he reappeared, spluttering. He clambered back.

'I've got to get up there!' he cried. 'Alice is in there. I've got to get her
out!'

Cyril didn't argue. Hurrying to the back of the cottage, they leaned the
ladder against the wall as far from the burning tree as possible. James

didn't notice the rain – only that the flames were consuming the rotted roof timbers like slivers of dry paper.

He climbed on to the rubble, scratching through it with his bare hands, tearing off broken bricks, slate and lumps of mortar. He knew where the bed had stood, where Alice would have been sleeping. He dug frantically, throwing the stones aside, unaware of the blood oozing from his fingers.

Suddenly he stopped. Sticking out of the rubble was a tiny shoe, trimmed with a silver buckle. Carefully, he lifted the blocks from around it. The doll, he had once chosen for a guy had not been burnt, nor had the pale hand clasping it. The scars it bore were from another fire.

The clang of the fire engine's bell grew louder, then stopped.

James held Alice's hand until she was finally uncovered. As they lifted her body down, he cradled the doll in his arms and cried.

Chapter 29

For Sale

'Shall I take it?' said Lucy.

James looked at her blankly and handed the doll to his mother.

'I loved Alice,' he said sadly. 'But I never knew how much till now.'

'I know,' she said.

'But why did she have to die?' he said. 'Like that – alone – afraid – and under all those flames.'

Grace put her arms around him and led him inside. 'There's nothing more you can do here. Come away.'

Early the following morning Lucy and Cyril drove the fifteen miles to Ilkley. Lucy hardly spoke in the car. Apart from giving Pansy the sad news of her daughter's death, Lucy was concerned about Rachel. What would become of the little girl now she was an orphan?

Pansy sensed there was something wrong when she opened the door and saw the expression on Lucy's face.

'It's Rachel, isn't it? Something terrible has happened to Rachel!'

'No Pansy, it's Alice.'

Pansy took the news quietly and appeared composed as Lucy told her what had happened. While the women talked, Cyril busied himself making tea and was pleased Miss Pugh was in good spirits and able to help him.

Pansy didn't touch her drink but waited until the others had finished before asking them to take her back to Horsforth. She was anxious to see where her daughter had died and the damage the fire had caused to the cottage she had lived in for many years.

On leaving the house, Pansy instructed her aunt to stay inside, lock the door and not let anyone in.

Miss Pugh hugged Pansy and planted a kiss her cheek. 'This war can't go on forever,' she said. 'Don't worry about me and the house. I'll make sure the door is locked. I'll be all right.'

No one spoke during the journey. In the back seat, Pansy stared blankly out of the window. Her eyes were glazed but her face showed no evidence of tears. But when the car stopped and Rachel ran into her arms, she wept. As Lucy and Cyril walked quietly away leaving the pair to grieve together, Lucy knew the little girl would be well cared for. Rachel would be going back to resume her life with Pansy and the poor demented Miss Pugh.

Less than a week later a telegram arrived from Pansy.

Desperately need your help. Rachel missing.

Lucy and Cyril set off immediately, calling in at the farm on the way. James was out in the truck, but Grace said she was sure he would follow them as soon as he got back. Despite Lucy's concern, Grace insisted the farm could manage without him for a while.

When Lucy and Cyril arrived at the tall Victorian house, Pansy was in a state of near collapse. She had not slept or eaten since the previous day and had spent the night walking the streets searching for her granddaughter. Her feet were wet and dirty, her clothes damp, but she refused either to change or go to bed.

'She went out to play yesterday morning,' said Pansy. 'To the park. It's only a hundred yards away. I didn't worry. She often went there on her own, but she always came back after an hour.' Pansy raked her fingers through her hair. 'When she wasn't home by dinner-time, I went out to find her. I looked everywhere. By tea-time I was at my wits' end and went to the police station. The constable was on his own and said he couldn't leave. But he told me another policeman would call around later.'

Pansy said she was out all that evening but presumed an officer had visited as Miss Pugh told her a soldier had called during the night.

'I sent the telegram this morning. I didn't know what else to do. I've searched everywhere. The only other places I can think to look are the moors and the river-bank. The places we used to go walking with Alice.'

It was some time before Pansy calmed down but when eventually she relaxed a little, her eyes quickly closed. Lucy didn't try to move her from the chair, instead she pulled a blanket over her and left her by the fire to sleep.

Though Miss Pugh appeared quite lucid and was worried about her niece, she was confused. She thought Lucy was her sister and, because so many people had called in to visit, believed it was Christmas Day. Her main concern was that she had made no preparations for the meal and could not remember where she had hidden the presents.

James arrived two hours later. After hearing what had happened, he and Cyril decided they should immediately set off across the moors from Heber's Ghyll to the Cow and Calf rocks. If their search was unsuccessful, the following day they would take the path which followed the river.

About four o'clock in the afternoon the two men found Rachel. She was huddled amongst a pile of fallen rocks at the base of the Cow rock, asleep. Apart from being cold and hungry and her legs scratched by the heather, she was all right. She couldn't remember walking over the open moors, or why she had made her way to the Cow and Calf. She didn't know how long she had been there, but told them she was waiting for her grandmother to collect her.

When they got back to the house, Rachel ran inside to Pansy's arms. As the pair held each other, Lucy could not hide her tears. Cyril excused himself, saying he would drive to the police station and give them the news.

The following day James arranged for a bulldozer to demolish what remained of the end cottage. After the pile of rubble had been cleared, James and Cyril chopped down the burnt-out trunk of the chestnut tree. After dragging the branches into the meadow they set them alight.

Because the wood was green, the bonfire smouldered for four days. James kept an almost constant watch and was not satisfied until every bough and branch had disappeared and all that remained of the spreading tree was a pile of ash.

Later that week, James told his mother he and Grace had decided to leave the cottage and move into the old farmhouse.

'Do you want to make the two cottages into one?' he asked his mother.

Lucy shook her head. 'I don't really want to live here any more,' she said. 'It's never going to be the same.'

That evening Lucy and Cyril agreed. They would move to Cyril's house in Kent. The two remaining cottages could then be put up for sale.

Cyril helped James move his furniture to the farm. After emptying his own cottage, James took some of his mother's things. There was little Lucy wanted to take with her to Kent.

The next morning, Cyril drove Lucy to Skipton where she paid a final visit to Proctor and Armitage, the solicitors who had served her well. Apart from instructing the firm to handle the sale of the Honeysuckle Cottages, she wanted to arrange for the money which she received to be added to the trust she had set up for Rachel. She wanted to ensure there would be ample funds for Alice's daughter to attend a good girl's school and, if she desired, to take private lessons in ballet or singing. Also, if Rachel proved to be as bright as Alice had been, there would be enough funds to support her through college.

Before returning to Horsforth, the pair stopped at a musical instrument shop and purchased a piano. Lucy arranged for it to be delivered to Miss Pugh's house in Ilkley.

'I hope Rachel's lessons won't drive the old dear crazy,' Lucy said, with a wry smile.

Lucy and Cyril spent their final day with James, Grace and Mr Fothergill at the farm. Before they left, James gave his mother the ebony box, inlaid with mother-of-pearl, the one he had found in the cottage ceiling. He also insisted she select some of Edward's fine china and ornaments from the glass cabinet.

'Take Constance too,' he said, as he handed her the doll. 'I remember the day Alice gave her that name. We never discovered where it came from, did we?'

Lucy took it. The dress was torn and dirty. The strip of goat skin was peeling from the head. 'Are you sure?' she said.

'She's yours,' he said.

Lucy took it and wondered.

When the Armstrong Siddely drove down the lane, the cottages looked bare. There was no lace at the windows. No smoke curling from the chimneys. No sound of children's laughter echoing from inside. And no tree. The only addition was a wooden sign, planted beside the gate in the front garden. Painted in bold letters across the top were the words: FOR SALE.

Lucy glanced at it for a moment as Cyril drove slowly past, then she wound up the car's window and turned her eyes back to the road.

Chapter 30

The Doll

The letter from Proctor and Armitage arrived only two weeks after Lucy had settled into Cyril's house in Kent. It detailed an offer on her cottage which the solicitors advised she should accept. Lucy replied by return mail. She wanted to close her affairs in Horsforth as soon as possible.

A week later she received a letter from Pansy.

My dear Lucy

I do not know how to thank you for what you have done for me and Rachel. We will be forever in your debt.

What a surprise it was when a lorry arrived with the piano. Rachel was delighted and is keen to start taking lessons.

You will be surprised when I tell you my dear aunt sat down and tried to play. I think, as a young woman, she may have played the church organ, as she knows a few hymns. Her fingers are not agile and do not work in time, but we can recognize the music. Rachel is encouraging her and they are enjoying each other's company.

Rachel has settled down quicker than I could have expected. She never talks about the fire or her mother, but at times I see her looking at the photograph of Alice on the mantelshelf.

The last few lines of the letter were smudged and hard to read. Lucy suspected her friend had cried a little when writing it.

Despite writing to James three times, Lucy had to wait several weeks before she got a reply. He apologized for not writing earlier, saying he had been too busy but that they had all settled in quickly at the farmhouse. Mr Fothergill in particular was happy to be home.

With the sale of his cottage already going through, James had arranged for some improvements to the house and the installation of a telephone. He said that on the farm the season was going well. Financially it would be their best year yet.

He finished his letter by saying Andrew and little Amelia Rose were well and added that Grace was expecting again. He sent his love and best wishes to them both. At the bottom of the page Grace added a few words of her own.

Lucy stood at the window and watched the summer shower as it passed. She knew it wouldn't last long. The sun was shining and there was a perfect rainbow stretching across the sky. The raindrops running down the pane were smooth and round like beads of quicksilver. On the wet grass a small bird splashed and fluttered as it bathed itself.

How lovely the summer is in England, Lucy thought.

Though Lucy had travelled across London from one railway station to another, she had never visited any of the famous places. Cyril, however, having spent many years at the Stock Exchange, knew the City well and was pleased to show her the sights.

They watched the boats from Westminster Bridge and wandered slowly through the Abbey. After feeding the birds in St James's Park they had strolled down The Mall. By the time they reached Trafalgar Square, Lucy's legs ached. It was a long time since she had walked so far.

'Seen enough?' Cyril asked, as they gazed up at Lord Nelson, the paving around their feet swirling in a sea of pigeons.

'Enough for one day,' Lucy said.

Cyril suggested they find a place which served tea and cakes before the long drive home.

As they headed down a narrow lane towards a small café, Lucy was attracted by a display in a shop window. A tall doll dressed in nurse's uniform was standing beside a miniature bed. Lying on the bed, covered in a white sheet, was another doll. Suspended above the setting was a sign. Printed in bold red capital letters were the words, DOLL'S HOSPITAL.

Cyril waited outside while Lucy went into the shop and spoke with the man behind the counter.

She looked pleased when she came out. 'The man said he would be interested to see that old doll I have. He thinks from my description it may be a French Bru. He said he doesn't see many. Usually only from private collections, but he said it could be worth some money if it's properly restored.'

As they walked along, arm in arm, Lucy was silent.

'Are you thinking about that doll?'

She nodded. 'Next time we are in the City, I will bring it with me.'

Not wanting to spend the winter in England, Cyril and Lucy had booked a passage on a steamer sailing from Southampton. The ship was calling at Madeira en route for the West Indies. Having heard the island offered a pleasant climate, they planned to disembark there and if they liked the place, they would stay until the worst of the English winter was over.

Three weeks prior to sailing, Lucy wrote to Captain Wainwright asking if they could visit and stay for a few nights in Tunbridge Wells. She explained she had business to attend to nearby. Wainwright replied by return mail. He said he would be happy to accommodate them and once again asked to be invited to join them on board, to take afternoon tea with them in their cabin before the ship sailed.

The first evening with Wainwright was very pleasant. Because Cyril had travelled extensively, he and the captain had much to converse about. They stayed up late talking about ships and foreign ports. Lucy was happy to listen, delighted the two men got on so well.

The following morning they breakfasted early. Lucy had planned the day's outing well in advance. She and Cyril were to drive down to Hastings, have an early lunch in the old town and then follow the coast road to Bexhill. If time permitted they would continue on to Eastbourne, arriving back in Tunbridge Wells before dark.

Wainwright declined the invitation to accompany them saying he was looking forward to visiting Southampton docks the following day. Lucy heard him whisper to Cyril about having shopping to attend to. Something about purchasing a bottle of champagne.

The sprawling house, perched on the cliff top near Bexhill-on-Sea, looked out across the English Channel. The azure sky reflected on the sea, its surface unbroken except for the white sails of passing yachts which dotted the water like wandering gulls. The breeze blowing from the land was light. It was not cold for the time of year.

From the main gate, guarded by a pair of reclining stone lions, the driveway to the house was bordered on both sides by a row of young poplars. Autumn leaves littered the gravel. On the east side of the house was a close mown croquet lawn and on the grass beyond, a set of swings, a see-saw and a child's wooden play house. On the cliff edge, a path and hand rail sloped down to the beach below. In front of the house, the driveway encircled a goldfish pond and fountain.

As the car tyres crunched to a stop, Lord Farnley came down the steps to meet them. He greeted Lucy with a kiss on the cheek.

'My husband, Cyril Street,' she said.

After shaking hands, Archibald Farnley invited them inside. Cyril collected a cardboard box from the boot of the car and carried it under his arm.

As the housekeeper served tea, Lord Farnley turned to Lucy, 'I was intrigued by your letter, wondering what it is you wanted to see me about.'

Lucy took the parcel and handed it to him. 'This is for you,' she said softly. 'Would you open it?'

Lord Farnley looked from her to Cyril before untying the string. Laying the box flat on the mahogany table, he lifted the lid and pulled back the sheets of tissue paper.

'My goodness!' he said. 'What a handsome doll!'

'Please take it out.'

Gingerly Lord Farnley lifted the doll to an upright position. As he did, the long eyelashes rolled back. A pair of luminous blue eyes gazed out at him.

'It's French,' said Lucy. 'Made in the 1890s. That is why her face has some fine lines. I think, like me, she is beginning to show signs of age.'

The doll's cape was folded at the back. Lucy reached out and smoothed it down. The velvet, in a rich shade of burgundy, felt as soft as the strip of ermine which edged it. Beneath the cape, the spun silk dress, trimmed with a yoke of Swiss lace, was decorated with tiny pearls. The pale grey wig shone with the lustre of pure mohair and was set into soft bouncing ringlets which fell to the doll's shoulders. The hat sported three pheasant feathers.

In one lace-gloved hand the doll held a turned wooden walking stick, its handle and ferrule tipped with silver. The kidskin shoes bore the original silver buckles, polished to a fine mirror finish. A tiny gold brooch decorated the neck.

'I thought perhaps your granddaughter might like it,' said Lucy.

Lord Farnley sat down. His face was pale.

'Are you all right?' Lucy asked.

'Yes,' he said, staring at the doll. 'There is something about it which reminds me of a doll I bought many years ago.'

Lucy paused for a moment. 'Did it have a velvet cape of peacock blue?'

'Yes,' he said. 'How did you know?'

'This is the doll,' she said kindly. 'You do not remember me. I was an upstairs maid at Heaton Hall. I was with your daughter when she died.'

Lord Farnley shook his head.

Lucy continued, 'Your housekeeper, Mrs Gresham, gave it to me. Told me to burn it. But I couldn't. I burned the clothes but kept the doll.'

'And you've had it all these years?'

'Yes,' said Lucy. 'But it was not right: I should not have taken it. It was never meant for me. And though I loved the doll, I always felt guilty. It was the only thing I ever stole. Now, I want to return it to you, so you may give it to your granddaughter.' She smiled. 'I'm sure Miss Beatrice would have wanted her to have it.'

Lord Farnley wiped his eyes.

'I'm sorry,' Lucy said. 'I didn't mean to upset you.' She glanced anxiously at Cyril as she waited for Lord Farnley to reply.

'Lucy,' he said, 'this doll means more to me than you can imagine. I never had anything to remind me of my daughter. No lock of hair. No pretty dress. No photograph. Everything she had was burned. And when she died I even lost her image in my mind. And though I tried, I could never conjure up her face, except occasionally in a dream, but in the morning she was gone.

'Now, as I look at this doll, I see the great bed, and I see my Beatrice in it.' His face lit up. 'And I see her face as clear as I see yours, smiling a soft smile, serene and beautiful.

'Lucy,' he said, the tears rolling down his cheeks, 'you have given me more than the doll, you have given me back the memory of my daughter.'

Lucy and Cyril did not wait to be seen out. When they left Lord Farnley he was still sitting in his chair. But he was not looking at the French doll sitting opposite him, he was gazing at the little girl whom Lucy had returned to him.